Praise for
A PEOPLE'S HISTORY OF HEAVEN

'Subramanian writes with empathy and exuberance, offering a much-needed glimpse into a world that too many of us don't even know exists. This is a book to give your little sister, your mother, your best friend, yourself, so together you can celebrate the strength of women and girls, the tenacity it takes to survive in a world that would rather have you disappear.'

Nylon

'The women are not there for our pity; they are there to be listened to. How refreshing.'
New York Times

'Subramanian's observations are sharp, witty, and incisive; her writing is consistently gorgeous.'
Washington Independent Review of Books

'A colourful, dramatic coming of age story.'
Ms. Magazine

'*A People's History of Heaven* does not reduce its characters to dozens of fists raised in the air, but instead gives a full account of the extraordinary lives that stand shoulder-to-shoulder in the wreckage of a wealthy city, ready to fight against the bulldozers upon the horizon.'
The Believer

'How can a novel about a group of daughters and mothers on the verge of losing their homes in a Bangalore slum be one of the most joyful and exuberant books I've read?… Each page delighted and amazed me.'

Heather Abel, author of *The Optimistic Decade*

'The power of these fierce young women shines in spite of their circumstances, and they prove just how beautiful and influential a strong, unconditionally accepting community is. Subramanian is a remarkable writer whose vibrant words carry a lot of heart. This inspiring novel is sure to draw in readers with its lyrical prose and endearing characters.'   *Booklist*

'A vibrant novel...a beautiful story of love, loyalty, and female friendship.'   *HelloGiggles*

'Wonderful... The stories of these young women...are full of emotion and drama, and also fierce power and hope. Their relationships and support for one another is inspiring, making this a beautiful testament to friendship and individuality. More LGBTQ+ novels about people of colour, please!'   *BookRiot*

'Spending time with this fearsome five is...just plain fun. Slum life is never romanticized. The narrator, an unnamed member of the girls' inner circle, delivers enough cynical wisdom and pithy commentary to show just how wise these girls are to their plight without dismissing how insidious cultural messages are.'   *Foreword Reviews*

'A girl power-fueled story that examines some dark social issues with a light...touch.'   *Kirkus Reviews*

'A strong debut... Subramanian's evocative novel weaves together a diverse, dynamic group of girls to create a vibrant tapestry of a community on the brink.'   *Publishers Weekly*

'Poetic... Subramanian's rich imagery conjures up the bustle of a diverse city where children live in poverty mere blocks from three-story homes where their mothers work as maids... As colourful as a Rangoli design, this bittersweet coming-of-age story will linger in the reader's mind.'   *Shelf Awareness*

'Perfect for readers who want to learn more about Indian and South Asian culture, or for readers who love stories featuring strong female friendships.'   *Reading Women* podcast

'What a thrill to read a novel as daring and urgent as *A People's History of Heaven*... I can't remember the last time I encountered a voice of such moral ferocity and compassion.'

Tania James,
author of *The Tusk That Did the Damage*

'Everything about *A People's History of Heaven* is wonderful: the lyrical, light touch of the narrator, the story, the humour, and most of all, the girls. Faced with bigotry and bulldozers, these girls know exactly what to do: stick together and help each other learn, love, see, fight. These are girls who save the world.'

Minal Hajratwala,
award-winning author of *Leaving India*

A People's History of Heaven

Mathanghi Subramanian

ONEWORLD

A Oneworld Book

First published in Great Britain, the Republic of Ireland & Australia
by Oneworld Publications, 2019

Two chapters previously appeared in slightly different form in the following
publications: "Banu the Builder" in *Hunger Mountain*, and "Half Wild" in *DNA India*
Published by arrangement with Algonquin Books of Chapel Hill,
a division of Workman Publishing Company, Inc., New York

ISBN 978-1-78607-676-2
eISBN 978-1-78607-677-9

Printed and bound in Great Britain by Clays Ltd, Elcograf S.p.A.

Oneworld Publications
10 Bloomsbury Street
London WC1B 3SR
England

Stay up to date with the latest books,
special offers, and exclusive content from
Oneworld with our newsletter

Sign up on our website
oneworld-publications.com

MIX
Paper from
responsible sources
FSC® C018072

For Swarna Narasimhan

The People of Heaven

Banu: A shy and talented artist who is the granddaughter of one of the first residents of Heaven.

Banu's *ajji*: Banu's grandmother (her father's mother), who comes from a traditional village where women are identified as "mother of" and "wife of" rather than by their first names.

Kadhir Uncle: Banu's father, who passed away soon after she was born.

Deepa: A gifted dancer and eavesdropper whose family pulls her out of school because she is visually impaired.

Neelamma Aunty: Deepa's mother, who, abandoned by her family at a young age, lived with relatives but was mostly raised by Banu's *ajji*.

Deepa's father: An auto driver who is one of the more respected fathers in Heaven.

Joy: The queen of the group and the top-ranked student in their class, who is transgender and has three older brothers.

Selvi Aunty: Joy's mother, a Dalit widow who converts to Christianity to escape casteism.

Rukshana: A queer, Muslim tomboy who is fiercely loyal and quick tempered.

Fatima Aunty: Rukshana's mother, a *hijabi* union leader whose husband left after their son died.

Rania: Rukshana's older sister, who eloped when Rukshana was young.

Padma: A migrant from the countryside who is the only literate member of her family.

Gita Aunty: Padma's mother, who suffers from untreated mental illness.

Padma's father: A night watchman known for his kindness.

Janaki Ma'am: The headmistress of the government school, who grew up in an orphanage.

Vihaan: Rukshana's neighbor and Yousef's best friend.

Yousef: Rukshana's cousin, who is in love with Joy.

Leela: A resident of Purvapura who falls in love with Rukshana.

A
People's
History
of
Heaven

PART ONE

Early Civilization and Settlement

1

Breaking the Sky

THE BULLDOZERS arrive on a Friday, orders of destruction in their glove compartments, construction company logos on their doors. Beneath their massive wheels, tin roofs shatter and cinder blocks crumble, wooden doors splinter and bamboo frames snap. Homes and histories disintegrate, ground into dust.

Our houses may break, but our mothers won't. Instead, they form a human chain, hijabs and dupattas snapping in the metallic wind, saris shimmering in the afternoon sun. Between the machines and the broken stone, our mothers blaze like carnations scattered at the feet of smashed-up goddesses. Angry, unforgiving goddesses, the kind with skulls around their necks and corpses beneath their feet.

The kind that protect their children.

That protect their daughters.

* * *

Ragged jigsaw of tilted tents, angry quilt of rusted roofs, maze of sagging sofas. Muddy monsoon squelch, dry summer hum. Jangle and clatter of gunshot tongues firing words faster than Rajni fires bullets. That's where we're from.

People who aren't from here? They think beauty is country colors. Rice-paddy green, peacock-neck blue. Sunsets gold and purple and pink. No one writes poems about pavement gray, road-roller yellow, AC-bus red.

People who aren't from here can't see past the sign stuck in the ground thirty years ago. "Swargahalli," it once said. English letters straight like soldiers. Kannada letters curved like destiny. Now it's been split in two, cracked by one of the bulldozers the city sent to erase us the first time—or maybe the second or the third. (After a while, we stopped counting.) All that's left is the word *Swarga*.

"Swarga?" people ask. "As in Sanskrit for Heaven? *This* place?"

"Heaven?" we say with them. "*This* place?"

Sometimes they laugh. Sometimes we do too. But most of the time, we don't.

Because the sign isn't right. But it's not wrong either.

* * *

There are five of us girls: Deepa, Banu, Padma, Rukshana, and Joy. Born the same year in the same slum. In the same class at school—until Deepa's parents pulled her out. Her mother, Neelamma Aunty, says it's because Deepa's blind, but we don't believe her. In Heaven, there are plenty of reasons to stop a girl's education. None of them are any good.

Every afternoon, we stop at Deepa's house on the way to our own. We like sitting with her in the sunlight that puddles outside her door, our hands busy peeling garlic bulbs or stripping curry leaves off of their stems. We like sipping the sugar-strong coffee Neelamma Aunty pours us while she tells us the day's gossip, rumors and stories we'll tell our mothers. We like answering Deepa's questions about our classes. What we learned, what she's missed. It makes us feel lucky. Smart. Important.

The afternoon of the demolition, though, Deepa and Neelamma Aunty aren't home. They're with the rest of our mothers, hand in hand, staring down the machines. The world smells like burnt rubber. The engines are off, but the air still hums.

Joy takes Deepa's hand, joins the chain, and asks, "What's going on?"

Deepa blinks her sightless eyes and says, "The city said we had a month. They lied."

"Same way they lied about getting us a water pump," Padma says, reaching for Joy with one hand and Rukshana with the other, "and about cleaning up the sewage behind the hospital."

"Where are the police? They always send police," Rukshana says, taking Joy's hand and reaching for Banu's. Rukshana's mother is always dragging her to protests, so she knows these things.

"The police? They left," Deepa says. "Told the bulldozer drivers not to run us over while they were gone."

"Are they coming back?" Padma asks.

"Who knows," Deepa says. "It's Holi weekend. I bet they're all off playing colors with their policewallah friends."

"Makes sense," Joy says, nodding. "They don't care about people like us."

"You mean they don't *see* people like us," Banu says. "That's different."

"You're right," Rukshana says. "It's worse."

"Whether they see us or not, this is our home," Deepa says. "The city can't just take it away from us."

"Sure they can," Rukshana says.

"Well, they won't," Deepa says. "We won't let them."

* * *

Once, when Deepa was watching Padma's brothers, an airplane cut a whirring path across the sky. Deepa couldn't see it, of course. But she could hear it roar.

"Wow!" Padma's brothers said, jumping up and down and pointing at the sky. "Wow, wow, wow!"

"*Akka*, what's that thing called?"

"An aer-o-plane," Deepa said, stumbling across the jagged vowels, the serrated consonants. The syllables sharp as shattered stones.

"It flies so high, *akka*," the youngest boy said. "Why doesn't it break the sky?"

"*Chee*! What nonsense. You can't break the sky."

"But that aer-o-plane looks so pointy," the youngest said.

"Like a screwdriver," the oldest said, "or a needle."

"If it did break the sky, I bet it would make a *big* sound," the youngest said, throwing his hands up in the air. "I bet it would be an explosion!"

"Don't be ridiculous. You can't break the sky," Deepa said again, more firmly this time.

But really, she wasn't so sure. What *would* it sound like, if you broke the sky? Would it be a jagged shattering of sharp-edged glass? A frayed ripping of overwashed fabric? Or would the sky break the way skin breaks, silently oozing, and smelling like blood?

This afternoon, when the bulldozers come, Deepa feels the air tremble, the clouds shudder. Hears the sounds of cooking pots and pressure cookers, lightbulbs and radios, table fans and kerosene cans being thrashed into pieces, being beaten into the ground.

Oh-ho, she thinks, so this is what it sounds like.

This is what it sounds like to break the sky.

2

Deepa Learns to Dance

DEEPA WAS BORN ON DEEPAVALI, the festival of lights—that's how she got her name. Hair soft and nervy as October's final skies. Screams shrill as the hiss of Indian-made sparklers, the screech of Chinese-made rockets. Toes red-brown as the clay lamps lining pensioners' windowsills, slum dwellers' doorways.

Our mothers filled Heaven with light that night. Portioning precious cooking oil, digging soggy matchbooks out from the corners of almirahs, the bottoms of plastic bags. Coaxing reluctant wicks into oily flame. But after all that scrimping and scrounging and lamping and lighting, they forgot to tend to the most important flames of all: the ones in Deepa's eyes.

Eyes tucked tenderly behind peacock feather lashes, freshly finished skin. Eyes that can only see the edges of things, the borders and tracings. Eyes that, at first, our mothers think are perfect.

Eyes that *are* perfect. Until you ask them to do their proper job.

Deepa the lamp, the light of our lives, the child of the flame, is, for all practical purposes, blind.

"Her womb is fine, though, isn't it?" Our mothers cluck. "Good, good. At least they'll be able to get her married."

* * *

Deepa's mother, Neelamma Aunty, was the first child born in Heaven.

Back then, Heaven was just a bunch of blue tarps strung up into haphazard tents in a clearing on the edge of a coconut grove. A for-now kind of place, not a forever kind of place. A square of dirt to tide a family over until something better came along.

Of course, for some families—for *our* families—nothing ever did.

Back then, no one knew Heaven would outlast the squat brick homes bordering the empty lot, the barely paved lanes where children played cricket and rode their bicycles to school. That those homes and lanes would flatten and crackle and burst into parking lots and shoe stores, breweries and offices. Into hospitals specializing in diseases contracted by people who eat too much, work too little.

"Even the diseases are posher than us," Banu's *ajji* said.

No one thought it was funny. Everybody laughed.

Everybody except Neelamma Aunty's mother. She was too busy instructing the midwife to hand Neelamma Aunty off to distant relations. What else was Neelamma Aunty's mother supposed to do? She already had four daughters and one son. She had no use for this tiny new scrap of life.

Particularly because it was a tiny new scrap of *female* life.

The relative that took Neelamma Aunty in had liver spots on his shaky hands. His wife was stooped and hard of hearing. Still, he did the best he could. Kept Neelamma Aunty fed and clothed and mostly in school. Gave her as much love as he had for as long as he lived. Which wasn't very long.

For the most part, Neelamma Aunty took care of herself. Grew up tough and lonely and watchful. Cultivated uncertain allies among the women who married their way in and out of Heaven. Women who were fiercely loved, cruelly abandoned. Who woke up every morning with fists clenched, knees tensed, ready to fight. Desperate to live.

Women who became our mothers.

* * *

Except for those eyes of hers, Deepa is just like the rest of us. Trains her fingers to fold the clothing her mother mends into perfect, even squares. Learns to fill the cook stove with kerosene, to rinse the breakfast dishes in half-filled buckets of water. Hums along to the film songs the neighbors play on the radio they got for free from a political party before the last election.

Normal things. Girl things.

We see Deepa all the time. Our teachers, though? They only see her on Annual Day. Which anyone will tell you is just a fancy name for pity day.

Every year, our maths teacher, Sushila Miss, goes around Heaven inviting out-of-school children to the function. Miss teaches us geometry, but she used to study dance. She's convinced that if she had just eloped with the nice boy from Bombay who proposed to her in the twelfth standard, she could've become a Bollywood backup dancer. Maybe even an item girl.

Instead she turned him down—or, more accurately, her parents turned him down—and she married an engineer with a bachelor's degree and a respectable score on the civil service exam. They settled into a government flat with a moldy roof, cinder-block walls. She learned how to pour coffee with her left hand while feeding a child with the right, how to serve breakfast without unraveling the razor-sharp pleats of her schoolteacher sari.

Three hundred and sixty-four days a year, she still plays the role of respectful housewife, devoted mother, government servant. But on Annual Day, she indulges herself in a different kind of performance. A performance of what could have been, had she done what she wanted to do instead of what she was supposed to do.

How she loves that three hundred and sixty fifth day.

When Sushila Miss gets to Deepa's house, Neelamma Aunty is delivering a batch of hand-stitched sari blouses to a rich lady who lives on the other side of the main road. Deepa's father is in his auto-rickshaw picking up the office workers who are his regular fares. Deepa sits in her doorway skinning carrots with a blunt kitchen knife. The peels twist off in red-orange spirals, like the inside of a firecracker before it explodes.

Sushila Miss says, "You poor thing. Do they always leave you here like this?"

"Who?"

"Your parents, darling," Sushila Miss says. Acts like she's rehearsed in front of the mirror. Which maybe she has. Sucks her teeth like this, tilts her head like that. All without loosening a strand of her tightly braided, waist-length blue-black hair.

("It's from a bottle," our mothers say. "She can't go this long with these children without any grays to show for it. Not possible.")

"So sorry, ma'am," Deepa says politely, "but I don't think I got your name."

"Sushila Miss. I teach maths over at the school," she says. "I'm here to invite you to Annual Day. There will be free lunch from the local leader. Last year we had *kichadi* and *basen ka ladoo*." She pinches the red-clay flesh on Deepa's arm and says, "Join us. Fatten up those skinny bones."

"That sounds nice," Deepa says. "Is there a program?"

"Your schoolmates—" Sushila Miss says, then catches herself. "Students will indeed be performing. There will be plays, dances, and recitations. How old are you?"

"Eleven."

"Ah, yes. Eleven. Fifth standard, then. The girls your age are dancing in a competition between the local schools. It's a tradition, you see. I'm choreographing. Coaching them too, actually." Sushila Miss leans in like she's telling a secret. Deepa inhales Miss's bouquet of cheap foreign perfume and sandalwood soap. "I was quite a good dancer when I was your age. Won awards." Caught up in her own generosity, she puts her hand on her chest, bats her eyelashes. When she remembers that Deepa can't see, she sighs a heavy sigh. "I'm doing my humble part to pass my gift on to them."

"How kind of you," Deepa says. Like she's hearing all of this for the first time. Like we haven't already cribbed about Annual Day, haven't imitated Sushila Miss's barked orders, her exasperation. Even warned Deepa about this very visit. "That sounds like something I would love to—er—see."

Sushila Miss laughs uncomfortably. She's not used to girls who don't apologize for who they are.

"You'll come then?"

"I'll come, ma'am," Deepa says. "And I'll be in the dance."

Sushila Miss laughs again, this time with confidence. Because really. A blind girl in the Annual Day dance competition? She can't be serious.

Can she?

Sushila Miss says soothingly, "Why trouble yourself?" She purrs like a kitten against a young child's knees. "Just come enjoy."

"Oh, I will," Deepa says. "I always enjoy learning new things."

"It's a dance *competition*," Sushila Miss repeats.

A competition our school has never won. Probably never will. But no need to admit that now, to this girl, who refuses to see what is right there in front of her sightless eyes.

"Which is why practice is so important," says Deepa, who understands perfectly.

* * *

In preschool, Deepa was Heaven's undisputed star. Counted up to twenty in English and Hindi, fifty in Tamil and Malayalam, one hundred in Kannada and Telugu. Recited multiplication tables like poems and poems like multiplication tables. Whenever a visitor came by to pass out a holiday lunch, Deepa was chosen to say the prayer before the meal. Tilted and turned her voice in all the right ways at all the right times.

We were only a little bit jealous. Especially after we figured out her secret: That she knew all of the words to the elephant rhyme, but none of the hand motions. That she could recite the Kannada vowels, but she couldn't write them down. That when she was at the front of the line, she didn't know which way to turn to take us to the toilets. Animals, birds, vegetables. Deepa could tell you their names. Their sounds, smells, textures. Just not their faces.

Deepa wasn't perfect. But she wasn't scared either.

Maybe that's why we protected her. Kept our hands on her shoulders when we marched in a line. Dragged her to the back of the classroom, far enough away that she couldn't be expected to point directly at anything on the posters at the front. We did a fine job too. So fine a job that it wasn't until just before the Dasara break, when Preschool Miss told us to get our slippers, that the adults suspected anything was wrong.

The problem was that we broke ranks that day. Rukshana's older sister, Rania, who hadn't eloped yet, dragged Rukshana into the corridor to yell at her about forgetting her water bottle in the schoolyard—which was really just an excuse for Rania to flirt with the dreamy Christian boy in the class-seven room next door. Banu's *ajji* hurt her back, so Banu skipped class to go on the morning *kolam* round, carrying the colored powders on her tiny, uncombed head. As for Padma, she still lived in the village, and Joy—well, she wasn't Joy yet.

All of this left Deepa alone on her hands and knees in the slipper pile. Nose pressed up against all those broken clasps and wet rubber soles. Squinting and sniffing and trying to decide which pair was hers.

"*Chee!*" Preschool Miss said. Yanked Deepa by the elbow, snapped her skinny body like an elastic band. "Naughty girl. Why are you putting your face in those filthy, filthy things?"

Rukshana left her sister standing in the hallway. Stuck her hands on her hips, and said, "Don't yell at her, miss. It's not her fault she can't see."

"Can't see? What nonsense," Preschool Miss said.

"It's true," Rukshana said. She turned to the doorway to get her sister's help, but Rania had already left, running across the compound after the Christian boy, who, thrillingly, stole the forgotten water bottle right out of her hand.

"Nonsense," Preschool Miss said. Pulled her hand back, deciding which of the girls to thwack first. "Just watch me beat the sight back into her, dirty thing."

Before Preschool Miss could deliver on her threat, our headmistress, Janaki Ma'am, appeared in the doorway. Silk sari shining, wire spectacles glimmering. Hair knotted severely at the nape of her neck. She settled Preschool Miss's hand by her side, and said, "Now, now, Yamini, you know corporal punishment isn't legal."

Then Janaki Ma'am knelt down so she was face to face with Rukshana and said sternly, "Tell me, child. What do you mean she can't see?"

"She can't see means she can't *see*, miss," Rukshana said.

"Ma'am," Preschool Miss said. "That's the headmistress. Call her ma'am."

"She can't see, *ma'am*," Rukshana said. "That's why she never knows where to sit. And why she doesn't know the dances to go with the rhymes. And why one of us always takes her a plate of food and then brings her plate to wash."

"Oh please," Preschool Miss said, "if Deepa couldn't see, don't you think we would've noticed by now?"

"But she *can't* see," Rukshana said. "And you *didn't* notice."

Like she's already run out of patience for adults and their seeing and not-seeing and saying and not-saying. Like Deepa's kind of blindness is the only kind of blindness that makes any sense at all.

* * *

After she visits Deepa, Sushila Miss goes home to tend to her family. To chop onions, fry mustard seeds, melt butter. To tuck clothing into drawers, sweep dust out of corners. An evening just like our evenings, except with a fancier stove.

In all those duties, she forgets her duty to the out-of-school children, especially to the girl who is blind in more ways than one. That is, until the next dance practice, which is also the last dance practice before the competition.

The rest of us are jittery and sulky.

"Why bother when we're going to lose anyway," Rukshana grumbles.

"What we *should* practice is how we'll look when they announce the winners," Joy says, "and they don't announce us."

"That we don't need to practice," Rukshana says. "We're used to it."

Except we're not used to it. You'd think we would be by now, since everyone in Heaven is always losing, all the time.

Sushila Miss claps her hands on our shoulders, pushes us into line. Presses the buttons on the brand-new battery-powered CD player donated by the local legislator.

"I didn't *ask* for a CD player," Janaki Ma'am had shouted when the thing showed up in her office, wrapped in cellophane the color of false promises. "I *asked* for new toilets."

"It's not so bad," Sushila Miss had said, trying to hide her excitement. "It might even be useful. For, say, Annual Day."

Last year, Miss played the music for our dance on the Nokia phone her husband got her from the black market behind the water tank. The song sounded like blue plastic. On the new player, this year's song sounds like electricity and money. Like moving up in the world.

Miss barks out our choreography like a military general. Shake those hips. Shimmy those chests. Seduce, seduce, seduce. All the things we are not supposed to do except when on school grounds, in our uniforms, once a year. Things that, at any other time, in any other place, in any other clothing, would get us kicked out of our houses for good.

When she sees us, Sushila Miss allows herself to hope. This year, maybe we have a chance. See Rukshana, right in front, her fair cheeks dimpling when she forces herself to smile. See Joy, in the second row, holding her head up like a queen. See those perfect lines.

But, what's this? What's happening there? Back in the third row. Yesterday, there was no third row.

Today, there is Deepa. And Deepa is a disaster.

Or, at least, Miss thinks so. Deepa's not doing any of the same moves as the rest of us. The blank, bright pupils of her unseeing eyes make her look like a ghost.

But the rest of us are impressed. Truthfully. How does someone who has never seen a Madhuri Dixit dance number know how to stretch her arms just so? How does someone who has never seen Kajol pout through a Tamil film know how to pucker her lips so perfectly? And how does someone who has never seen, well, anyone know how to keep her back so straight, her neck so long?

"She's better than all of us," says Rukshana. "Better than Joy."

"Well," Joy says, "almost as good maybe."

"She's not deaf," says Padma, who knows all the ways women can be broken.

Sushila Miss makes us do the dance ten times. Fifteen. Adjusts an arm here, a hip there. Pretends not to see the girl who can't see.

"Tomorrow, be here," Miss says. "Nine a.m. in the morning. Sharp. If anyone is late, she doesn't dance."

"We'll be here, miss," says Deepa.

"Oh, darling," Sushila Miss says with her why-didn't-I-elope sigh. "It's one thing to practice. It's another to perform." She puts a hand on Deepa's skinny shoulder and says, "Tomorrow you just come watch—um—attend. Okay?"

Deepa pats Miss's hand. Padma takes Deepa by the shoulder. Holds onto her the whole way home.

* * *

Deepa wanted to stay in school. Maybe not our school, but *a* school—any school, really. It's Neelamma Aunty who pulled her out.

After Rukshana made her see things properly, Janaki Ma'am visited Deepa's house. It was a gray November morning, an hour or two after sunrise. Janaki Ma'am wore scratchy socks with her sandals, a chunky red cardigan with her sari. The air smelled like wood fires and wind.

"Come in, ma'am," Neelamma Aunty said. Janaki Ma'am stepped inside the house, taking in the neatly stacked pots, the newly hung shelves, the straw floor mat with the fraying edges. In the corner, Deepa's father sat silently, careful not to involve himself. Deepa was there too, wearing a dress made out of fabric left over from the cotton sari blouses Neelamma Aunty stitched on her Singer sewing machine. Sleeves two different shades of maroon, skirt a chaos of pink and green and stamped-on gold. Neckline copied from the photo of the blue-eyed baby in the window of the Kodak shop in the main market. Technically, the dress was new. Not a hand-me-down. Which is more than can be said for most of the clothes on most of us girls in Heaven.

"So, you're Deepa's mother," Janaki Ma'am said approvingly. "I've seen you around."

"Yes, ma'am," Neelamma Aunty said.

Unlike our mothers, whenever Preschool Miss called a meeting, Neelamma Aunty dropped what she was doing and went. Memorized what she heard, repeated it over and over again as she walked home, then did exactly as she had been told. Made Deepa sweets stuffed with palm sugar and *dosas* fried with spinach, sang songs in as many languages as she could, kept Deepa's injection card in a plastic bag locked in an almirah. Retrieved the checkered paper every month on the exact date when her daughter's next vaccination was due.

Neelamma Aunty thought no one had noticed. She didn't yet know that Janaki Ma'am notices everything.

"Did you go to school?" Janaki Ma'am asked her.

"Yes, ma'am," Neelamma Aunty said, then, blushing, added, "Not very long. But some."

"I wasn't headmistress, was I?" Janaki Ma'am asked. Took the metal tumbler of coffee Neelamma Aunty handed her and held it gratefully between her chilly fingers.

"No, ma'am, you joined after I left," Neelamma Aunty said. A mere month after, actually. Neelamma Aunty often thought that if she had just held out another few days, Janaki Ma'am would've helped her find a way to at least study up to tenth.

But no use wondering about that now.

"That's a shame," Janaki Ma'am said. Like she was thinking the same thing. "Well, I must say, your daughter is quite bright. One of our brightest."

Neelamma Aunty nodded shyly. "You take good care of them, ma'am," she said.

"I'm not taking care of her yet. She's still at the *anganwadi*, at least for a few more months. Then she'll be old enough to be admitted into kindergarten."

"Yes," Neelamma Aunty said eagerly. "We have her birth certificate. Her vaccinations are up to date. We're ready to enroll her."

"The thing is," Janaki Ma'am said—she cleared her throat, not sure how much of what she was about to say was new, and how much Neelamma already suspected—"your daughter can't see properly. In fact, she can't see much at all."

Neelamma Aunty nodded again. Glanced at Deepa's father. A look passed between them, its meaning transmitted through the secret language of spouses.

"There *are* schools that can help her," Janaki Ma'am said. "Schools with teachers trained to work with the blind. At a place like that, Deepa would shine."

"That sounds like a private school. We don't have the money for fees," Neelamma Aunty said. Gathered Deepa up in her lap.

"We have *some* money," Deepa's father said. Even though he knew he probably shouldn't. Children, after all, are women's business.

"It doesn't matter how much money you have. You see, there is a scheme," Janaki Ma'am said. "It pays for hostels, and—"

"Hostels?" Neelamma Aunty asked. "What do you mean 'hostels'?"

"The schools are residential," Janaki Ma'am explained. "I was in a similar situation growing up, actually. I know it sounds risky but—"

"Unless it's in this neighborhood, we're not interested."

"I know it feels like too much. But I really believe you should consider—"

"There's nothing to consider," Neelamma Aunty said. Her words clanged like a slamming door. "I'm not sending my child away. That's final."

"If you'll just hear me out," Janaki Ma'am said. "Your daughter has such potential—"

"That's right. *My* daughter," Neelamma Aunty said. Squeezed Deepa so tightly she gasped. "*I'm* her mother. *I* know what's best for her."

"She needs an education," Janaki Ma'am said.

"She needs her mother," Neelamma Aunty said. Neelamma Aunty with her eighth-standard pass, her vocational certificates. Neelamma Aunty, who pretended she had a bank account instead of a wad of cash locked up in her almirah. "She needs me."

"She'll still have you," Deepa's father said gently.

"You're not a woman," Neelamma Aunty said, turning on him. "You don't know."

When Janaki Ma'am left, Deepa slid off Neelamma Aunty's lap and onto the floor. Pulled the fabric of her dress over her nose and inhaled deeply. It smelled like starch and thrift and perspiration and caution. And, around the neckline, a little bit like fear.

* * *

On the morning of Annual Day, we go to Deepa's house and dress her in a government school uniform. Plait her hair with state-issued ribbons. Tuck her feet into a pair of Rukshana's old shoes. There's a hole in the bottom of the left sole, but Deepa says the toes don't pinch, so it should be fine.

"What are you lot up to?" Neelamma Aunty calls through the doorway. We can hear her sewing machine buzzing. She's set it up on a wooden table on a grassy patch just outside the door. She says it's because she likes the air, but Deepa thinks it's so she can watch us while she's working. So she can keep up her role as the head of our mothers' not-so-secret police.

"Don't worry, Aunty," Padma yells out the doorway. "We're only taking Deepa to school." The rest of us giggle.

"School?" Neelamma Aunty asks. "What for?"

"Annual Day, Aunty," Rukshana yells.

"Free lunch, Ma," Deepa yells. "*Basen ka ladoo.*"

"Stop moving," Joy says, batting Deepa's shoulder. "Now look. I have to redo your plait."

"Annual Day? All these functions you girls have," Neelamma Aunty says. The machine's whir stops as she readjusts the needle. "Don't they teach you anything at school anymore?"

"They've taught us how to dance," Joy says. She comes outside and pops her hip so Neelamma Aunty can see. "If we don't pass our tenth, we can be in films."

Neelamma Aunty laughs. We love it when she laughs. She doesn't snicker guiltily behind her hand, like the rest of our mothers do. Neelamma Aunty's laugh is throaty and generous and kind. Just like Deepa's.

"Is Janaki Ma'am still running things over there?" Neelamma Aunty says.

"Yes, Aunty," Padma says.

"Tell her I said hello," Neelamma Aunty says.

"We will, Aunty," Joy says.

"Don't forget," Neelamma Aunty says. We all tumble out the door, and she adds, "And bring my daughter back safely."

"Of course, Aunty," Rukshana says. Puts her hand on Deepa's shoulder, the way Deepa likes it. The way we've been doing it since we were four years old. "You can trust us."

"I know," Neelamma Aunty says. But only after we're far enough away that we can't hear her.

* * *

Before Deepa was born, Neelamma Aunty lost babies. All of our mothers lost babies. But Deepa's mother lost more than the rest of them.

They died early, these babies. Slipped away in fat clots of red-brown blood, cramps she might've missed if she didn't realize what was happening if it hadn't happened so many times before. Droplets of endings too small to merit the enormous, scraping grief they left behind.

"It happens," our mothers told her. Sometimes, they said it when they were full with child themselves. Rubbed their bulging bodies and said, "And just see now. Just see."

"Those others? Not even children. Call them accidents."

"*Your* child has not come to you yet. Be patient."

"*Pukka.* And then, once it comes? You'll wish you were childless and carefree."

The last baby—the one before Deepa—almost made it. Formed fingers and nostrils and feet that kicked when Neelamma Aunty ate palm-sugar-laced sweets. When the pains started, Rukshana's mother, Fatima Aunty, ran to the new slum on the other side of the airport to get the midwife. Banu's *ajji* boiled water. Joy's mother, Selvi Aunty, chased Neelamma Aunty's husband out of the house.

A few hours later, the midwife, whose blue-black skin smelled like soap and toddy, placed the baby in Neelamma Aunty's arms. It was a boy. Eyelids wrinkled and transparent as jasmine petals. Purple lips pinched together like carnations.

"Isn't he supposed to cry?" Neelamma Aunty asked. Felt his fingers clutch her hair, his feet knead her thigh, his chest struggle and wheeze. Didn't know he was burning through life quick as a piece of camphor.

When her son stopped breathing, when his heart stopped beating, Neelamma Aunty started shaking. Selvi Aunty took the baby from her arms. Fatima Aunty went to tell the father. Banu's *ajji* held Neelamma Aunty for hours and hours and hours, all through the night and the next morning too. Held her until the she sat up and asked for a bucket of water to clean the blood off the floor.

For weeks after, Neelamma Aunty did not flinch. Instead, she grew stiff and watchful, bracing herself against the memory. Forced herself to ignore the sandy-haired children on the main road selling pens and flowers to passengers in auto-rickshaws and cars, the beggar women carrying emaciated babies whose mascara-lined eyes fluttered with drug-induced sleep.

In Bangalore, there's always someone worse off than you. Even if you do live in a place like Heaven. We may not have much, but we do have roofs and floors and walls. And childhoods.

A few months later, when Neelamma Aunty started showing again, Banu's *ajji* took her aside and said, "Darling, this time will be different. This time, you go to a hospital."

"Those places are dirty," Neelamma Aunty said. "I hear they put rags in your mouth to keep you from screaming."

"Not one of those rubbish public places," Banu's *ajji* said. "There's another place now on the main road. A private place."

"And who is paying for this private place?"

"The government. There's a scheme."

"What kind of scheme?"

"The kind that keeps your baby alive," Banu's *ajji* said, clutching both of Neelamma Aunty's hands.

Neelamma Aunty stared at Banu's *ajji*'s fingers twined around her own. And nodded.

* * *

When she sees Deepa with us, Sushila Miss's eyes go round and her knees go crooked. She glides across the compound, her face twitching.

"So glad you came, darling," she says to Deepa. Her voice sounds like fluttering eyelashes. "Come. Let me find you a seat."

"She doesn't need a seat, miss," Rukshana says. "She's dancing with us."

"Don't be silly." Sushila Miss laughs nervously. "She doesn't know the steps."

"Of course she does," Joy says. "She's come to practice, hasn't she?"

"But—"

"Tell us, miss," Padma says. "Where should we line up?"

When she can't get past us, Sushila Miss turns to Janaki Ma'am. Like that's going to work.

Janaki Ma'am is sitting with the Member of the Legislative Assembly, whose gold-embroidered sari costs more than the entire budget of the dance itself. When she fidgets her feet out of her strappy high-heeled shoes, we can see that even her toenails are painted gold.

The MLA has pots and pots and pots of money to her name. Some pots are legal. Some are not. Those illegal pots? She has to get rid of them somewhere. Might as well be our school.

When the MLA sees Deepa, she touches Janaki Ma'am's shoulder with her manicured fingers.

"A blind girl in the dance?" the MLA asks. "How lovely. What generous people you government-school teachers are."

"It's our job, isn't it?" Janaki Ma'am says. Even though she is not a teacher. Even though she runs a school, which is a completely different thing. A much harder thing.

So when Sushila Miss creeps over, Janaki Ma'am brushes her off before she can even speak. "Inclusion, Sushila," Janaki Ma'am says. "It's what you're paid to do."

"But, ma'am—"

"No buts. That girl wants to dance, so you let her dance. Make it work."

* * *

A week before Neelamma Aunty was due, Banu's *ajji* took her to the private hospital. The doctor was busy, the nurse told them, but she could help.

"How far along are you?" the nurse asked.

"Far along?" Neelamma Aunty asked.

"How long have you been carrying?" the nurse said. A little bit mean. Like she was reminding them who was in charge.

"Eight months," Neelamma Aunty said. Firmly. "Almost nine. Nine next week."

"How nice," the nurse said, full of false cheer. She put her hands on Neelamma Aunty's belly without asking her. As though she knew what was happening outside the womb, Deepa kicked the nurse's hand. "So what are you doing here, then?"

"I want to deliver here," Neelamma Aunty said. "Why else do you think I came?"

"There's a scheme, no?" Banu's *ajji* said, before Neelamma Aunty had time to get mad. Before she had time to change her mind.

"You want the scheme?"

"If it's possible."

"Of course it's possible," the nurse said, opening a squeaky drawer. She ruffled through a pile of papers and pulled out a form the pale blue color of Bangalore skies. Started writing neatly in each of the blank boxes. Banu's *ajji* answered even though Neelamma Aunty was right there.

"Name?"

"Neelamma," Banu's *ajji* said.

"Age?"

"Twenty-three."

"Address?"

"House number—"

"What is it, exactly?" Neelamma Aunty asked. "This scheme?"

"You know, you look ready to deliver," the nurse said. "I think we could do it for you tomorrow. Deepavali. An auspicious day."

"What is the scheme?" Neelamma Aunty repeated.

"You get four thousand rupees," the nurse said.

"That much?" Banu's *ajji* was suspicious now. "For what?"

But Neelamma Aunty's doubts fell away. She and her husband could do so much with four thousand rupees. Put in a new roof. Pay off the house. Put it toward buying an auto-rickshaw, so they wouldn't have to rent anymore.

Besides, the hospital was full of screams. Not mothers' screams: babies' screams.

Neelamma Aunty needed the money. The hospital needed to deliver babies. This scheme felt like her first stroke of luck in a long, long time.

"You say you can deliver my baby tomorrow?" Neelamma Aunty asked.

"No, no, hold on," Banu's *ajji* said. "No one just gives away four thousand rupees. What do you people take in exchange?"

"You and your baby will both be safe," the nurse said. It wasn't an answer to Banu's *ajji*'s question. But it was exactly what Neelamma Aunty wanted to hear.

"Where do I sign?" Neelamma Aunty asked.

Forty-eight hours later, Neelamma Aunty woke up with a terrible pain throbbing through the part of her body where her baby had been. She clutched Banu's *ajji*'s right hand. Banu's *ajji*'s left hand—arm, really—was clutching Deepa.

"Darling," Banu's *ajji* said softly. "There's something you should know."

"First, my baby," Neelamma Aunty said. "Give me my baby."

The second she held Deepa, whole and healthy and unapologetically loud, her body fell away from her. All she could feel was her daughter's weight, her will. The fact that she was breathing and kicking and fighting. That she was alive.

"A survivor," she whispered in Deepa's ear. "Just like your mother."

When Neelamma Aunty tried to sit up and nurse, her body

shattered into sharp, aching shards that pierced her back, her side. Her womb.

"*Kanna*," Banu's *ajji* says gently. "I need to tell you what they've done to you."

"Did they give me the money?" She gasped.

"Yes," Banu's *ajji* said, hesitating. "Yes, that they've done."

"And they've given me the baby? And a birth certificate? Did you tell them her name is Deepa?" Later, Neelamma Aunty was proudest of this part of the story. From the beginning, she thought of Deepa as someone with a long life. An educated life. Someone who would need papers in her name.

"Yes," Banu's *ajji* said, swallowing. "They've given you all this. But they've taken something too."

Before Banu's *ajji* could explain, the nurse told them to leave.

"She's awake, is it? Good. The bed is needed for the next person."

"But I don't know if I can walk," Neelamma Aunty said, wincing.

"You can," the nurse said, propping Neelamma Aunty up so quickly that she gasped. "You're strong, you people. You'll be fine in a few days."

"You people?" Neelamma Aunty tried to say. But the pain was so intense that it squeezed her throat closed. It was only when Neelamma Aunty was limping home, leaning against Banu's *ajji*, that she learned that she didn't undergo just one surgery, but two. The first was a C-section to deliver Deepa. The second was a sterilization.

With expenses deducted, she received 2,332 rupees.

* * *

Since our school is hosting the competition this year, we are the first to dance. Sushila Miss sends up prayers to every god and goddess in heaven and Heaven and all the other worlds too, just for good measure. Fixes her features like Kajol. Her hips like Madhuri. Gives a speech about using the new "sound system" that was "gifted by" the MLA. Throws out terms like *generosity* and *community*. English words Janaki Ma'am has told her to use.

Then she presses the button on the shiny silver stereo, and the music starts. We all move in perfect unison—all except for Deepa, who shimmies and shakes her way through a choreography all her own.

It's not that she's bad—her movements are more graceful than ours, her neck more swan-like, her hips more seductive. It's just that she is doing what she wants to do. She won't fall in line. Can't, actually, because she doesn't know how.

Then, things really get bad. And it's not even Deepa's fault.

The stereo that has been so reliable for so many practices wheezes and squeaks. The music screeches and slides, squawks and stutters. Grinds to a halt.

Well, not completely to a halt. That would've been manageable. Instead, it gets stuck on one phrase that repeats over and over and over, like a prayer chanted by a deranged god-man.

Sushila Miss frantically beats the side of the stereo. Blinks back tears and swallows, curses in all the languages she knows. Shakes the thing and hits the top with the heel of her hand. Like the stereo is a student, the tape deck the raw knuckles of a pair of naughty hands.

One more thwack, and it goes silent. We go silent. And still.

All of us except for Deepa.

* * *

One morning a few months after Deepa was born, a health worker gathered whichever of our mothers were home and made them form a circle around the broken sofa in front of Selvi Aunty's house. Our mothers wouldn't have come except they heard the worker was passing out free samples of something or other.

"What's this?" Neelamma Aunty had asked, taking a bottle and turning it in her hand. The brown glass felt chilly and smooth.

"Oil. It's useful for many things. Baby massage, for one," the health worker said. Even though her voice was young, she had the face of an older woman, brown and pockmarked as a peanut shell. "You take the oil and work it into their limbs. Slowly, slowly, like this." The health worker took Neelamma Aunty's arm and squeezed up and down, her hands rough, fleshy, and cozy. Warmth flooded Neelamma Aunty's limbs. Still, she shrugged the touch off, careful to keep her eyes away from our mothers.

"After that, leave the child out in the sun. They get vitamins that way. Good for the bones," the worker said. Then she wagged her finger at our mothers and said, "Boys and girls. Both need it."

When the health worker left for her next stop, Neelamma Aunty looked at the bottle and muttered, "Useless, these people."

"Exactly," Selvi Aunty said. "Like we don't know about this oil. Or massages."

Neelamma Aunty looked up.

"She's from the next slum over, you know? The new one that's just come up," Fatima Aunty said. None of our mothers knew which slum, exactly, but Fatima Aunty's meaning was clear: the health worker was newly arrived, poor, and probably from a village. In other words, she was less than us.

"Coming over here acting like she's telling us things our mothers never told us," Fatima Aunty said. "Or like we haven't raised our brothers and sisters."

"Or our daughters and sons. Or *their* daughters and sons," Banu's *ajji* said. She cackled, her laugh clotted with the ashes of too many funerals.

"Remember when she came last week with the eggs?" Selvi Aunty said, rolling her eyes. "Like we don't know the age to stop our milk and start giving them food."

"These people come and talk to us like we don't know anything," Fatima Aunty said, laughing. "Waste of bloody time. When they start telling us something new, then I'll listen."

Of course, Fatima Aunty didn't know that in a few years, her husband would leave her, and she'd become a health worker too, telling women the obvious, handing out free rations. But that's another story.

Neelamma Aunty listened to our mothers talk. She didn't disagree with them. But she also didn't admit that she *didn't* know. She never had a mother to teach her about oil or eggs or milk or sunlight. She never had brothers or sisters to diaper and feed and push off to school. She only knew what the health worker told her, and even then she gauged what to do and not to do more from our mothers' facial expressions than from the actual information she received.

As Deepa slept, Neelamma Aunty replayed the scene in her mind, her fingers pushing piecework under the Singer's murmuring needle. What age did they say about solid food? When was it all right to start eggs? Deepa was seven months old, and she was already giving her mashed up rice and dal. Was it too early? Or too late?

A tiny mewling interrupted her. Looking up, she saw Deepa crawling slowly and clumsily across the few feet of dirt separating her from Neelamma Aunty. She felt her way along with her hands, whining quietly.

"Oh, darling," Neelamma Aunty exclaimed. "You're crawling!"

When she heard her mother's voice, Deepa's face stretched into a tiny smile.

Neelamma Aunty felt then the crushing weight of this child's need for her, and her alone. Neelamma Aunty, who, her whole life, had fended for herself and no one else. Who had trusted no one, loved no one, relied on no one. Who had known no one and allowed no one to know her.

This child, though. This tangle of brown limbs, loose curls. This jumble of babbles and cries. Neelamma Aunty knew her. Knew her in a way she knew her own flesh, her own heart. Knew when she was hungry or tired, curious or frightened, joyous or pained.

Neelamma Aunty had always thought of motherhood like marriage: a set of duties and obligations, a series of defined tasks. But clutching Deepa to her chest, she realized it was something more. Something she would have to learn. Not the way she had learned tailoring to bring in money but the way she had learned to raise herself.

For days, she waited for the gravity of her epiphany to weigh her down. But all she felt was lightness.

* * *

For the rest of us, music is something that comes out of phones and stereos and auto-rickshaw speakers. Out of mouths and throats and pirated CDs and ringtones.

But for Deepa, the girl who listens her way through life, every sound is precious. The world is a symphony that keeps her out of the paths of goats and scooters, vendors and grandparents, traffic and rain. Bangalore speaks to her boldly, precisely. Urgently.

So when the rest of us stop dancing, Deepa keeps listening. Keeps hearing. Keeps moving.

"*Kaaa, kaaa, kaaa*," she sings with the crows, spreading her arms like they are black-feathered wings.

"*Haaa, haaa, haaa*," she sings with the motorcycles honking and revving on the main road.

"*Tamaataaaar, thakaleee*, tomatoooo," she croons along with the vegetable vendors pushing their carts through the alleys and lanes. Swerves her hips. Rattles her anklets. Bends her elbows just so.

We notice Deepa's performance before the grown-ups do. We push her into her own front row and whisper, "Sing louder. Go slower. We'll follow you."

Deepa, light of our lives, girl of the shadows, stands in front and leads us all, face bright as a burning candle. She isn't beautiful, exactly. But she is sure. Happy.

Early on, we girls learn that life owes us nothing, that womanhood is a spectrum of nuisances, heartbreaks, and tragedies. When Deepa sings and dances, though? It's like she's got her feet on the string between sadnesses. Like she can stop time with the force of her joy.

When the MLA notices the local newspaper photographer pointing his lens at her, she puts her hand to her mouth and sighs.

Expertly coaxes one or two crocodile tears out of her almost-green eyes. Dabs them with the golden corner of her sari.

"So beautiful," she whispers, but loudly enough for the press to hear.

Perhaps even Deepa hears. Probably she does. But she doesn't let on. She just keeps singing and keeps dancing. To the moo of the cow sorting through the garbage piled along the school's compound walls. To the yelps of the dogs pestering the cow. To the cry of a baby passing by the gate. To the bronze ring of temple bells, the silvery echo of the mosque's *azaan*. To the shuffling of the audience who have never seen a blind girl dance.

We copy her moves. But mostly, we try to listen. Try to hear what she hears. For a minute, we live in a world that squawks and honks and sighs only to keep us safe. For a minute, our city becomes something new. Something raucous, but kind. Something a little bit beautiful.

* * *

The day after Deepa was born, the world smelled burnt. Gangs of boys burst leftover firecrackers on street corners. The air was dense with reminders that another year had passed. That nothing and everything had changed.

Neelamma Aunty knew she was supposed to feel something. Rage, sadness, frustration. But all she felt was an overwhelming love for this life that is her daughter's. That is also hers. A feeling that whizzed and popped louder than any unspent cracker or undone holiday.

The day she came home with their daughter, Neelamma Aunty told her husband that they would never have another child. A few months after that, a health worker shone a flashlight in Deepa's motionless pupils and told them their daughter was legally blind.

After the worker left, Deepa's father took Deepa into his arms and stared directly into her eyes. Neelamma Aunty watched him surreptitiously, all the while pouring *dosa* batter onto the pan.

Her husband might stay another week, she figured, another month. But certainly not another year. Not with a wife who has given him a blind daughter, a dead son. A wife whose womb was now unable to sustain any more life. Sustain *male* life.

Figures turned in Neelamma Aunty's mind. She'd completed a sewing course. She had clients and a sewing machine. She could handle the rent on her own. As for a dowry, she wasn't sure they'd be able to get Deepa married. Perhaps she could send her to one of those new vocational places for blind people, the ones that advertised in the paper. Deepa could learn how to make handicrafts. Clay lamps, beaded jewelry, that sort of thing.

The dough sizzled and fried. Absently, Neelamma Aunty flipped the crispy-edged *dosa*s onto a steel plate, her mind whirring. When Deepa's father placed his hand on her shoulder, she jolted.

"Come," he said, still cradling Deepa. She was chubby back then, her cheeks round and fat as *idlis*. "See what I did today."

"The *dosa*s will get cold," Neelamma Aunty said.

"Five minutes," he said. "That's all I need."

Neelamma Aunty followed him to the empty patch where he parked his auto for the night. Land that, in a few months, would be the space where Joy's parents put up tin walls, a tarp roof. He stopped in front of the fender and looked at her expectantly.

"What does it say?" he asked.

At first she didn't understand. Searched the rickshaw's canary yellow back, the glass window lined with the "Jai Hanuman" sticker. Until she saw a slogan painted in English above the bumper. The paint smelled fresh and new.

She gulped, "It says we two. Ours one."

"Good." He nodded, pleased. "That's what I wanted. I haven't studied like you, so I didn't know if they did it properly."

"Do you know what it means?"

He wrinkled his eyebrows and his forehead. "It means that in our country, two people should only have one child. Is that right?"

"Yes," she said.

It's happening, she thought. Now he'll lay out my failures. He'll say my uterus—the thing he married me for, the thing every man marries every woman for—is useless. Impudent. Disrespectful. Had the audacity to bring a girl into the world. That too, a blind girl.

This is when he will say that it is his right to find another wife. A wife who can give him one child. A son. A son who can see.

Neelamma Aunty took a deep, blameless breath. She would let him go. After all, this is how men work. How marriage works.

But instead, he said, "We have our one now. We're finally complete."

She was so startled that she blurted out, "So you're not leaving?"

"Leaving?" he said, sounding just as startled as his wife. "Why would I leave?"

"Because of the one I gave you," she said. "She's a girl. And that too, she's—"

He didn't let her finish. "I'm not leaving," he said. Kissed Deepa's velvety cheek. Their baby—their blind baby girl—giggled and smiled.

For the first time in her marriage—maybe in her life—Neelamma Aunty allowed herself to imagine what it would be like to be part of something lasting. Something she's heard others call love.

* * *

Deepa makes a final twirl, presses her hands together, and bows. So do we. Our dance is done.

The audience bursts into applause. Hindi folks yell "*Vah vah*" and "*Kya bath hai.*" Southerners whistle and stomp their feet. Some even stand up.

When the prizes are announced, and we are not chosen, the whole audience boos.

"What nonsense is this?" they shout. "Didn't you see Ambedkar school? Or are you lot blind as well?"

Joy squeezes Deepa's hand and says, "Thank you."

"For what?" Deepa asks.

"For this," Joy says. Gestures at the audience, even though she knows Deepa can't see.

Sure, we protected Deepa. Kept our teachers away from her when we could, warned her when we couldn't. Whispered the secrets the older girls told us about bodies, marriage, love. But over the years, Deepa's done more for us than we've done for her. Fed Padma and Banu countless dinners. Slipped Rukshana extra rotis when hers came out crooked. Hid Joy's makeup collection in an old pouch. Made us read the paper to her and talk about what we read. Made us pay attention to the world. To each other.

It's funny, being a girl. That thing that's supposed to push you down, defeat you, shove you back, back, and farther back still? Turn it the right way, and it'll push you forward instead.

"It's not like we won or anything," Deepa says.

"We didn't win," Rukshana says, "but for once, we didn't lose either."

3

Uninhabitable Planets

A DRIVER STEPS OUT of the bulldozer closest to us, reeking of sweat and machine-warmed air. Pulls his ringing phone out of his pocket and looks at the caller ID, chewing on the inside of his cheek. Balances the phone between his shoulder and his ear as he lights a bidi, its ashy musk curling between the words sputtering from his nervous mouth.

"Yes, Madam Secretary, thank you so much for returning my call. Very generous of you, very generous. Yes, yes, I know admissions season is over. But please, try to understand my side," he says. Stuffs his local accent behind a wall of words he's read in the newspaper but has never said out loud, inflections he's heard on the radio but has never tried with his own tongue. "We've been calling and calling, my wife and I. For months we've been calling, but only just now have we gotten a response."

"Sounds like he's trying to get his son into private school," Deepa says. "Poor man."

"Poor *him*?" Rukshana says, rubbing her sweaty palms on her pants. "What about us? Standing out here in this heat for hours and hours. Why did the city have to do this in March?"

"Don't blame the weather. You're the one wearing trousers," Joy says.

"They've done it today because Holi's on Monday," Deepa tells us.

"Bloody north Indian holiday," Joy grumbles. "Nobody in Bangalore even celebrated Holi until all those Hindi engineers showed up."

"You mean *Hindu*-Hindi engineers," Rukshana says. "There's no Holi in Islam."

"So how come I saw your Muslim cousin-brother filling up balloons with powder?"

"You know Yousef. When it comes to mischief, he's fully secular."

"Fine, so it's Holi," Padma says. "But what does that have to do with anything?"

"It's a public holiday," Deepa says. "That means all the government offices will be closed for three days. Courts too. We have no one to complain to and no way to get a legal stay."

"One minute, one minute," Rukshana says, shaking her head. "Are you saying that because of this festival that none of us celebrates, during the height of summer, we're going to stand out here for three days and either melt or get our homes destroyed?"

"Yes," Deepa says.

Rukshana groans.

Joy sucks her teeth and says, "Oh, stop it, Rukshana. Look how many people are here. Do you see any of them complaining?"

Joy's right. Sometime between school letting out and the sun creeping up, our neighbors have joined us. Single mothers with broken bits of straw from used-up brooms clinging to the bottoms of their saris. Old ladies with hands shaking from throwing dirt on graves, frankincense on funeral pyres. Girls with evil-eye spots smudged onto their cheeks wearing clothes that used to be ours. We never knew where all those shirts and pajamas and dupattas went. Then again, we didn't know where they came from either. Only knew they had been worn before.

"These people live here?" Rukshana asks. "I've never seen them before."

"Of course you have," Padma says. "Banu's got them in her notebooks."

* * *

If you open *our* school notebooks, you'll see they're full. Full of passages copied from English textbooks, figures calculated on counted fingers, facts we will rewrite word for word on our next geography exam.

Technically, Banu's notebooks are full too. Except they aren't full of passages and facts and figures like they're supposed to be.

They're full of people. Drawings of people. Or, more specifically, the people of Heaven. The thin-lipped knife sharpener who smells like toddy in the evenings and metal in the afternoons. The trash collector who pairs chunky plastic-gold earrings with her fluorescent government-issued vest. The vegetable vendor's daughter, who runs in front of her father's cart yelling, "Spinach! Fresh spinach! Best prices, just for you!"

Banu's drawings are full of details—the dimples on chins, the calluses on fingers, the grass stains on knees. Scars left behind by struggle and disappointment and pain. Her sketches make our world feel intricate, significant, precious. Like a work of art.

Poverty might make our lives ugly. But in Banu's drawings, our survival is full of beauty.

*   *   *

"You girls need to stay hydrated," Joy's mother, Selvi Aunty, tells us. She trudges toward us, arms loaded with plastic bottles of the sugary orange juice they sell in tea stalls next to the tamarind candies and the masala chips. "Drink this."

"Did everyone run out of water?" Rukshana asks.

"We're trying to save it," Selvi Aunty says. "Especially since the pump wasn't working this morning."

"Thanks, Ma," Joy says, taking a bottle from her mother. She tilts her head back, tips the liquid into her mouth in a thin, steady stream, all without touching the bottle to her lips.

"Banu, darling, how are you? Have you and your *ajji* decided what to do about your house?" Selvi Aunty asks.

"What do you mean, Aunty?" Banu asks. "What happened to my house?"

"Oh, *kanna*," Selvi Aunty says, cupping Banu's cheek with her hand. "You better go see before it gets dark. The rest of you lot, go with her."

"Why, Ma?" Joy asks.

"Just go," Selvi Aunty says, squeezing her daughter's arm. "Take care of your friend."

*   *   *

If you want a people's history of Heaven, just look at the houses.

The newest buildings are only thatch. Woven walls listing and tilting, not yet anchored to the ground. The oldest homes are solid, stubborn. Brown brick walls, red shingled roofs. Wooden doors streaked with rainbows of waterproof paint, warped from years of Bangalore's monsoons.

In between are all the other houses, the ones still waiting for more time, more money, more hope. Padma's house is a precarious tumble of asbestos siding, its entrance a gaping, empty hole. Deepa's house has a real wooden door but only two real brick walls; the other two are pieces of aluminum donated by an NGO. Rukshana's roof is a ramshackle layering of plastic, tin, tarp, and extra-thick cardboard, while Joy's is a waterproof mosaic of red ceramic tiles.

Before today, Banu's house was the oldest. Cinderblock walls painted blue, roof shingled red. Wooden shelves lined with steel pots that held rice, oil, and palm sugar before Banu's mother left, before her father died. One window with real glass that opened and closed and didn't even leak when it rained. Materials and improvements painstakingly acquired over three decades, three generations, pieced together from countless hours of prayer and labor, strategy and luck.

All of it was destroyed in a matter of seconds, crushed beneath a bulldozer's wheels.

Now, Banu's half of Heaven is an uninhabitable planet. Wood frames of houses jut out of the earth like broken bones. Wires twist out of the rubble like severed limbs. Banu kneels in the dirt, excavating her former home like it's a grave site.

"You can fix it, Banu," Padma says.

Banu pushes aside the pebbles and sand and broken glass. Holds up half of a red and black Rakshasa mask her *ajji* once hung on a wall to repel bad fortune.

"She's right, Banu. You can fix *anything*," Rukshana says. "Even this."

Banu pieces together the cracked remains of a shelf she built using a tool set borrowed from a bicycle mechanic whose shop was near our school.

"We'll help you," Joy says. "Just like before."

She uncovers a sepia-toned snapshot of her parents' wedding. Her father's face is pierced through with a rusty nail. Banu pokes her finger through the father-size hole.

"Okay," Banu says, in a voice that sounds like she knows nothing will ever be okay again.

4

Banu the Builder

THE LAST TIME BANU SAW HER MOTHER, she was boarding a plane to Dubai. She had bought a plane ticket and working papers and a live-in nanny job from a fast-talking man with bruised knuckles and Brylcreemed hair. Sent money home on the thirteenth of every month, starting the month that she landed.

It wasn't much, but it was enough. Enough to give Banu's *ajji* hope that they could move out of Heaven. Rent a flat with a window or two, a place breezy enough to dry clothes inside when it rains. A place with a shady veranda for afternoon coffee, with cool linoleum floors for afternoon naps. Naps Banu's *ajji* planned to take when her daughter-in-law had put enough away that they could both stop working.

Banu's *ajji* never stopped working, though. Neither did her daughter-in-law. But the money did.

Three years after the payments stopped coming, a human rights lawyer asked if Banu's *ajji* would like to investigate what happened. Apparently, there was some kind of fund set up for legal cases of women who disappeared in the Gulf. Banu's *ajji* was grateful but still respectfully declined. She'd heard enough to know that some stories are better left untold.

When word got around that her mother had disappeared, Banu's teachers started shooting her looks of deep concern. Over and over again, Banu told them that she was fine.

"I live with *Ajji*," she said, "father's mother. She's an artist. She's got magical hands."

That's not true, of course. Banu's grandmother is just like the rest of us.

Banu's *ajji* is a *kolam* lady. Walks around posh neighborhoods with tins of colored powder on her head. Clatters gates and yells out "*KOOOO-lam, ran-GO-leeee*," sharp as a mynah bird's cry. For a reasonable price, she squats on the concrete on her leathery heels, funnels red-yellow-purple-green fistfuls of powder into lotus petals and starbursts and shapes without names, turns driveways and temple floors into the insides of kaleidoscopes, into pinwheel blades spinning in the sun.

She tries to teach us sometimes, at Pongal or Onam or Ugadi or Deepavali, when Hindu houses welcome the gods. How to move our wrists with straight, sure movements. How to draw our imagination out of our mind and onto the ground. When *she* does it, it looks like she's grinding rainbows out of Bangalore's gray-blue sky. But all *we* get are piles of chemical dust.

So maybe Banu's grandmother isn't quite like the rest of us. But maybe she's a little bit like Banu.

* * *

In fourth standard, when we were twelve, the airport started hiring more and more construction people. We thought they were making the place bigger, shinier, newer—just like the rest of the city. Turns out they were taking it apart. Building a new airport in some village where a potbellied politician bought a lot of land and promised impossible things.

We should've known back then that nothing in Bangalore was built to last—least of all Heaven.

Before they packed it all in, the airport was close enough to Heaven that every time a jet took off, the sides of our houses shivered and tilted, the air crackled and rushed. At night, red and yellow wing lights out-blinked the stars.

Banu's house was closest to the runway, just on the other side of a falling-down wall that people from the north were getting paid to tear down. Some afternoons we climbed up on Banu's roof, lay on our backs, and watched the planes cut shiny silver paths through the sky. Watched so hard that we stopped feeling the corrugated tin against our skin, the jagged nails in our hair.

"Why don't they crash?" Banu asked.

"Because they're full of rich people," Rukshana said.

"One day I'm going to be one of those ladies who works on planes. The ones with the fancy hair and short, short skirts," Joy said. She folded her hand like she was carrying a tray. "I saw it in a film once. They bring people drinks and snacks and they wear lipstick to make their smiles look bigger."

"I'm not going to *work* on planes," Rukshana said. "I'm going to be the one they *serve* on planes. I'll make them give me hot, hot bhaji and then massage my feet."

"No one will massage *your* feet," Joy said. "They're too smelly."

Rukshana pretended to hit Joy. But we all heard her giggle along with the rest of us.

"Anyway, come on, *yaa*. Giving people drinks and snacks? All the way up in the air like that?" Rukshana said. "Not possible."

"They built something that goes in the sky," Banu whispered. "Anything is possible."

We used to stay up there until somebody's mother or older brother or cousin saw us and told us to stop acting like monkeys. Or boys.

"What is this sky-watching nonsense?" our mothers said. "Waste of time. Better you all learn how to live on the ground."

Except learning isn't Banu's style.

* * *

The mothers in Heaven all work. Make their money sweeping other people's floors, cooking other people's meals, pressing other people's machine-washed, ready-made clothes. Filling out government forms for other people's rations, giving injections to other people's children. In the evening they come home with mouths full of questions, eyes full of suspicion. Show up at times they think we won't suspect it, even if it's just for an hour. How else will they know if we're sneaking into dirty movies or doing unmentionable things with boys? If we're memorizing curse words instead of Kannada verses, polishing off cheap whiskey instead of problem sets?

If our mothers don't check on us when school lets out, they send their spies. Grandmothers, cousins, sisters-in-law, aunts. Sons can wander and roam and get into all sorts of delicious trouble. Boys will be boys, after all. But daughters are not to be trusted. When you are a girl in Heaven, someone is always watching.

Unless, that is, you're Banu.

Once, before we were born, Banu's *ajji* was the head of maternal intelligence, a master of womanly espionage. That's how she raised Banu's father. In a way, that's how she raised our mothers too. Found them dowries and leant them jewelry when they married the right husbands. Hid them in her house to escape the wrong ones. Squeezed their hands through birth, death, abandonment.

Now, though, Banu's *ajji* is tired. She's buried too many children: the one she bore, the many she raised. Choked down too many untold secrets, too much unspent grief. When she laughs, the sound dissolves into a hacking cough, her body folding in on itself in pain.

At night, and lately, sometimes, during the day, she curls up in the home she thought her daughter-in-law would one day help her vacate. Sometimes Banu lies beside her, breathing deeply, searching for the talcum-powder aroma her grandmother used to carry around in the folds of her sari, the hollow of her neck. These days, Banu's *ajji* smells like flowers after a puja: sweetly wilting, rotten and brown.

On bad nights, Banu tries to cheer her *ajji* up by practicing *kolam*. She doesn't do the usual designs, though—dots and curves and flowers and pots. Instead, she does a city. Skyscrapers, airplanes, roads. Bridges and bullock carts, motorcycles and Metro rails. Her *ajji* watches. Places her hand on Banu's arm, laughs quietly.

"You mad child," she tells Banu. "What's going to become of you?"

When our mothers talk about Banu's *ajji*, they say, "What's gotten into that woman? So many years of telling us not to give up, and now look at her."

"Her granddaughter is growing and growing, and she can't even take her own advice."

"*Chee*! Why should we worry? We have our own daughters, don't we?"

"Not to mention our sons."

We don't know if Banu knows what our mothers say when they are together. Or, for that matter, what they say when they are alone—how Banu's *ajji* helped Rukshana's mother get her union job, helped Selvi Aunty enroll Joy in school without a proper birth certificate, helped Neelamma Aunty deliver Deepa at a real hospital with real doctors.

Whenever Banu shows up in the evenings, just in time for dinner, our mothers make her a plate with an extra *dosa*, a second helping of sambar. After she leaves, they tell us, "Next time you tell that girl to eat at her own house. You understand?"

We understand. Which is why we never say anything to Banu. And our mothers never turn her away.

* * *

For a while, the grown-ups thought Banu was slow. Not slow in the feet. Slow in the head. For a long time, we thought so too. We're not even sure how she's still in our class, she's failed so many subjects so many times. Ask her to add two plus two, and she'll say anything but four. As for the ABCs, we're not sure if she ever got past B. Not sure if she can write the second half of her own name.

So no one is surprised in sixth standard when Banu starts skipping school to go to construction sites. We figure she must have gotten bored with studying and started having an affair. Because what else is there at a construction site? The chaos of jackhammers? The rattle of steel pans and broken stones? The smell of ten thousand village dreams burning to the ground?

Banu's fallen in love, it's true. But not with a person. With a trade.

Banu has fallen in love with building.

Every afternoon, Banu comes home with pockets full of rocks and sand and nails and metal rods. Everything she takes is bent or broken. Most of us don't notice. We're too busy memorizing seven times eight equals fifty-six and Gandhiji was born on October 2 and "Johnny Johnny Yes Papa." Sometimes, when we walk home with her, we wonder about a thumping or a rattling or a crunching coming from the inside of her school bag. But we don't think much of it. This is Banu, after all.

While we memorize, Banu builds. Goes off behind the bushes, between the roots of the tallest and sturdiest banyan trees. Constructs an empire along the banks of Heaven's very own river of hospital sludge.

Builds a fort with steel spikes and pebble towers, a moat big enough for a dragon. A palace with windows made out of broken bottles and a gate that slides open and closed. A farmhouse with a wire fence and two bedrooms, a kitchen with the fixtures for one of those brand-new ignition stoves. Roads stronger and straighter and wider than any Bangalore's ever seen.

In fact, her whole city is stronger and straighter than Bangalore. Makes Bangalore look like it was stuck together with cheap glue and broken promises.

We don't know how. She just does it.

It's not that she builds to show off either. We only find out because Yousef steals Joy's bag, and we chase him into the clearing. Run into his back when he stops.

It's like walking in on the earth goddess when she's becoming the world. Banu's no goddess, though. Stares at us with eyes as wide as potholes.

Joy says, "Banu, you're a builder."

Rukshana says, "I told you there was no boy."

Yousef says, "All this time you never said anything."

Not that it matters. In Heaven, everyone finds out everything eventually.

* * *

In Bangalore, posh kids go to private schools. Which means they have a lot of things that we don't have: Textbooks. Electricity. Toilets. Water for the toilets. Water to drink. But there's *one* thing we government-school kids have that they don't.

Rats. Lots and lots of fat, juicy, scurrying, burrowing rats.

You know what rats like to do?

Eat.

You know what rats like to eat?

Everything.

The radishes in the school garden. The registers on teachers' desks. The pipes at the water pumps. The *pais* the little kids sit on.

These rats? They're clever, mostly. (Definitely didn't go to government schools.) We wouldn't have even noticed them if not for a bite mark here, a dropping there.

Gradually, they get bolder. We hear them shuffling behind the walls, catch their pink noses poking out from cracks in the plaster. A flash of paw, a twitch of whisker. Fuzzy behinds disappearing into burrows they dig along the edge of the compound wall or in the sand where the oldest, nastiest boys play cricket after stopping by the liquor store. These rats, they have stealth. Patience. Restraint.

But even the most disciplined rodents can't hold out forever.

Especially when they smell the holiday meal donated by the rich guy who went to our school and miraculously made good. *Besan ke ladoos* and chicken biryani. Proof that he didn't forget the rest of us. Even though he probably wishes he could.

Those rats smell the crumbs left on the silver foil plates and slurps left in the metal tumblers. Grow incautious. Arrogant.

In the middle of the day, they run across the room, humans be damned. And they feast. If they have to cross a desert of feet to get there, scrambling over a terrain of bare toes with their cold, pointy claws, then so be it.

And if ten of those toes belong to Sushila Miss?

Well, charity *ladoos* are worth the risk.

When she feels those toes on her toes, the fur against her ankle, Sushila Miss jumps onto her desk. Hitches her sari around her bare belly in a most undignified, un-Sushila-Miss way. Doesn't care that the desk has been known to collapse when piled with a quarter of her weight. Shrieks a multilingual noise that is pure, unadulterated fear.

"Rat!" She screams in English. And then in Kannada. And then in Tamil and Hindi. And then in English again, just to be sure. "*Ili! Perichali! Chua!* Rat! Rat! Rat!"

Our headmistress, though? She's not afraid of rats.

She's not afraid of anything.

Janaki Ma'am flies into the room, eyes blazing with the fire of a thousand vermin funerals. In her hand is a stick she's pulled from the tree outside her flat. Wielding her weapon, she hits the wall with a thwack. Leaves a mark by the hole where a rodent rump has just disappeared.

It's enough to make you believe that all those enormous stone

Kalis aren't enough to hold the fury lying dormant in a single woman's heart.

Janaki Ma'am turns around, silver hair falling into her face, arms shaking.

"This," she says, "has gone too far."

* * *

In Bangalore, schools are run by men with mustaches like hairy caterpillars, bellies like rubbery balloons. They skim money off the textbook fund—that is, when they bother to check the budget. Stop by the building every now and then to curse the students in all of Bangalore's official and unofficial tongues.

Our school is different.

Our school is run by Janaki Ma'am, who is a headmistress, not a headmaster. Hair the color of wishes, eyes cut like broken stones. She knew our mothers, and sometimes even our mothers' mothers. We know because she told us.

She tells us other things too. When our mothers and our mothers' mothers aren't around and the boys aren't listening. (Which is most of the time.) Truths flat and round that fit in your palm like five-rupee coins.

"They'll say you have to marry. But you don't."

Truths that make our aunties cringe, our sisters giggle.

"See these? Put them in your underpants when you start to bleed. And stay away from boys—especially after the blood starts."

Janaki Ma'am lives by herself in a flat with air conditioning in the bedroom and bookshelves in the hall. On certain puja days—not all of them, but some of them—she doesn't even pray. Instead, she takes a holiday. Reads novels. Makes chocolate cake in her pressure cooker. When she does laundry, she hangs her petticoats and bras on the clothesline right outside her balcony window. Where everyone in the neighborhood can see.

When we ask her about it, she says, "They'll tell you secrets keep you safe. They're wrong. Nothing safe ever needs to be hidden. Nothing hidden is ever truly safe."

We don't just listen to Janaki Ma'am. We watch her too. If we want something, we act like her. Fold our arms and narrow our won't-back-down eyes. Flash our give-me-money smiles.

"They'll say you can't have what you want," she tells us. "But you can."

When other people tell us, we don't believe them. But Janaki Ma'am?

She makes us believe.

* * *

"These rats think they run the place," Janaki Ma'am says, shoving her loosened silver hair behind her ear.

"Might I suggest an exterminator, ma'am?" Sushila Miss squeaks from on top of the desk. It wobbles and shakes. She looks down, calculates. Decides it's safer up there than on the ground.

"With what money, Sushila?"

Even Janaki Ma'am can't hold off a vermin scourge with a government-school budget.

"I can help," Banu says.

"Who's that?" Janaki Ma'am asks.

"I'm Banu," she says.

Now, don't pass judgment. It must be the third or fourth time

Banu's spoken in class. Ever. So how are Janaki Ma'am and Sushila Miss supposed to know what she sounds like? The scrambling scratch of rat feet is more common than the whisper of Banu's voice.

"*You?*" Sushila Miss asks, probably remembering the score Banu got (or didn't get) on our last exam.

"I can build something. To hold the records. To fence the radishes. To block the burrows."

"Please," Sushila Miss scoffs. "This one can't even recite her times table. Tell me, child, what is seven fives? Eight sixes? Thirteen twos?"

Banu doesn't say anything. How can she when she doesn't know the answers?

"You see? Worthless." Sushila Miss starts to wave her hand, and the desk tilts almost all the way to one side. She bends her knees to steady herself. Doesn't fall off. Doesn't get down either.

Janaki Ma'am says, "Quiet, Sushila. Speak up, child."

But Banu doesn't speak up. The silence grows scaly as a rat's tail. The rest of us can't stand it.

"She might not know her times tables, ma'am, but she knows this," says Joy. "Building, I mean."

"It's true, ma'am. You should see the way she builds."

"She's clever, she really is. Just not at school."

"Why do we need times tables anyway?"

Janaki Ma'am holds up her hand. We go quiet again. Like we are the orchestra and she is our conductor. "How much will it cost?" Janaki Ma'am asks.

"Nothing, ma'am," Banu says. "I'll source the materials myself. And the team too."

"Then name your team," Janaki Ma'am says, "and start today."

* * *

The team is obvious—if you need something done, you ask us girls. So Banu becomes our forewoman, our school becomes a construction site, and we become construction workers. None of us is afraid of rats—we've protected each other from much worse than a bunch of overachieving fur balls.

So we build. And we build and we build and we build.

We build a fence around the kitchen garden with long pieces of wire Banu finds in the garbage pile behind the showroom on 100 Feet Road. Banu brings us new pipes for the water pump, sand to stuff into the burrows on the compound grounds. We install shelves using pieces of wood and metal Banu drags from the slum they're bulldozing behind the posh flats made of glass. It feels a little wrong, taking from our own like that. But not wrong enough to make us stop.

Our feet are dusty and our backs ache. Our cheeks are coated in grime, our hands are scraped and rough. Our hair smells like paint and plaster. The seasons turn and the weather gets cold. In the mornings, we come to the work site in hats our mothers knitted and sweaters our cousins outgrew. Bits and pieces of debris catch in the chunky yarn.

"Where'd you get all this stuff?" Rukshana asks.

"Behind the hospital," Banu says.

"In the waste?"

Banu shrugs.

"Doesn't that spread disease?" Rukshana asks.

"Probably to the rats," Banu nods.

"But what about us?"

"Stop it," Joy snaps. "We're builders now. Don't question. Just build."

"Builders? What, like those kids who live at construction sites?" Rukshana asks. She's talking about the migrant kids who have started appearing at our school, skinny waifs with empty bellies and hollow eyes that follow their parents from site to site, hauling and hammering the stone and sand and glass that are transforming Bangalore from a village to a town to a city.

The kids never stick around for long—most don't even claim their free school uniforms, instead showing up every day in the same clothes, pilled from not enough washing, from too much sun. We make fun of their ashy elbows, their bare feet. Their accents, their naïveté. Convince ourselves that we are better than them. Different.

Except now that we're Banu's building team, we're becoming more and more like them. We stop coming to school in our uniforms. Tie old bath towels around our heads, button men's shirts over *salwar* suits. Observe our arms and backs and legs become ropey and taut and tan from lifting and hauling beneath the Bangalore sun.

"This better work," Rukshana grumbles.

"Don't worry," Banu says. "It will."

* * *

One afternoon, at the midday meal, the school ayah smiles and splashes a piece of radish onto Banu's plate. A week later, she gives the rest of us some too.

The preschool teacher convinces the local councilor to buy new *pai*s for the littlest kids, on the condition that she takes the *pai*s home every night to protect them. The first time she forgets, she finds lines of bucked-tooth bites along the red and green stitched seams. The second time she forgets, nothing happens. The bamboo pleats look exactly the same.

The space behind the walls goes quiet, then silent. Sushila Miss goes back to leaving her shoes outside before coming into the classroom. (After the incident, she insisted on wearing closed-toe slippers, even when the rest of us had to go barefoot.)

Even though things are improving, Banu doesn't rest. So neither do we. She brings us plaster to seal up the cracks in the walls and along the floors, paint to cover it all up. She makes us go to the school compound at dusk to fill the newly dug rat holes with more sand.

"We have to stop sometime," Joy says, squinting in the looming dusk, nails black with sand. "Or we'll never go back to class."

"What's wrong with that?" Banu says.

"I'm just saying this can't go on forever," Joy says. Like we all don't know she's worried she's going to lose her first rank. Which, by the way, is about as likely as our school getting new books this year.

"She's right. Look at us," Rukshana says. Holds up her blistered hands, pulls at the yellowed collar of her shirt. There's a hole in the sleeve from where she caught it on a nail. Her elbow peeks out like a cat's nose. "We look like those construction site kids."

"Who's there?" Janaki Ma'am asks. Shines a flashlight at us, and we stand up and blink.

"It's us, ma'am," Rukshana says.

"Ah yes, the extermination team. What are you doing so late at night?"

"Filling rat holes," Joy grumbles.

"Good," Janaki Ma'am says, nodding. "Conscientious. I like that."

Rukshana asks, "What does *conscientious* mean?"

"It means—" Janaki Ma'am stops for a minute and thinks. The silver streaks in her hair shimmer in the flashlight beam. "It means you are a group with a promising future."

That night, all of us work so late we get in trouble for missing dinner.

* * *

A few days before the end-of-year exams, Janaki Ma'am calls us to her office. Most of us have only been inside to collect our free uniforms or to bring our mothers to sign papers that Janaki Ma'am makes us read out loud to them. Sometimes they put their names or, sometimes, their thumbprints.

We've never looked around before. Never noticed the gold-framed picture of Saraswati on Ma'am's desk, face dotted with kumkum, feet lined with freshly picked flowers.

"Goddess of wisdom and learning," she tells us. Like we don't already know.

We've never noticed the steel almirahs full of leather-bound registers with yellowing pages, the drawings from students pasted over water-damaged spots on the walls. Some of the drawings are Banu's.

The power, which has been off all morning, suddenly comes on. The dusty ceiling fan jerks to life. Strains and pushes against the scorching summer air. Janaki Ma'am takes a handkerchief out of the blouse of her sari and wipes her forehead, her neck. Tucks the salty-wet cloth back into her blouse, and tells us, "There's a terrible rat infestation down at the new shopping mall. The one they built next to the airport." Pushes her lips together, sticks out her hand to Banu. "Such a shame, don't you think? About the rats, I mean."

Banu grins and takes Janaki Ma'am's hand. Squeezes it proudly.

Because this, of course, is the surest sign of victory: the rats have given up on Ambedkar Government School. They have moved on to posher places. Places that would throw us out.

Where they went is not the point. The point is that they went, and it's all because of Banu, and her builders.

It's all because of us.

* * *

That afternoon, a straw-haired girl in a faded skirt-and-blouse set shuffles into our classroom. Feet flat and dusty and too big for her legs. Like her body was meant to grow more but just didn't have the strength.

"New student?" Janaki Ma'am asks.

"Yes, ma'am," the girl says.

"Is that another of those construction site kids?" Yousef says. "Or is it a rat?"

Joy smacks Yousef across the face.

"What?" Yousef turns red. Maybe from Joy's hand, but probably from her eyes.

"Don't call her a rat. Here, new girl," Joy says, patting the chair next to hers. "Come sit with me."

"Are you . . ." the girl asks Joy.

"I'm a builder," Joy interrupts her. "Just like you. Now tell me your name."

"Padma," says the girl.

Who, from that day on, was one of us.

5

Frangipani

WHEN WE FIRST MEET PADMA, she's at *that* age. That *useful* age. That age when going to school is not as necessary as working for a living. According to her parents.

Not according to the state. But then, the state isn't interested in people like us.

While Padma dreams of sliding her feet beneath slanted wooden benches, her parents dream of piling her head high with tins full of rocks. Sure, she would only earn 150 rupees a day when a boy would get 200. But even an extra 150 could be enough to send her younger brother to school. A proper school, where teachers speak English. Where graduates get jobs answering phones, typing up letters. The kind of jobs that leave your back straight, your lungs clean.

"Education is the reason we moved to the city in the first place," her father tells her mother. "We never had it. Our child deserves it."

By *child*, of course, he means his son.

* * *

Padma's from way up north of nowhere. (Not that we're from somewhere, exactly. But it's a lot more of a somewhere than

Padma's place.) We know it before she tells us. Can see it from the way her heart thumps like a trapped rabbit's back leg, the way her body curls and tenses like she's still got the jungle wrapped around her bones.

Padma's parents got married a year before she was born. The other families in their village whispered about how Padma's mother, Gita Aunty, could've done much better. Gita Aunty was poor but beautiful, with hair as straight as a freshly pressed sari and eyes the brown-green color of crumbling leaves. When Gita Aunty found out who her parents had chosen for her, though, she wasn't disappointed: Padma's father wasn't rich or influential, but he was kind, never striking her, always asking her opinion before making a decision. He owned a tiny patch of land and, after a few years, rented a tiny bit more. Back then, the soil was rich and fertile, fed by the healthy waters of the river that formed the borders of what little they owned. The land bore enough to keep Gita Aunty and her husband comfortably fed and clothed. When Padma came along, they had enough for her too.

What they didn't have were connections. Or schooling. So when the head of a prominent family gave them a contract to sign, saying that the whole village was going in on a moneymaking scheme, they couldn't read it, but they also couldn't say no.

Which is why they didn't understand why the city men in their growling yellow trucks arrived at their few meters of shoreline and demanded help filling the backs of the trucks with river sand. Couldn't predict that the river would die, and so would the soil. Couldn't know that they and all the other families who signed the agreement would lose their livelihoods, becoming so desperate for cash that, one by one, they'd leave for the city, looking for jobs that would pay them enough money to save their land. Green, vibrant, faithful land that, after generations of giving, had turned as rocky and lifeless as hate.

Gita Aunty agreed to go with her husband to Bangalore mostly because she had heard that there were decent schools. Decent, free schools. Maybe her children could learn to read. At worst, they wouldn't make the same mistakes she and her husband had made. At best, they would know enough to undo whatever she and her husband had done—a thing that, even now, she wasn't sure she could explain.

* * *

One afternoon, Padma and her mother straggle home from the construction site, leaving Padma's father to work an extra shift of overtime. Padma asks, yet again, if she can go to school.

Normally, Gita Aunty would say no. After all, she and her husband have agreed that Padma, who is the oldest, and also a girl, should be a wage earner, not a student. But today, she is tired. So tired. Of everything, but especially of that word. *No.* Tired of hearing it said to her. Tired of saying it to her daughter. Her daughter, who is so much more sensible than she has ever been.

Putting the girl in school, she knows, means more growling stomachs, blistered feet, throbbing shoulders. Less money for rice, lentils, salt. For quilts to spread over the endless parade of concrete floors that has become the rhythm of their lives.

Then again, they are poor. They have always been poor. Which means that they are used to pain. With so many ways to suffer, she thinks, might as well choose the way that hurts the body more than the heart.

"All right, fine. We'll ask your father. But we'll need some divine intervention to make this work," she says. She points to a tree in front of a three-story house wrapped in terraces. "See that tree? The one with flowers shaped like stars? Bring me as many as you can. We'll do puja with them. The blossoms will give our prayers power."

As soon as she speaks, Padma's mother wonders if she's made a mistake. But it's too late—her daughter has already set off for the tree.

Padma knows about uncertainty, about the way time can tip the universe in and out of your hands as easily as river water over rocks. Knows that there is nothing more uncertain than a mother's promise to a girl who is almost a woman.

* * *

The tree's roots begin below the pavement and sprawl beneath the boundary wall of one of the neighborhood's poshest houses, a redbrick bungalow with a shiny blue Toyota parked in front. The tree's branches extend over the railing of the balcony of the house's upper floor, showering blossoms onto the wicker outdoor furniture, the ledge of the double-paned window, the crevices of the details carved into the traditional wooden door.

"Foreigners call it frangipani," the aunty of the house says when she and her husband welcome their friends inside. "We call it the flower of the gods. Auspicious. Lucky."

"Modern house, traditional values," her husband says then. Always on cue, perfectly in sync.

Today, in the second-story sitting room, Aunty laughs to herself, thinking of her husband's odd humor. Runs her fingertips along the mantel where she keeps figurines from Odisha, Kerala,

Bengal. Checks if the maid left any dust. Glances out the window, expecting to see the usual leafy, flowery tableau, reassuring and pristine.

Instead, she sees Padma.

* * *

Although she is surrounded by pavement and walls and locked-up doors, when Padma climbs Aunty's tree, she feels her body dissolve into the textures of home. Bark coarser than piled-up flagstones. Branches stronger than concrete. Leaves softer than piles of stolen sand. It makes Padma happy enough to hum to herself as she places flower after flower into the shopping bag she pilfered from the guava vendor. The plastic crinkles and sighs as though it is singing along to Padma's song, a song she used to sing with her mother and the other women when they worked together in the golden-blue paddy fields, harvesting rice.

A girl making noise? Obviously *that* isn't going to end well.

Sure enough, Aunty throws open the doors and barks, "Stop that racket. And stop your stealing. This tree is private property."

The air stiffens with the moneyed musk of brand-name perfume, purchased duty free in Dubai. Padma startles, her gaze flying into the house, which looks as posh as Aunty smells. Turquoise walls, red-brown floor. A black plastic rack stacked with shoes beside the doors. High heels and sneakers. Floaters and flats. More pairs than she can count.

Padma has never owned *one* pair of shoes. Never considered the possibility of owning more. Has never spritzed glass-bottled fragrances with unpronounceable names on the insides of her wrists, the hollow of her neck. But now, looking at this rack, smelling this perfume, perched on this tree, she thinks that maybe, someday, she can.

"Don't look into other people's homes," Aunty commands. Her Kannada is fresh and sticky, like a new coat of paint.

She can, that is, if she goes to school. If she learns whatever Aunty learned. Another alphabet. Another tongue. A language spoken by women like Aunty, who live in houses with sky-colored walls, earth-colored floors.

"Didn't you hear me? Get down from there," Aunty yells. "Who knows what disease you'll give my tree with your dirty, dirty feet."

* * *

Aunty has been married for thirty-nine years. She and her husband own three cars, two houses—this one and one in the mountains—and a stretch of undeveloped farmland just outside the city limits. They have two children: one daughter, one son.

Before her marriage, Aunty was accepted into a medical school, one of the best in the country. She wanted to go, but her now-husband, then-fiancé, told her she couldn't.

"It wouldn't do to have a working wife," he said. "What would the neighbors say?"

She understood, of course. Her husband had allowed her to attend college, after all. Best not to push it.

Years later, her daughter announced she was doing a PhD program abroad, even though she was already ten years older than Aunty had been when she got engaged.

"What about your marriage?" Aunty said.

"I'll find a husband after," their daughter said. "Or I won't."

While her daughter was away, Aunty began making inquiries

about eligible boys in their community. All of the conversations ended in polite regrets. When one of the suitors—a fair-skinned engineer who had a job offer from Infosys—told her, "It would be difficult to manage someone more educated than I am," she knew she had to intervene.

"Stop this and come home," Aunty told her daughter over the phone. "This PhD is ruining your prospects."

"You mean my professional prospects," her daughter asked, "or my personal ones?"

"You're almost thirty," Aunty said. "Plus you have dusky features. With two strikes against you, why would you add one more?"

"So you think my dark skin, advanced age, and doctorate all make me inferior?"

"I'm your mother. I know what's best for you. You quit this degree, or you quit this family. It's your choice."

That was five years ago. They haven't spoken since.

* * *

"What's going on, Aunty?"

While Aunty stares Padma down, a group of children clusters on the pavement beneath the tree. One clutches a wooden cricket bat. One adjusts his spectacles. One pulls the earbuds out of her ears. One rolls back and forth on pink shoes with wheels at the heels.

"She's taking my flowers," Aunty says. Glowers at Padma's tangled hair, obsidian eyes.

The youngest of the children—branded glasses, digital watch, plastic Crocs—asks, "Why?"

"Don't ask me," Aunty says. "Ask this one. Little thief."

The child, who still takes everything literally, yells up in Kannada, "Hey, you! Why are you taking Aunty's flowers?"

"So I can go to school," Padma whispers.

"You don't go to school?" asks Earbuds.

"Lucky," says Cricket Bat, who still does not understand.

"Don't be stupid," snaps Wheel Shoes, who does.

"But what are the flowers for?" Spectacles asks.

"Puja," Padma says. Although they are all speaking in Kannada, she feels like she is talking in a foreign tongue.

Except maybe she isn't. Because down below, the children nod.

"My mom says those are the best puja flowers."

"It's true. If you use those, you get whatever you ask for."

"Why can't she have them, Aunty?"

"Because the flowers are mine," Aunty says. Still imperious. But maybe a little less sure.

"You have extra, though," Cricket Bat says.

"That's not the point," Aunty says, gesturing at Padma furiously. "What this girl is doing is wrong. She needs to learn. She can't take things from people without asking."

"But you let my mom take flowers," Wheel Shoes says. "She took some just this morning, and we never asked you."

"That's different." Aunty balls her fists.

"Why?" Earbuds asks.

"It just is," Aunty says. How can she explain to these children, whom she would never begrudge a blossom or two, that in the game of life there are two teams: rich and poor? That she and these children are on one team, and Padma is on the other?

"Just let her take some."

"It's for school. Grown-ups love school, right Aunty?"

"That's enough," Aunty says.

The children think so too.

"Hey, you," Cricket Bat yells.

It takes a minute before Padma realizes they are talking to her again.

"Yes, you. How many do you need?"

"What?"

"*Hugalu*," Wheel Shoes yells. "*Flowers*. How many *flowers* do you need?"

Inside her chest, Padma's wanting flickers and flames, her wishing catches and burns.

"All of them," Padma says. Louder this time.

"What?"

"All of them," she says again. Her words taste like sparks. Like smoke.

"The whole tree?"

"The whole tree. And then some."

"Okay," Earbuds says, shaking her head. "Boy, you must really want to go to school."

* * *

Padma watches these children who are her age but nothing like her. Who seem both older and younger than her, wiser and more naive. Who seem to come from another galaxy, another world. A constellation of privilege.

These children who wear T-shirts printed with American superheroes. Sing along to songs by pop stars born in countries the color of ice. Songs that glitter like diamonds. Like gold.

These children who, today, hook plastic bags over their wrists. Hitch themselves onto branches. Fit designer shoes into nooks and crannies. And harvest.

Today, Padma learns more than she will ever learn at our school.

(Because she does, eventually, end up at our school.) She learns to ask. To want. To hope. Learns the feeling of responding to a hunger that lives not in her belly but somewhere else in her body.

But of all of the things Padma learns today, the one she will always find the strangest is this: that city children know how to climb trees.

* * *

There are five frangipani trees on the block. After an hour, not a single tree holds a single blossom.

"Take them," Earbuds says, handing Padma sixteen bags full of flowers.

"I still don't see why you want to go to school," Cricket Bat mumbles.

"Forget him," Spectacles says. He reaches up and helps Padma swing down from the tree. Padma's bare feet slap the pavement, braid swings like a pendulum. The plastic bags full of flowers crunch as she lands.

Before she lets go of Spectacles' hand, she asks, "Why did you do this for me?"

Spectacles looks at Earbuds. Earbuds looks at Wheel Shoes. Wheel Shoes looks at Cricket Bat. Cricket Bat shrugs and says, "I don't know. Just because."

Because in the game of life, there are two teams: adults and children.

Sometimes, the children win.

6

Finding Joy

AN ORANGE BULLDOZER looms over the ruins of Banu's house, mechanical arm still stretched. Like a tiger interrupted mid-pounce. A driver leans against the door of the steering compartment, chattering into a flip phone stuck to his ear. When he speaks, he worries a bulging black wart on his chin.

"What to do? These women lay down in front of me. Right here on the dirty, dirty ground. Can't continue without killing one of them. What's that?" He spits a wad of chewed-up betel out of his mouth. It crashes to the ground like a bullet. "Correct, correct, but these bosses won't see it that way. Me, I say a body here, a body there. Teaches these people a lesson. That's why I'm the one up for a promotion, *na*? I think like a manager."

In his blue plastic sandals and pleated khaki pants, he looks like our fathers. Like our brothers and cousins and neighbors. Like he's from a place that's just as fragile as ours. Where the threats are just as powerful.

* * *

Tears trace soggy paths through the dust layering Banu's cheeks. Her eyes and mouth stay perfectly still, like they're not even a part of the rest of her body.

"We have to distract her," Padma says. "Look at her. She's falling apart."

Banu kicks at the wooden beams that used to hold up the walls of the house her grandfather built. Walls that, for almost thirty years, never once had reason to fall.

Deepa says, "Are you hungry, Banu? Do you want to come over and eat?"

"Or you could draw in your notebooks," Rukshana says. "We could sit really still and pose for you if you want."

Banu tries to smile. Curves her mouth into a shape hollow and empty as a steel pot.

"That's even worse than the crying," Padma whispers.

"Enough. Come, everyone. Let's go," Joy says briskly. Strides off the way people do when they know that they'll be followed.

* * *

Joy takes us to her church, which is really just the old community hall with a new roof. Inside, spiders with striped and bulbous bodies weave webs between the heads of crooked nails. In the center of the room is a table covered in flaming candles. Bumpy wax rivers drip down their sides, honeying the air with a fiery sweetness.

"What are those for?" Padma asks.

"Wishes," Joy says. Digs under the table until she finds a damp cardboard box full of unlit candles. Hands them out to us, one by one. In our hands they are as solid as thunder, as pure as rain. "Light one and ask for something. Make sure you say a prayer too."

"That's who we pray to?" Banu asks, gesturing to a crucifix at the front of the room. A long-bearded Jesus sags off of the cross, pewter eyes turned skyward.

"Pray to whoever you want," Joy says. "That one doesn't mind."

Joy lights Rukshana's candle with the flame of one that is already burning. Rukshana takes it and prays: "Allah, I like being a woman. I do. But do I really need these breasts? Maybe make them a little flatter? Just a bit? Oh, and if you could do something about this demolition. Please."

Rukshana lights Padma's candle. Padma takes it and prays: "Please, someone. Anyone. Vishnu, Siva, Parvati—whoever is out there. Stop these bulldozers. Because if you don't, then my father will leave. And if he leaves, then I have to stay. Because who will take care of my mother and my brothers? How can I leave if he doesn't stay behind?"

Padma lights Deepa's candle. Deepa takes it and prays: "Vishnu, Shiva, whoever you are and wherever you are. I'm getting married. I don't want to, but I don't have a choice. So, now that I've accepted your will and everything, can you make sure the boy turns into a good man? Maybe becomes someone like my father? Someone I can handle, please."

Padma helps Deepa light Banu's candle, but Banu is too busy looking at the renovations put in by the local leader. Instead of praying, she thinks: "This roof might fall at the next rain. If we added a few frets, it would be much stronger. Maybe I can do that at my house too." After a minute, she adds, "I mean, maybe I *should've* done it at my house. Maybe then we'd still have a roof."

Joy takes our candles from us, one by one. Lights their bottoms so the wax becomes liquid, like glue. Sticks them onto the table in a neat line. The rest of us shut our eyes against the heat of other people's wishes. As though wanting is only allowed in the dark.

Finally, Joy lights her own candle, closes her eyes, and prays: "Our Father, who art in Heaven, hallowed be thy name. Father, we both know I'm a woman. So can't you make me one? If you're going to take away my home—my neighborhood, my friends, my house—can you at least make my body a place I want to stay?"

* * *

Joy is the girl you can't miss. Eyes large as a calf's, long-lashed and velvet. Hips like palm fronds that billow and sway. Hair black and glittery, like a strip torn off of midnight's double-color sky.

Joy. The girl of your dreams. Our unofficial queen.

Now, that is. Back in fourth standard, Joy wasn't Joy at all.

She was Anand.

* * *

Anand was never like his brothers. Grew his hair long enough to pin it back with garlands of orange and white jasmine. Made perfectly round chappatis copying the movements of his mother's quick, sure wrists. Stole his mother's kohl and painted his eyes like a film star's. (A 1970s film star, of course. Not one of these taste-less girls you see now, with their bare stomachs spread across the billboards on Mahatma Gandhi road.)

At school, we girls don't care much about what Anand thinks he is or isn't. Even with his braids and his makeup, Anand is much more sensible than Yousef or Vihaan or any of the other boys we know. Besides, he's promised that after he learns how to do thread-ing, he'll sculpt all of our eyebrows for free.

In the mornings, when we're walking to school, Yousef runs behind us and pulls the ribbons tied around Anand's plaits. Won't give them back unless Anand catches him.

"Idiot," Anand says, government-blue ribbon safely back in his hands.

"If you're going to be a girl like us, then you better get used to it," Rukshana says.

"I'm not *going* to be a girl like you," Anand says. "I already *am* a girl like you. Just in the wrong shape."

"Yousef seems to like your shape just fine," Rukshana says.

* * *

Anand's mother, Selvi Aunty, is not like the rest of our mothers. Selvi Aunty is from a district in Tamil Nadu that we always misspell on our geography tests. Tirunelveli? Tiruppur? Tiruchirappalli? A place where people speak a language as cratered as the studs they wear on both sides of their noses.

Anand doesn't have a father—or, at least, a father who's around to protect the house and yell at his wife and do all the other things that fathers are supposed to do. Unlike our fathers, though, Anand's father did not abandon Selvi Aunty for a peg of liquor or a younger woman. Anand's father died in a construction accident, which, after the insurance payment, left Selvi Aunty with two precious things: money and dignity.

But here is the biggest difference of all: Selvi Aunty gave birth to no daughters and four sons.

No one criticizes her lazy womb. No one blames her unclean habits, her unpure heart. No one whispers that her husband is a saint for putting up with this useless lady uselessly bringing more and more useless girls into the useless world.

Selvi Aunty knows that by the standards of Heaven, she is lucky. Mostly, she is grateful. But sometimes, secretly, she wishes she was just a bit unlucky. Not unlucky enough to be married to a drunk, or to be unemployed, or homeless.

Just unlucky enough to have a daughter.

So when Anand learns how to blow the skin off the milk in one perfect breath, to plait his growing hair into coconut-oiled ropes, to keep his face still, his eyes forward, ignoring catcalls and marriage proposals and accidental-on-purpose touches, Selvi Aunty knows she should stop him. She knows she should remind him that he is a boy who will one day be a man who will one day be married to a woman he may or may not abandon. Should stop the quiet notes of speculation that she recognizes as the prelude to a symphony of pain.

But she can't help but think that maybe, just maybe, the gods (and goddesses) have heard her wish. Maybe, just maybe, she will be lucky one more time.

* * *

"Anand is running wild," our mothers say. "Selvi better get him under control before it's too late."

"Too late for what?" we ask.

"You'll understand when you're older," they say. Which is what adults say when there's nothing to understand at all.

Anand is the opposite of wild. He is careful. Deliberate. We see him watching us, measuring, memorizing. The way our hips move when we walk. The way we unleash anger, hold back tears. The unwritten rules of our lives.

All the things the rest of us dread, hate, flee? Anand chases them like Bollywood dreams.

As if the lock that binds us is the one that sets Anand free.

Locks are funny like that.

If Anand is any kind of wild—and we're not saying he is—he's wild like one of those birds rich people keep in cages. The ones that fling themselves against the bars until the door flies open. Or until they break their necks.

Wild like something rare and beautiful and fearless and desperate. Something trapped.

* * *

Fourth standard is an election year. A local leader with a fat mustache starts building a community hall. Tilted walls, leaky roof. Stuck together with sand stolen from the banks of the rivers where our families once farmed.

While it's being built, our mothers tell us not to go inside. So naturally we do, sneaking in after they catch the early buses to work. Anand follows us.

"Hello!" Rukshana shouts. Back comes her voice, "Hello hello hello."

"Who's there?" Deepa yells. Back comes her voice, "There there there."

Then we all start. Singing songs in Kannada, Hindi, Telugu, Tamil, Malayalam. Chanting rhymes we learned in school. Imitating our aunts and teachers and grandmothers. Our echoes tangle and catch and knit themselves into a fabric of sound.

"Which one is mine?" Deepa asks.

"You can't own an echo," Banu says.

"You can own anything." Rukshana rubs her fingers together, wiggles her eyebrows like a shopkeeper. "At the right price."

"Forget the price. That's just philosophy," Deepa says. "I made it, so it's mine."

"Our mothers made us, but we're not theirs," Rukshana says. "We belong to whoever we marry."

She's trying to be funny, but none of us laugh.

"So what you're saying is," Anand says, "that girls can be bought, but echoes can't?"

"Yes," Deepa says. "That's exactly what we're saying."

"You *want* to be a girl?" Rukshana asks Anand. Like she's just remembered he's here.

"I don't *want* to be a girl," Anand said, straightening the skirt he's started wearing to school. "I *am* a girl. I already told you that."

The next day, the monsoon begins. The community hall collapses, caves in like wet newspaper. At least there was nothing inside, the grown-ups say. A few plastic chairs, maybe. Some pots to catch the leaks. Nothing worth anything.

"Nothing except our echoes," Anand says.

We pretend we don't hear him.

* * *

Not long after the election (which the local leader wins) a man in a black robe comes to Heaven.

"Swarga," he says, reading the broken yellow sign outside our slum, tapping the Kannada letters.

"Swargahalli, actually," Banu's *ajji* tells him. "The sign's just split in half."

"Ah, I see," the man says, nodding. "But still and all. This is a place named after the Hindu heaven."

"Are there other kinds of heaven?" Neelamma Aunty asks.

"Oh yes. Yes, there are many kinds. Much kinder kinds," the man says. "Kinds that require just one rebirth."

"What kind of rebirth?" Fatima Aunty says. Straightens her hijab just so he knows that whatever he's about to say, she won't believe him.

"Jesus's kind," he says. "Mother Mary's kind."

The next day the community hall that has no working walls (so it isn't really a hall) and no interested people (so it isn't really a community) is reborn with a big blue cross, a brand-new roof. A sign saying God's Love Prayer Hall in five different languages. Letters crowded and pushed up against each other, like they're elbowing for space.

Selvi Aunty sneaks into the community hall after she knows the rest of our mothers have left for work. On her way inside, she passes a truck full of heavy wooden benches. The man in the robes—who, it turns out, is a priest—is helping some workers unload them.

When the priest sees Selvi Aunty, he stops and says, "Welcome, sister." He wipes the sweat off his forehead with the back of his rolled-up shirt sleeve.

Selvi Aunty likes that. It makes him seem less godly. More human.

"You Christians have holidays?" she asks.

"Christmas and Easter and St. Mary's feast," he says. "We have prayers to say and hymns to sing. We have salvation. We have comfort. We have joy."

"What about schools and colleges?"

"Schools and colleges we have. Scholarships too."

"Reservations?" Selvi Aunty asks. "Special quotas for university, for jobs? For my sons, I'm asking. It's too late for me."

"That and all we have," the man says, smiling his purse-full-of-paisa smile. "That is no problem. No problem at all."

"I see," Selvi Aunty says.

The priest asks, delicately, "Do your children have reservations now, sister?"

"We are SC," Selvi Aunty says. "That's what you're asking, no?"

"Ah, Scheduled Caste," he says. "I see. Well, sister, caste is one thing we Christians don't have. At least not at this church. After rebirth you won't be any caste at all."

When Selvi Aunty doesn't say anything, the priest asks, "Are you interested in joining the flock, sister?"

Yes, Selvi Aunty thinks to herself, definitely. But to the priest, she says, "*Chee*! I only came to see what all the fuss was about."

* * *

When Selvi Aunty was a teenager, her cousin eloped with a Brahmin girl. Selvi Aunty had seen the girl at a function once, sitting with the family that owned the land that Selvi Aunty and her family farmed. Diamonds dripped from the girl's ears, wrists, nose. Rubies and emeralds sparkled along the center parting of her hair. Even her heavy silk sari was embroidered with gold.

"It's all a bit over," Selvi Aunty's mother had said. But Selvi Aunty knew she was just jealous.

The night the two ran off, Selvi Aunty's father woke their family and pushed them out the door and into the paddy fields, urging them to be as silent as possible. They sloshed through the puddles, bent and frightened, their footsteps muffled by the distant shouts of angry landowning men, their breathing choked by the smoke coming off of her cousin's burning home. For hours, they hid in the muggy night, swatting mosquitoes and watching their neighbor's house smolder. Even though they must have been too far away for it, Selvi Aunty remembers the heat against her skin, the curses flying off of the arsonists' high-caste tongues. After sunrise, when the noise died down and they were finally able to go home, the air tasted burnt and broken and defeated. It tasted, Selvi Aunty thought, like hate.

Before breakfast, the whole village knew that the boy's house was a pile of ash. That his parents and his brother and his twin sisters were nowhere to be found. Side by side, crouched over the paddy fields, the women whispered what they knew.

"If you go through the ashes, you'll find the bones," they said. "No question."

But when the police made inquiries, no one said anything.

Selvi Aunty tried to ask her mother about it. But her father interrupted and told her to be quiet. To focus on being grateful that this time, it was only the one house. Warned her that if she ever tried "something like those children did," he would murder her himself.

To his wife, he said, "We need to get this girl married before she makes any stupid mistakes."

"He only wants to protect you," Selvi Aunty's mother told her later. But Selvi Aunty knew her father was only interested in protecting himself.

* * *

In Bangalore, Selvi Aunty's neighbors tell her that caste doesn't matter. Just see how we're all living in the same place, together, all kinds of communities and languages and religions. That would never happen in your village, would it?

Selvi Aunty knows they are wrong. Notices how these same open-minded neighbors keep a separate cup for her in the corner of their kitchens, separate mats for her to sit on, all to save themselves from her pollution. How social workers speak to her tenderly about overcoming the "backwardness" of her "community." How when there's a theft or a murder or a rape in the area, the police come to the Dalit houses first. Make their false arrests. File their false reports.

You don't have to light a match to burn a family's life to the ground.

* * *

At the water pump, our mothers confer.

"They say that priest has fixed the hall nicely," Neelamma Aunty says. "Tin roof and all. Have you seen?"

"Why should I bother?" Fatima Aunty asks. "I've got my religion. I'm not out shopping for another one."

"People like that have come before," Banu's *ajji* says. Groans when she lifts the full drum to her hip. "All of them leave. This one will go soon too. Just watch." She's older than even our mothers are. So when she says things like that, they believe her.

"What about you, Selvi?" Neelamma Aunty asks, taking the drum from Banu's *ajji* before lifting up her own. "No interest?"

"No interest," Selvi Aunty says.

They're all lying, of course. Even we girls know that much. How could they not be interested? Strange men don't come to Heaven every day. Especially strange men with big blue crosses and purses-full-of-paisa smiles.

* * *

Selvi Aunty knows about conversion. Back in the village, her cousin-sister eloped with a Muslim boy. Accepted Islam before they ran away. She still writes to Selvi Aunty now and then. Turns out they did well for themselves. That husband of hers got a computer science job and a flat with a water purifier, a working lift. Both of their children—one son, one daughter—go to college abroad.

Which just goes to show something. Doesn't it?

Then there was Selvi Aunty's grandmother's sister. That would make her what? A great-aunt. After years and years of trying and failing and trying and failing to conceive, the Virgin Mary came to her in a dream. Told her to eat a bowl of cashew nuts under a full moon.

"Plenty of ghee, the blessed Virgin told me," the great-aunt said later.

Six months after her divinely ordained feast, she conceived. Twin boys, no less. Now she wears a cross around her neck and goes to church on Thursdays and Sundays. Still keeps black stone statuettes of Ganesha and Mariamma in her kitchen cupboard, right next to her statue of the Holy Mother.

Then there was Selvi Aunty's youngest brother, the one who was able to study the longest. The first time he came home from university, he announced he was an atheist. Which, if you think about it, is another kind of conversion.

"It's all in here," her brother said, waving a red-spined paperback that smelled like wet fingerprints. The cover had a black-and-white photograph of a man with a long, tangled beard. "It's by a man called Periyar. A genius, this man. He's opened my eyes to caste oppression."

"Hinduism is ancient," Selvi Aunty's father said, echoing

something a Brahmin priest had recently said at a puja. "Its wisdom is timeless."

"What kind of wisdom keeps you cowering in the paddy fields like wild animals in the middle of the night?"

"Why do you come home and start trouble?"

"*Start trouble?*" her mother said. "There's already *been* trouble. He just wants to cause more."

Then, even though Selvi Aunty was only sitting in the corner, cataloging questions she wanted to ask once her parents left, her brother pointed to her and said, "See how this sister of mine struggles. What kind of religion allows such injustice? Periyar says women deserve equal rights."

When he heard that, Selvi Aunty's father sent her to bring water from the next village (her family wasn't allowed to use the local well). She hoped this new version of her brother might offer to go in her place. Or at least come with her and tell her more about all that he'd gone away to learn. Instead, he asked their mother to make him another cup of coffee.

By the time Selvi Aunty got back, a barrel of water on each hip, her brother was gone.

But forget politics, religion, romance. Forget money and jobs, marriage and murder. Selvi Aunty does not need to be pregnant, to please a forbidden suitor. Is not political, exactly, although she feels she could be in the right company.

Above all, Selvi Aunty is a survivor. She is raising four boys— well, three boys, at least—without a husband. Boys who are clothed, fed, and in school. She is doing just fine.

But maybe she and her children deserve more than fine. Maybe we all do.

* * *

When she returns to the priest, Selvi Aunty takes Anand with her. Asks, "What about daughters?"

"Sorry?" the priest smiles.

"How do Christians feel about daughters?" She pulls Anand closer. He buries his face in the folds of her sari, inhales her sandalwood-soap and floor-polish smell.

"All children are the children of God, sister," the priest says. "Daughters, sons. We love them equally, as any good soul would."

Selvi Aunty nods. Presses the top of Anand's head. Traces the center parting between his plaits.

Becoming a Christian won't change the way her neighbors treat her. Selvi Aunty knows that much. Knows that thousands of years of caste oppression cannot be erased by something as simple as a change in faith.

But maybe becoming a Christian isn't about the way her neighbors see her. Maybe it's about the way she sees herself.

At home, she tells her three oldest sons, "Tomorrow we are getting reborn. Wear something clean and pressed. And comb your hair."

She doesn't have to tell Anand. He already knows.

* * *

The next morning, Anand stops by the Home for Destitute Women and Girls. The building is on the main road behind another slum—the one where our mothers say all the useless, no-good thugs live.

He runs up the concrete steps to the first floor, where the nuns have their offices and the destitute girls sleep. Passes through the

empty hallways reeking of bleach and overcooked rice and mil-
dewed laundry. Streaks across the stripes of sunlight that filter
through windows cracked with age.

Anand doesn't know where the destitute girls have gone, but it
doesn't matter. He knows where *he* is going, and that is enough.
Before they can tell him that boys are not allowed, he bursts into
the nuns' offices, lined with donated steel almirahs and portraits of
the Virgin Mary and Jesus. Announces that his family is migrat-
ing again—this time, to a new faith.

The nuns embrace him. Declare that God is good. Praise Jesus.

"A dress is needed," Anand says. "For my sister."

"Lovely," the nuns say. "How old is this sister of yours? How
broad, how tall?"

"Just hold the dress up to me," he says. "We're the same size."

The nuns know just the thing. They pull out the donation bins,
push aside the *salwar kameez* with the broken drawstrings, the
cotton saris faded from drying in the sun. Brush past the collared shirts with torn pockets, the T-shirts with English words
that nobody in Heaven can read. They hold up a dress the color
of snow. Lace and tulle and gatherings. Tight and narrow at the
waist. The perfect fit for someone with palm-frond hips. With legs
as long as coconut trees.

Anand says, "Thank you. This will do nicely."

Then he says, "Praise Jesus. Praise Mary. Praise the church."

"Such a nice boy," the nuns say as they watch him leave. "His
sister is a lucky girl, isn't she?"

Except Anand doesn't have a sister.

* * *

Sometimes a dress is more than a dress. Sometimes a dress is a parachute, a promise of a hurtling fall, an uncertain journey. A soft landing.

On the road behind the children's home, Anand pulls off his T-shirt and shorts. Inhales the tulle overskirt, the lacey sleeves. It smells like starch and talcum powder and mold.

Anand feels eyes on his back and looks up to find Banu dangling her feet over the compound wall.

"You're going to get in trouble," Anand says.

Banu shrugs. "You're the one running around in your underwear," she says.

Anand ignores her. Pulls the fabric over his head, pushes his arms through the sleeves. Reaches around himself to find the cool metal zipper, the line of silver hooks.

Banu jumps off the wall and says, "Hold your tummy in, like this." When he obeys, she pulls up the zipper. Smooths out the skirt, fastens the hooks. Ties the sash, adjusting the bow so the long strings are even, the loops the same size.

"Are you going to that function today? The one where they're making people into Christians?" Banu asks.

"None of your business," Anand says.

A stray dog with patchy fur and a stick-straight tail charges the end of the compound wall, barking hysterically at a palm squirrel. The squirrel scales the wall, leaps onto a tree branch, springs to safety. Once it reaches a high branch, it begins to squeal. Its body inflates and deflates like a balloon, its mouth rounds into a scandalized o. The dog gets bored and trots away, tail wagging.

Anand has been told in science class that when squirrels scream, it is a warning. But to him, it sounds like victory. Like the whoop of a creature who has, against all odds, survived.

Banu pushes herself back on top of the wall and asks, "You don't actually believe in all that Jesus Christ stuff, do you?"

"I don't know," Anand says. "Does it matter?"

Banu shrugs. "I don't think so."

"I have to go," Anand says.

"Okay," Banu says. Before she swings off the wall, and back to wherever she was hiding, she adds, "They dunk your head in the water. I've seen it. Whatever you do, don't swallow. It's holy and everything, but my *ajji* says it'll give you the runs."

Then she leaps off the wall and is gone.

* * *

A few hours later, Anand's mother and brothers line up in the community hall. Fingernails clean, shoes polished, hair oiled. Ready to be reborn. But mostly ready to not be. To not be scheduled caste. To not be reincarnated a hundred times. To not be a version of themselves that they cannot control.

Anand is missing.

"Where is that brother of yours?" Selvi Aunty asks. Her other sons shrug.

Anand's family watches a girl in a white dress kneel before her new God. Her skirt puffs around her like a comet, a cloud. They watch the priest push her face into a drum full of water that may or may not be clean. Watch her raise her head and gasp, stand on her toes to whisper in the priest's ear. Watch the priest smile his purse-full-of-paisa smile.

"Rise and be reborn, child," the priest says. "Now your name is Joy."

When Joy turns to her family, they gasp.

* * *

Selvi Aunty calculates. This morning, she was scheduled caste. This morning, she had four sons.

This afternoon, if she says the word, she will have salvation, comfort. Hymns, holidays. Scholarships. Someday, she may have more than this: Money. Respect. Freedom. A new God who honors her deepest secret, who is willing to grant her most scandalous wish. A God who does not punish women for wanting daughters instead of sons.

If she says the word, she will have Joy.

So she says the word.

"Come, Joy," she says. "Come and stand with your family."

And the word is good.

7

Free

"COME ON BANU," Deepa whispers, after our candles are lit, our wishes are made. She clutches Banu's elbow, picks her way across the cratered ground. Feels for her usual footholds, only to find that they've been covered with rubble and dust and stone. "Let's find your *ajji* and get you to my house."

"She's right," Padma says. "You need rest."

Banu shrugs. Stares straight ahead, her pupils shattered by the ragged reflection of the wreckage.

Padma and Joy and Rukshana exchange a look. If Deepa could see, they would've shot their eyes at her too.

"Banu?" Joy asks. "What are you going to do?"

"What are *you* going to do?" Banu asks. Meaning all of us, not just Joy. Although wherever Joy goes, we go, so it amounts to the same thing.

"We're going back to the protest," Joy says.

Rukshana groans, but Joy elbows her in the stomach. It turns into a hiccup.

"I'll go too," Banu says.

We probably shouldn't let her come with us, but we do. After all, we understand.

They say mothering makes you strong. Turns out daughtering does too.

* * *

Back in the path of the machines, our mothers aren't happy to see us. Mumble about who's going to make dinner, about how we girls will do anything to avoid our homework, our chores. But they don't ask us to leave.

At least if we're in front of them they can watch us. Make sure we don't use the demolition as an opportunity to sneak around with a boy. Which, in their eyes, is a bigger disaster than these bulldozers.

Rukshana's mother, Fatima Aunty, paces back and forth, yelling into her phone. In her blue and green hijab, she looks like a planet bobbing in a shattered sky.

"What do you mean you have other work?" Fatima Aunty yells. "Our *lives* are at stake. How many times have I come out for your useless causes? Come out for us and do something worthwhile for once."

"She's got all these so-called friends who she's always helping," Rukshana says. "Feeding them, giving them clothes, going to their protests. And now when she needs help? These people are nowhere to be found."

"I don't have charge left on my phone," Fatima Aunty calls out. Runs a finger under the chin of her headscarf, like she does when she's anxious.

"Here, take mine," Neelamma Aunty says. Unravels a plastic phone from the waistband of her sari. "My husband says he topped it off yesterday."

"And you believe him?" Banu's *ajji* asks. Slaps her bony knees beneath the cloth of her white widow's sari, growls out a laugh that creaks into a racking cough.

"Oh, shut up," Neelamma Aunty says playfully, rubbing the old woman's back. "My husband's a good one. You know that."

"Who are you calling now, Fatima?" Selvi Aunty asks. She's a widow too but doesn't dress like it. Lines her eyes with kohl, her wrists with bangles. Wraps herself in saris the colors of hibiscus blossoms.

"The local leader," Fatima Aunty says. Flips through a spiral bound notepad filled with cramped Urdu letters. "My union gave me the number. It's just here."

"*Chee*! Don't waste your money on that call," Neelamma Aunty says.

"She's right. Politicians in Bangalore are fully crooked. Won't do a thing," Selvi Aunty says.

"Besides, you think the local leader is going to take a call from an unknown number?" Banu's *ajji* says. Points at our mothers, finger smudged with *rangoli* powder. "Let's go to the office. Show up in person. Only then will they take us seriously."

"What rubbish are you saying, Aunty? The second we're gone from here they'll finish what they started," Neelamma Aunty says. "If we leave, we won't have any homes to come back to, I'm telling you."

"You all go," Joy shouts. "We can stay."

"No," all our mothers say. It's the one thing they agree on.

"We have to ask, and we have to do it now," Fatima Aunty says. She glances over at the drivers, now huddled together on the ground, backs against a bulldozer's warm rubber wheels. "Those people are conspiring. They'll find some way around this quickly."

The drivers, though, don't seem to be thinking about us. Really, they don't seem to be thinking about anything except themselves.

"I thought getting my daughter educated would *reduce* the dowry," one is saying. His skin is a patchwork of red and white, a discoloration that we're sure cost him *his* choice of bride, back when he was looking. "But every family that expresses interest acts like they're doing me a favor for taking her off my hands."

"This is why I'm glad I have just the one son," the other driver says. He's the one we heard on the phone earlier, talking to a headmaster about private school. "Getting him educated is hard enough to pay for. Bribe for admissions, and then tuition. And then all the fees they ask for field trips, books, supplies."

"We paid all that for my daughters. I'm telling you, it's nothing compared to the dowry," the first driver says. Leans his head back against the bulldozer's hubcap and sighs. "You're too, too lucky, only having a boy. Here I am cursed with not one but two girls."

"Idiots," Deepa mutters.

"Ma, calm down," Rukshana says to her mother, "they're not conspiring. They're waiting, just like we are."

"Hush, Rukshana," Fatima Aunty says. "How many of these protests have I taken you to? You think I don't know how this works?"

"Fine, fine, Fatima," Neelamma Aunty says. "You're the activist, no? Tell us what to do and we'll do it."

Fatima Aunty doesn't answer. She's already back on the phone.

* * *

Fatima Aunty is in a union. Sometimes she takes us to protests in Freedom Park. We like to watch the protestors in red saris wind their way down the park's sandy lanes, overstuffed luggage on their head.

"Those women? They've come from all over the state—Gulbarga, Dharwad, Bagalkote," Fatima Aunty tells us. "Sometimes they travel for three days, even though the strike will last just one. At night, they sleep over there, on that lawn."

"By the side of the road?" Rukshana asks, wrinkling her nose. "Ew. Why?"

"Because they are part of something bigger than themselves," Rukshana's mother says. "Because they *believe* in something bigger than themselves. They believe in the struggle."

"But Fatima Aunty," Padma says. "You've been doing this struggle since before we were born. Don't you get tired?"

"If we stay together, victory will be ours," Fatima Aunty says. Which, with Rukshana's mother, is the closest thing we'll get to an answer.

* * *

Our mothers whisper about everything Fatima Aunty *used* to have. A father—until he started a new family with a new wife, house, village, and land. Left Fatima Aunty and her mother and a pack of sisters alone to fend for themselves. They panicked, until they realized they had been doing most of the work already. Plus, the money was easier to manage without a man to gamble it away.

Fatima Aunty had an older daughter, Rania. Still has her, technically. The problem is that she eloped with a Buddhist boy, a Dalit convert who found a job as a driver for an NGO. Not the kind of NGO that sets up offices in falling-down flats either; the kind that gets enough money from foreigners to put ads on the radio asking for *more* money from foreigners. Rania calls sometimes using free Airtel-to-Airtel minutes. But since Fatima Aunty hasn't forgiven her, when they speak, they don't say much of anything at all.

Fatima Aunty had a son who died from a fever that the government hospital doctors said would go away overnight. They were wrong. No one remembers his name. Fatima Aunty refuses to say it out loud.

Fatima Aunty had a husband who wasn't any better or worse than any other husband—except he left her, so maybe he was a little bit worse.

Fatima Aunty says her union has taught her to focus on the present, to value what she has: Her tenth-class pass. Her job, her faith. Her daughter, Rukshana, who hasn't left her. Yet.

When she talks about it, she wobbles her head in that yes-no way and says, "What I have? It's enough."

That's a word we never hear our mothers say. Especially about themselves.

* * *

Rukshana remembers her father's burnt cotton smell, the sharp prick of the whiskers on his sunken cheeks. Remembers how he screamed at Fatima Aunty the day Rukshana's older brother died. Called Rukshana's mother useless, careless, heartless. Accused her of killing her only accomplishment, their son. *His* son.

Our mothers say it would have been better if he had scuttled off in the night like all the other worthless husbands did. Silently. Carelessly.

"When it comes to men leaving," they say, "it's best not to know why."

When Rukshana's father left, Fatima Aunty discovered fissures and craters and cliff-edges inside of her that were never there before. Piled her daughters onto the last bus to her mother's house in the village. Away from Bangalore's splitting pavement, melting tar. To a place where the landscape was even, stable. Whole.

Back then, Rukshana was as frantic as a just-hatched dragonfly, shimmering and eager to test her brand-new wings. The second they set foot in the village, she joined a pack of boy cousins and ran wild. Climbed trees, swam streams. Built castles out of pebbles and mud, slingshots out of rubber bands and twigs. The soles of her feet grew dense and calloused, her arms muscled and tan. After she got lice, and an aunt shaved her head, no one could tell *what* Rukshana was—girl, boy, or something in between. Sometimes, thinking she was a boy, they gave her extra portions of eggs and chicken and dal. Sometimes, thinking she was a girl, the aunts scolded their sons for coming home muddy and bloody and bruised but forgot they had to scold her too.

Rukshana's city memories began to fragment and fade. She forgot the vicious burn of pavement on her bare feet, the defeated rattle of blue wooden vegetable carts crossing ripped up sidewalks, the salty odor of exhaust spewing from the tail pipes of local buses. Forgot that she was a girl governed by a set of rules, a being doomed to honor, silence, submission. Forgot who she was supposed to be. Became, instead, who she really was.

It was perfect.

During the day, at least.

It was different at night. Long after the river breeze loosened summer's chokehold on the starlit air, Rukshana lay awake, listening to the sounds of her mother's grief. Not the stifled gasps that ended alcoholic fights; not the howling wails that followed the burial of a child; not the desperate weeping that trailed a father's retreating footsteps. This was an almost silent sobbing, a shaking originating along deep and secret fault lines, a quaking primal in its need.

A sound that Rukshana vowed she would never, ever make.

*   *   *

One ferocious village morning, when the boy cousins were being punished, Rukshana—who had escaped again, forgotten—sat cross-legged under a tree, sucking on a tamarind pod and watching her mother and her grandmother snap laundry onto a clothesline.

"Enough now," Rukshana's grandmother said. "You've been here long enough. Go back to Bangalore. Put these girls in school."

"How?" Fatima Aunty asked. Cheeks shiny with tears, neck shiny with sweat. "I can't support them. I can't face the community. I can't even face myself."

"Of course you can," Rukshana's grandmother said. "We are women. Sometimes our husbands leave us. Sometimes they die. Sometimes they're there and we're *still* alone. Yet every one of us has survived. What makes you so special?"

Rukshana looked up at her grandmother then. Sunlight bounced off the mirrors embroidered in the cloth wrapped around the old woman's head, making the bits of glass shine like stars. Like the whole universe.

A few days later, Rukshana and her sister and her mother boarded a city-bound bus. Carried a few dresses they'd had stitched by a neighbor, a short stack of rotis wrapped in a torn sari. A phone number of a politician and a stack of crisp new thousand-rupee bills high enough to pay a union leader a reasonable bribe. (Borrowed from another neighbor at a reasonable rate.)

Rukshana's mother wore a black dupatta around her head. Now and then, when she was distracted, she pulled the edge over the bottom of her face, so all Rukshana could see was her mother's kohl-lined eyes.

"Why are you wearing that, Mummy?" Rukshana asked.

Fatima Aunty said, "Because it helps me feel like a part of something. Something bigger. It makes me feel free. And brave. For you girls. For me. For all of us."

Other daughters would've been inspired. But Rukshana just rolled her eyes.

* * *

Rukshana may have forgotten she was a girl, but back in Bangalore, the whole city is ready to remind her. When she tries to sneak away with Vihaan and Yousef and the other boys in the afternoons, one of our mothers always catches her.

"Hey, Rukshana! Naughty girl! What do you think you're doing?" they say. "Go home and help your mother."

"*You* help her," Rukshana says. "I want to play."

"You want *us* to help her?" our mothers say. "Oh-ho! That's a good one. If we help, who will make dinner and do the wash and sweep the floor at *our* house? Who will do the dishes and make sure that all the children come home?"

"You mean the *boy* children?" Rukshana says.

By the time she finishes arguing, Vihaan and Yousef are already gone. There's nothing left for Rukshana to do except drag herself home. She tries to pretend that washing dishes in buckets of soapy water is the same as catching water bugs in the river. That making the dough for rotis is the same as splashing in the mud.

"The work is bad, but the rules are worse," Rukshana grumbles, imitating our teachers, our mothers. "Keep your knees together when you sit. It's so sunny, take an umbrella so you won't get dark. No, no, don't speak up. Just do as you're told."

"It's the way things are," Padma says. "Might as well accept them."

"Plus, it's better than being a boy," Joy adds.

"Is it, though?" Rukshana asks.

* * *

Things get worse in sixth standard, when Rukshana's body begins to bubble and rise. Every day there is some new bulge to deal with, some unexpected change.

In the winter, Fatima Aunty pulls Rukshana out of school to go back to the village and help with a family wedding. On the walk from the bus stop to the farm, Rukshana feels her legs and arms and stomach and heart coiled and ready. Her braid swings back and forth, back and forth. Like even her hair cannot contain its pent-up energy.

But when she gets to the farm, instead of sending her out into the field, Fatima Aunty hands her a bowl full of unshelled peas. "Do these," she says.

Rukshana, too shocked to reply, looks up at her mother with round tamarind-pod eyes.

"Don't worry," Fatima Aunty says. Just as Rukshana is relaxing, she adds, "I'll get you some tea. To keep you awake after the ride."

Rukshana does her work beneath a tree whose high branches

used to be her favorite hiding place. Now, even in its shade, she feels cruelly exposed. While she works, she watches. Watches the younger boys play cricket and fight kites and catch fat black horse-flies with their bare hands. Watches the older boys leave the house on bicycles and two wheelers, smelling like cheap body spray. Watches them come back smelling like wind and music and other people's cigarettes.

Rukshana's aunts hand her an endless stream of chores and chai. After the peas are done, she soaks coriander and mint from the garden in bowls of water from the tank where she learned how to swim. Peels the skin off of gourds from the gardens where she used to chase rabbits and build stick forts. Strips curry leaves from the wooden stems she and her cousins used to use as swords. The leaves fall into the metal colander with a hollow rattle. When she washes the dishes from the meals that she helped prepare, she studies the callouses on her fingers, wondering if they're the same consistency as the ones she got climbing trees and fighting kites.

The day before the wedding, Rukshana's mother brings her a piece of black cotton and a set of pins. Holds the fabric across her palms like a dagger.

"It's not just us, you know," she tells Rukshana. "These Marathis? They're Hindu, and they cover using the ends of their saris. And I read somewhere that some Jews do also. In America."

"Why?"

"Because it makes them a part of something bigger. And that makes them brave. Sets them free."

"Makes them brave?" Rukshana repeats. "Sets them *free*?"

"When I cover, I am more than myself. I am all the women who covered before me. I'm the ones who cover now. So all the things the world wants me to be, wants me to do? That *men* want me to be and do? I don't have to *be* any of them. I don't have to *do* any of them. Because I'm not just myself. I'm more than myself. I'm everyone. And that's what makes me brave. And free."

"I already know how to be brave," Rukshana says. And she does. Fearlessness quivers inside of her like the pulled-back string of a hunting bow. As long as she can remember, that's how it's been.

Rukshana doesn't care about being any braver than she already is. What she cares about is being free. Not the kind of free Fatima Aunty wants. Rukshana wants—not something more, exactly. But something different.

Bravery, she thinks, belongs to girls. But freedom belongs to boys.

* * *

Fatima Aunty doesn't make Rukshana wear a head scarf to the wedding. But that doesn't mean it's over. When they get back to Bangalore, she starts again. "Just try it," Fatima Aunty says. "You can wear it around your hair only, like your grandmother."

"Skirts are bad enough. Now you want me to wear this too?"

"I only want you to try. See what it's like to be a *part* of something."

"Part of something like your union, which has never gotten you a single raise?" Rukshana asks. On especially bad days, she adds, "Part of something like your marriage, which you couldn't hold onto?"

"Strength isn't about holding on," Fatima Aunty says, pretending not to notice how badly her daughter wants to hurt her. "It's about letting go."

Rukshana thinks of the kites she used to make with the boy cousins. Flimsy newspaper cut into diamonds, clumsy twine looped around splintery sticks, bits and pieces of glass woven into the deadly tails. The feeling of catching the wind. The feeling of opening her palm, releasing the string. Watching the cheap paper flap and whirl into the vastness of the sky. A sky that makes everything else feel small.

Her fingers twitch, imagining tying her world to a kite string. What would it take to untether, to let go? To be free?

"It's not that I don't *want* to be a part of something bigger," Rukshana says to no one in particular. "It's that I want to be *myself* first."

This morning, she pilfered a pair of scissors from Janaki Ma'am's desk. Blue plastic handles, blades sharp and shiny. If she holds them open at a certain angle, they make the shape of a kite. The shape of a decision.

Rukshana combs her hair and fastens it into one long plait. Hair that, since that time with the lice, she's never cut. The braid swings across her back when she bowls cricket balls or chases after the ice cream cart. The boys at school say it's the only thing about her that is beautiful.

She knows that they are wrong.

In two fast motions, she cuts. When the braid falls, she thinks it will sound definite, stubborn. Final. Instead, it crunches and crinkles like fireworks. Like something about to happen. Like something flaming and free.

* * *

Fatima Aunty finds Rukshana standing in front of the almirah with her hair cut short, her lopped-off braid curled around her feet.

"What are you doing?" she says, gasping.

Rukshana looks up, startled. Checks that she is not, in fact, hovering above the ground.

"Letting go," she says.

Rukshana's mother takes the braid. Feels the soft ends unraveling. Thinks of all of the years of her daughter's life she is holding in her hands.

"Your beautiful hair," she whispers. But even as she says it, she knows that something about her daughter's life—something more than this long hair—is already done.

Fatima Aunty rifles through the almirah until she finds a clean plastic bag. Holds it open so Rukshana can drop the hair inside. It falls in with a quiet crash.

"Tomorrow I'll sell it. We'll have enough for cooking gas and provisions. And fabric."

"Fabric?"

"For a new skirt for your uniform. Yours is getting short. And tight."

"Trousers," Rukshana says. "I want trousers."

Fatima Aunty looks outside the open door of their hut, where a bunch of boys play cricket with plastic bats donated by the local rotary club. There is a thwack, a scream. The sound of pounding feet, of bodies moving beneath the falling ball.

"That's a six! That's a six!" one of them says.

Another yells, "Catch it! Catch it!"

They are so loud that Rukshana almost doesn't hear it when her mother says, "Fine."

Her mother, who has lost a father. Lost a husband, a daughter, a son. Once, not so long ago, she thought she might lose herself. Somehow, after all of this loss, she survived.

Losing Rukshana, though? That she could never survive.

Fatima Aunty decides that her daughter's choice to cover her legs is not so different from the choice to cover her face. That cutting her hair is not so different from hiding it.

Sometimes, the smallest decisions are the most important.

"Now stop your daydreaming," Fatima Aunty says, "and help me put the clothes outside to dry."

Outside, mosquitoes buzz, auto-rickshaws honk. The boys playing cricket run past, chasing each other and fighting over the score. Rukshana's mother hands Rukshana blouses and towels and scarves and a plastic bucket full of clothespins. When Rukshana snaps the fabric on the line, the air smells of blue soap and sunshine. Of secret languages. Of beginnings.

PART TWO

Development and Expansion

8

Perfectly Clear

THE SUN SLIDES DOWN THE SKY, dragging the heat with it. Timid breezes poke their heads up from the depths of Bangalore's dying lakes, pawing at the air and puffing at the sparse remains of clouds. Dulling the edges of the unforgiving day.

Beyond the borders of Heaven, men and boys fill the street. Suck bhang lassis through plastic straws the color of zinnias, moonshine from bottles the color of moss. Laugh and scream, their speech syrupy with ganja and liquor, their words as mean as riots.

The women, though, are just like us. Housewives with their hair tied up in towels, their hands sticky with caramelized milk and almond paste. Daughters with their arms slick and soapy from scrubbing away dirt, yelling at their younger siblings above the wail of pressure cookers and bubbling pots. Trapped inside their homes the same way we would be if we weren't so busy trying to keep our homes from falling down.

All of us, that is, except for Banu, who can't afford to be like the rest of us. She's gone out to do her *ajji*'s *kolam* route. Tips of her fingers stained red and yellow, forehead smudged purple and green. Pockets of her *salwar* pants stuffed with ten- and twenty-rupee notes, crumpled with fingerprints the colors of Holi.

She's already gone to her *ajji*'s regular houses and done the traditional designs her *ajji*'s taught her, the kind that usually bore her
with their rules and lines, their formulas that feel suspiciously like
school. Tonight, though, Banu doesn't mind the predictability, the
symmetry, the sameness.

Tonight, she wants at least one thing that she can control.

Banu takes the long way home, hoping for some new clients.
Balancing her *ajji*'s powder basket on her head, she calls out,
"*Rang-o-lee! Rang-o-lee!*" Her voice is thin, pastel, a hue too weak
to penetrate the riotous rainbow of sound that spangles the night.

Unless, of course, someone is listening with X-ray ears.

"Banu? Banu, darling, is that you?"

Banu looks up and realizes she is underneath Janaki Ma'am's
balcony. Janaki Ma'am, who can't be bothered with holiday prepa-
rations. Who, instead of taking care of a family, like all the other
women in Bangalore, is taking care of herself. She sprawls on a
weather-beaten wicker chair on her veranda, feet propped up on a
stool, fingers around a cup of coffee. Peers over the top of her wire-
less reading glasses at a Kannada novel borrowed from a friend.

"Yes, ma'am," Banu says, "just doing my *ajji*'s route for her."

"Are you on your way back to your house?"

"Yes, ma'am," Banu says again. Then, remembering that she no
longer has a house, she adds, "Something like that."

"What do you mean, something like that?"

"They're demolishing Heaven, ma'am," Banu says, gulping.
"They brought bulldozers."

"What are you saying? When?"

"This afternoon."

"*Chee!* Shameless people," Janaki Ma'am says. "The notices they posted said we had another month. This city, I tell you. Need them to do something, they drag their feet. Need them to drag their feet, they do something."

"That's what Fatima Aunty says, too," Banu says. "They're all out there protesting. I was too. I didn't want to leave, but—it's just—we need the money. They destroyed our house. And my *ajji's* medicine was inside, so I need to buy some more."

"I see," Janaki Ma'am says. Chews the inside of her cheek. The sunset turns the lenses of her spectacles lavender and gold. "Sounds like I should get over there too. Before we both go, though, why don't you come up for a minute. There's something we need to discuss."

* * *

In the summer of 1975, the orphans in the Home for Destitute Women and Girls began clanking like jars of marbles. Hacking, coughing, rattling. Jangling and clattering their way toward the light. And not the good kind of light.

Doctors crinkled their foreheads and knitted their eyebrows, filled manila folders with scribbled patient records that rustled with defeat. Walked halfway up the orphanage stairs, hesitated, retreated. Whispered words that thirteen-year-old Janaki Ma'am did not understand. Antibiotics. Tuberculosis. English syllables that knocked against each other, hollow and hard.

The nuns lined the girls up oldest to youngest. The youngest pinned jasmine to what was left of their closely cut hair. The oldest wore half saris over frayed petticoats and sun-faded blouses. Everyone clung to each other and tried not to be afraid.

"Where are we going, *akka*?" a little one asked.

"We're getting chest X-rays," the older one said.

"That sounds like it might hurt," someone else whispered. The girls shuddered with memories of the sharp prick of injections, the slow burn of lice shampoos. The littlest ones started to sob.

"Don't worry, darlings," an older girl said to the younger ones. Used her thumbs to roughly rub tears from a crying girl's eyes. "It's just a machine that snaps a photo of your inside."

"Like the inside of my tummy?"

"No, the inside of your chest. Your heart, your lungs. Like that."

"We're getting a picture of our hearts?" Janaki Ma'am asked, her voice feathery and small.

The older girl nodded, misunderstanding. Placed her hand affectionately on Janaki Ma'am's head. "Like a magic camera. Don't worry. It's over in one two three seconds, just like that. Doesn't hurt at all."

But Janaki Ma'am was not *that* kind of worried.

* * *

Banu sets her basket of colors on the floor outside of Janaki Ma'am's door, next to the rack where she would leave her sandals if she owned any.

"Ma'am?" she calls out softly.

"Come, come. I'm in the kitchen," Janaki Ma'am says. "I'll just be a minute."

Banu steps inside and looks around. Janaki Ma'am's flat is a boxy jumble of cluttered rooms lined with bookshelves and framed folk art, a kitchen in the back, a toilet on one side, a bedroom on the other. In the kitchen, dishes rattle, a burner lights with a hiss and a pop.

"Have you studied for your exams?" Janaki Ma'am calls through the doorway.

"Yes, ma'am," Banu says. Wiggles her dirty toes on the immaculate red tiles lining the hallway floor. "But I don't think I'm going to pass."

"I see," Janaki Ma'am says. Comes out of the kitchen and hands Banu a steaming steel tumbler of buffalo milk mixed with some kind of protein malt. Horlicks, probably. Or Ovaltine. "Have you thought about your future, then? What you'd like to do after tenth standard?"

"My future?" Banu puts her lips to the rim of the metal cup, takes a drink. "I haven't thought much about it."

"Why ever not?"

"They bulldozed my house," Banu says, "and my *ajji* is dying."

It's the first time she's said the words out loud. She feels them float up in the air, like the hissing of spray paint before it hits a wall. She waits for Janaki Ma'am to deny them, to say that everything will be all right, that the worst will never come.

Instead, Janaki Ma'am says, "I know, darling. Everybody knows."

"What am I supposed to do?" Banu asks. "I'm all alone."

"What's so wrong with being alone?" Janaki Ma'am says, gesturing around her flat. "I've been alone my whole life. And my life's not so bad, now, is it?"

* * *

Janaki Ma'am was the Sisters' favorite. Or, at least, everybody thought she was. Why else would the nuns pool their money to enroll her, and only her, in the convent school across the street from the government school where the rest of the motherless girls studied for free? Why else would they allow Janaki Ma'am to skip chores two afternoons a week to spend time in the head office, flipping through books the director's nephew sent from the United States?

The books. Oh, the books. Not the battered old textbooks they hand out at government schools or the overly polite textbooks they hand out at private ones. These books had dense covers and woven bindings. Smelled like secrets and wisdom and ink. In Janaki Ma'am's hands, they felt heavy and sturdy as promises—the kept kind, not the broken kind.

Janaki Ma'am's favorite book was an illustrated guide to the human body, its pages sprinkled with English letters, curved and juicy as Karnataka grapes. Each thin, delicate plate peeled away a layer of skin, muscle, blood, bone. The nuns helped her sound out the captions. Epidermis. Scapula. Appendix. Words that tasted strange and hefty and important.

"You'll be a doctor someday," the nuns said. "You'll go study at Vellore. They make lady doctors there."

Like it wasn't a question. Like abandoned girls topped the medical school entrance exams every day.

Janaki Ma'am tried not to get her hopes up. Tried not to believe them. But she couldn't stop herself from studying, memorizing. More syllables, more words. Circulation. Respiration. Digestion. Swallowed up a world in which everything could be illustrated, reasoned, explained.

If I read enough, she thought, I'll be able to understand everything. There won't be any mysteries left.

Of course Janaki Ma'am didn't want to understand *everything*.

She only wanted to understand one thing: how she could be so fiercely accepted, so intensely protected, so effortlessly adored by so many girls, so many women—regular girls like the other orphans, extraordinary women like the Sisters—but not by her mother.

Her mother, who left Janaki Ma'am on the doorstep of the children's home mere hours after giving birth. Who used whatever love she had for her daughter to entrust her life to the goodwill of strangers.

Her mother, who may or may not have loved her but is not around to say which one it is.

Where are the words to explain that?

* * *

Banu can do things that the rest of us can't. She can fix a broken bicycle using only leftover cooking oil, a bent wrench, and a tarnished chain filched from a junk pile. She can sketch our entire neighborhood from memory, down to the number of branches on the tree leaning over Padma's door, the exact angle of the paths we take to Deepa's house, the changing level of water in the drum that Joy's family keeps on their front stoop. She can break the world down into colors and patterns and structures that the rest of us can't even picture.

But for some reason, she cannot do school. In her books, the letters twist and tangle, the numbers tumble and churn. When she is supposed to memorize a passage about our independence movement, or solve a multiplication problem, she can't focus. Finds herself noticing the texture of a piece of wood, the contours of a piece of metal. The way sunlight streaming through an open window gathers and pulls the shadows into new lines. New planes.

It never bothered her much. She doesn't have a mother like our mothers, someone who pictures her having a better home, a better life. For Banu's *ajji*, the hut she owns in Heaven *is* a better life— better than the village where she slept on dried grass and packed mud, better than the joint family farm where she was treated more like a servant than a wife.

Except now her *ajji*'s home is gone. Soon her *ajji* will be too.

"I imagine your troubles seem endless right now," Janaki Ma'am tells Banu. Rifles through stacks of papers balanced precariously between piles of notebooks and unread novels. Underneath, Banu sees the contours of a desk. "Insurmountable."

"Insur-what?" Banu asks.

"Insurmountable," Janaki Ma'am says. "It's an English word. It means an obstacle that is impossible to overcome."

Banu nods and says, "Yes." Because that is exactly how things seem, even though she'd never tell anyone that. Not even herself.

Even now, she says, "I have my *ajji*'s *kolam* route. And I can do construction. I hear they give women 150 rupees a day. It's fine."

"The thing is," Janaki Ma'am says, recovering a glossy pamphlet from the tumble of books and papers, "life can be so much more than just fine."

* * *

Janaki Ma'am was not like the other students in the convent school. Those girls had mothers and fathers and uncles and aunts and grandmothers and grandfathers and cousins and brothers and sisters. Those girls were tethered to a glorious chaos of blood and bone.

Janaki Ma'am, though? She wasn't tethered to anything.

In the children's home, girls like Janaki Ma'am asked the nuns for explanations.

"Where is *my* family?" they asked the Sisters before falling asleep at night.

"In your heart," the Sisters would say, smiling and pressing their palms against a dozen orphanage-issued cotton nightgowns, their brown knotted fingers like tree roots in concrete.

The other girls thought hearts were imaginary. Like princesses or Rakshasas or promises exchanged between heroes and heroines in the films the older girls acted out when the nuns weren't listening.

Only Janaki Ma'am—ever-studying, ever-sciencing Janaki Ma'am—understood that the heart is a real organ, an actual muscle that actually beats in everyone's chest. Understood that the heart is not just a thing but also a place. That the heart has tunnels and hollows and caverns, a million tiny nooks and crannies where blood is stored and released. Where secrets and mysteries can hide.

If the heart could hold blood, Janaki Ma'am reasoned, it could hold other things too. Why not?

Janaki Ma'am understood anatomy. She understood evidence, experiments, truths. She did not understand lies. Or, more specifically, she did not understand that the cruelest lies are meant to be kind.

So, every night, while her convent school classmates lay down on sun-faded sheets, squeezed between cousins and siblings and parents; while her fellow destitute girls stretched out next to her on the floor in the main hall of the children's home, Janaki Ma'am put her hand on her chest. Started to believe that her mother sat cross-legged inside of her, in a heart-shaped cavern pulsing with blood. Pictured her mother's braid swinging as she rocked back and forth, back and forth, singing a song the color of turmeric in warm milk. Felt a tickling buzz of melody somewhere at the bottom of her throat. Imagined her body illustrated in paper-thin plates, her mother's outline visible on the page.

Not that she thought she'd ever see her body sliced thin that way.

Until the day the doctors took the girls to a magic camera designed to reveal the insides of chests, the insides of hearts. Uncover the room where her mother has been singing, rocking, hiding her whole life.

How much will I be able to see? Janaki Ma'am wondered. The color of my mother's skin? The curve of her smile? The tilt of her eyes?

Or maybe, Janaki Ma'am thought, maybe the camera is so powerful that I will see inside *her* heart too. Maybe I will see her secrets. Her longings. Her regrets. The hollowed-out place that formed when she gave me up, the piece she carved out of herself like a tiny crescent moon. Or maybe, I will just see her shadow. Whether she is fat or thin. Whether her hair is curly or wavy or straight.

Whatever it is, Janaki Ma'am thought, it will be enough. It will be mine.

* * *

Janaki Ma'am hands Banu the pamphlet. Banu runs her hand over the cover. Studies a photo of a cluster of students in a courtyard. Girls in jewelry carved out of silver and wood, boys in trousers knit from handspun cotton. Together, they lean over easels, charcoal pencils darkening their fingertips.

"The school of fine arts," Janaki Ma'am says. "It's a government program. Admission comes with a scholarship. Just pass your tenth, and then your twelfth, and leave the rest to me."

Banu runs her finger over the yellow Kannada letters. Turns the pages and listens to them crackle crisply, hopefully. Traces the stapled edges of the pamphlet with her finger. When she was younger, the staple would have cut her. Now, her hands are calloused from building, drawing, *kolam*-ing. They feel armored, impenetrable.

Insurmountable, Banu thinks. Even though she knows that isn't what the word means.

"You're acting like everything is ending," Janaki Ma'am says, "but your life is just beginning. You're fifteen, for God's sake."

"Sixteen," Banu says. "Last week I turned sixteen."

"Still young," Janaki Ma'am says. "Too young to give up. You've survived more than most girls your age, I'll give you that. But we both know that you've done far more than just survive, haven't you? Your drawings. Your buildings. Your—other activities."

Banu blushes and looks out the window at the street below. At the bare driveways that, tomorrow, will be covered in color. Some of it will be hers.

"You have a gift, Banu," Janaki Ma'am says softly. Lays her hand on Banu's shoulder. Banu realizes then that she's been trembling. Beneath Janaki Ma'am's palm, she feels her body still. "You owe it to your *ajji* to do something about that gift."

* * *

The lady doctor smiled at Janaki Ma'am and said, "Such a brave girl."

Janaki Ma'am took off her *salwar* and put on the sea-green hospital gown that smelled like other people's worries. Stood in front of a boxy robot with metal arms and asked, "This will take a picture of my chest?"

"Yes, *ma*," the lady doctor said, "your chest and everything inside."

"So that means my lungs. And also my ribs," Janaki Ma'am said. "And also my heart?"

"So smart." The doctor cupped Janaki Ma'am's chin, kissed her nose. "They've been teaching you quite well in that school, *na*?"

"After it's over," Janaki Ma'am asked, "do you think I could look at the X-ray, Doctor Aunty?"

"No, *ma*. We don't let you girls see."

"Someday I want to be like you, Doctor Aunty," Janaki Ma'am said, widening her eyes. "I want to be a doctor. So I can help people."

The lady doctor's cheeks dimpled and blushed. "Well. In that case. I suppose we could make an exception this time. Only because you are such a smart little girl."

Janaki Ma'am smiled. Did she get her smile from her mother? In just a few minutes, she would know.

The lady doctor left the room and told Janaki Ma'am to take a deep breath.

"You won't feel a thing. Don't worry."

Janaki Ma'am puffed out her chest. And started to worry.

What if, she thought, my mother is not alone? After all, she hadn't asked Sister about her mother specifically. She'd asked about her whole family. And ever-studying, ever-sciencing Janaki Ma'am knew the value of precision.

Who else, Janaki Ma'am wondered, is in my heart?

The way the Sisters tell it, Janaki Ma'am's mother was a martyr, and Janaki Ma'am's abandonment was an act of love. They focus on the details: The perfect roundness of the black mark on Janaki Ma'am's cheek, drawn to ward off the evil eye. The care with which red plastic bangles had been placed on her wrist, silver anklets hooked around her legs. The softness of the pink silk-cotton dupatta wrapped around her otherwise naked body. The pillow tucked under her head in the straw basket woven the way they do in the countryside.

"Your mother knew we would love you from the minute we saw you there on the doorstep," the nuns said, pinching Janaki Ma'am's cheeks. "And we did. You have always been our precious daughter."

Janaki Ma'am had seen the evidence. Had run her fingers along the inside of the basket, held the pink silk-cotton dupatta in her hands. Kept one of the red bangles in her pencil box. Believed the story, believed that her mother is, at most, loving, and is, at least, kind.

But what about the rest of her family? What did she know about them?

Janaki Ma'am thought about the other girls at the orphanage, the ones who ran away, who whispered stories to each other about the lives they left behind. Stories of uncles and brothers and fathers with hands that wanted too much. Of aunts and grandmothers and great grandmothers desperate to feed babies that wouldn't stop growing, wouldn't stop being born. Of cousins and sisters and sisters-in-law who spat rumors and venom to protect themselves from the lives they were almost leading.

In the sunlight, those girls shimmered with hope. At night, they simmered with rage.

Janaki Ma'am had not thought much about the rest of her family. But now, in the face of the magic camera, she began to imagine them. A father with quick fingers, a chin rough with half-grown beard. A brother whose friends aim X-ray eyes at the wrong part of her chest. An aunt with a tongue sharper and more bitter than any vaccine. Imagined the shoulders and elbows and ankles and earlobes of the people who convinced her mother to abandon her.

Were they in her heart as well?

And what if, Janaki Ma'am wondered, it *is* just my mother. What if she hates me for being born, for making her into a woman who abandons children? What if she's forgotten me altogether?

The room flashes with purple light.

The doctor was almost right. On the outside, Janaki Ma'am felt nothing but the hot wet tears rolling down her cheeks. But inside, she ached and ached and ached.

* * *

Janaki Ma'am takes the empty cup from Banu's hand. Banu's whole body feels liquid and full, tingling and warm. She's not sure if it's the drink, or the idea that Janaki Ma'am has given her. The idea that after everything precious in her life is destroyed, there could be something left. The idea that she, herself, is something precious.

"Will you think about it, at least?" Janaki Ma'am asks.

"Yes, ma'am," Banu says. "But right now, I should go back. Are you coming?"

"I'll come, but not now. I need to make a few calls first."

"Okay," Banu bends down to pick up her basket of colors. As she does, her back brushes the garland of dried mango leaves Janaki Ma'am strung around the door frame, probably for a celebration, or maybe just for good luck. The leaves crackle and Banu leaps away, startled. But when she turns around, she sees that they're still intact, unbroken. Whole.

* * *

When the doctor finally called her into the X-ray room, Janaki Ma'am was a mess of swollen eyes, twitching mouth. The lady doctor, who grew up surrounded by parents and grandparents and uncles and aunts and cousins, who knew family only as the people who wanted the best for her, was not trained to recognize these symptoms. Symptoms triggered by the past.

Thinking only of the future, of Janaki Ma'am's healthy future, she said, "Don't worry, darling. The X-ray is clear."

"Clear?" Janaki Ma'am asked.

"*Perfectly* clear," the lady doctor repeated, speaking of bacteria and cloudy lungs. Speaking of pain that can be eliminated with a course of drugs. Speaking of people whose families are real and present.

Janaki Ma'am thought of all the other places where memories could pool. The insides of ears. The edges of eyes. Ran her finger inside her collarbone, the curve where her neck met her chest. Pictured her heart as just a heart, her chest as just a chest, her body as a place where only she resided. A place holding only herself. A place that is her very own.

"There's nothing there?" Janaki Ma'am asked, just to be sure.

"Not a thing. Just look. It's right here."

The lady doctor smiled and showed her a gray sheet that looked like a collection of shadows. Pointed to a smudge in the corner and said, "This is your heart. And these—"

"Are my lungs," Janaki Ma'am said. She began to use words her classmates have never heard: Thoracic. Bronchial. Aorta. Pushed her nose close to the film. Searched the shadows for a shape like a body, like a sari, like a hanging braid.

"You know, there are scholarships for girls like you," the lady doctor says. "I bet you could get one."

No one would find Janaki Ma'am a husband or plan her wedding. No one would stay home to make sure she studied for her exams. No one would tell her the secrets mothers tell daughters, would fight for her the way our mothers fight for us.

But no one would tell her to quit studying to get married either. No one would tell her that sending a girl to college is a waste of money. A waste of time.

Maybe no one would tell her she could do anything she set her mind to. But no one would tell her she couldn't either.

The road ahead was perfectly clear.

* * *

Janaki Ma'am leans over the veranda railing and watches Banu. The girl's curly hair is clumsily plaited, the ends dry and split. Banu's collarbones jut out beneath the jagged cut of her *salwar* blouse—a shirt that Janaki Ma'am is sure used to belong to Joy— like a pair of calcified wings.

Janaki Ma'am, who never had a mother. Never had siblings, neighbors, friends that might as well be family. Janaki Ma'am, who is nothing like the rest of us.

But who is maybe a little bit like Banu.

9

Walls

JUST BEFORE DUSK, the drivers step out of the bulldozers and into the graying evening buzzing with mosquitos. Oily hair, thick mustaches. Teeth stained brown by bidis and tea. Vests with fluorescent stripes, "BBMP" painted in the front in bold capital letters. Seeing them all together, here, we notice they are different only in the tiniest details. One has those maroon patches around his eye and down his cheeks. Another has a wart on his chin. The last one limps, which is maybe why he wears scuffed-up sneakers instead of plastic sandals.

Before they lumber off, the one with the wart says, "We'll be back in the morning."

"So will we," Fatima Aunty yells, throwing her fist in the air like her union taught her to do.

"If you come back tomorrow, we'll call the police," the one with sneakers says. "We've had enough of your nonsense."

"Useless people," the one with the wart says. "What do you think you're going to do, stop the city?"

The one with the wrong skin is gentler. He says, "Don't waste your time on this. Move out of your house, find somewhere else to stay. Somewhere better."

"Somewhere *else*? Somewhere *better*?" Selvi Aunty says, snorting. "If we had somewhere better, you think we'd be living here?"

"Then get yourself new husbands," the one with the wart says. "Men who work like we do and take care of our families."

"My husband would *never* do what you do," Neelamma Aunty says. Out of all of the mothers here, she's the only one with a husband left to defend. "Destroy people's lives for money? We'd rather starve."

"Starve then. We're leaving."

The drivers float away, our mothers' curses pelting them like asteroids.

* * *

Without the drivers there to argue with, we get quiet—except for our stomachs, which growl like rusty engines. None of us women have been home long enough to massage flour into rotis, sizzle batter into *dosas*. To conjure chutney out of curry leaves, curry out of vegetables paid for with counted-out change.

"I'll make something quickly, quickly," Neelamma Aunty says. "*Ajji* will help me."

"Don't be silly," Fatima Aunty says. "I went shopping this morning. Why bother yourself when my kitchen is full?"

"*Chee*! Today of all days I can't suffer through your bland, healthy food," Selvi Aunty says. She's not wrong—ever since Fatima Aunty got a job as a health worker, it seems like she's forgotten all about ghee, oil, and salt. Masala too. "I'll make us some spicy, spicy curry. Like they make in my village."

"By the time they're done arguing, we'll starve to death," Deepa mumbles.

"Maybe not," Padma says, sniffing the air. "Doesn't it smell like chicken?"

Banu runs up then, finally back from her *kolam* route. "They pulled up in a big white bus," she says, panting. "They have pots and pots of something. Biryani, I think. Chutney too."

"What are you saying?" Deepa asks, stiffening. "The city brought us dinner?"

"No, not the city," Banu says, "the engineers."

* * *

If you ask us girls, we'll tell you Bangalore's a city with too many problems. Too many bars packed with too many men. Too many women with too many children. Not enough roofs and too much rain.

If you ask our mothers, they'll tell you Bangalore has just one problem: engineers.

When our mothers were younger, they couldn't walk ten meters without stumbling into a lake or a garden or a two-hundred-year-old banyan tree. Electronic City was a vast and sprawling pasture, a sleepy shepherd's grazing ground, a village where farmers' wives went hunting for grass for their cows, husbands for their daughters. Even the air force camps and the research parks had more leaves than bricks, more green than gray.

Then the engineers who worked for the air force and research parks started inventing this, programming that. Founding this company, buying that one. Towering glass buildings sprouted in the grass where sheep used to graze. Highways paved over the husband-hunting grounds.

We heard our mothers complain, but we never understood. How could we, when we'd never seen an actual engineer? To us, engineers sounded like wild animals, exotic birds, a species not entirely our own. Visitors from foreign planets who spoke in clipped and angry tongues laced with furious consonants, with frantic vowels.

In eighth standard, we found out they were people, just like us, but richer. People who showed up at our school two or three times a year. Handed out T-shirts that we gave to our mothers to tear up into rags. Passed out chocolates we gave to our younger siblings when there wasn't enough food at home. Played games with us that were supposed to give us confidence. Since they talked mostly in English, we didn't know what they were saying, or what we were supposed to do. Which didn't make us confident at all.

* * *

Tonight, in the shadow of the bulldozers, there are no games or clothes or candies. Instead, there are tall metal pots of aromatic rice, shiny silver stacks of crimped foil plates, plastic tubs of raita made with mint and cumin and salt.

These engineers are mostly women. Kumkum in their hairlines, bindis on their foreheads. Matching strands of jasmine fastened to their pinned-up hair. They wear T-shirts with company logos over tight, pressed jeans. Sit cross-legged on the pavement by the main road and serve us orange and yellow biryani dripping with juicy pieces of chicken, fat chunks of carrot. We mix the rice with spicy green chutney and plain yogurt that we squeeze from plastic bags. Push burnt black cloves and cardamom pods to the sides of our plates, pop the chilis in our mouth spicy and raw.

"This is a protest," Fatima Aunty mutters. "Not a picnic."

"Hush, Ma," Rukshana says. "It's free food. Just eat."

"Lucky thing they came, isn't it? I don't know how we would've managed otherwise," Neelamma Aunty says, pushing some of her raita onto an empty spot on Padma's plate. When Padma objects, she says, "Eat, eat. It's good for the bones."

"That's true," Rukshana says. "How did they know?"

"I told them."

That voice. We know that voice.

"Janaki Ma'am!" Joy says.

"If you think this is an excuse for skipping your tenth-class exams, you're dead wrong," our headmistress says. She reaches into the hemp bag slung over her shoulder and pulls out a handful of water bottles. The good kind with the green lettering, the kind we've seen foreigners drink on the street outside of five-star hotels.

"Seriously?" Rukshana says under her breath.

"I heard that, young lady," Janaki Ma'am says, handing Rukshana a bottle. Rukshana looks down at her feet. Janaki Ma'am is the only one who ever makes her feel guilty. "How do you think you're going to survive crises like this without an education?"

"All the mothers in Heaven are surviving," says Deepa, who doesn't go to school, "and they barely studied at all."

"I know, darling." Janaki Ma'am kisses Deepa on the top of her head and says, "I was their headmistress too."

* * *

Bangalore used to be a place where things grew. Trees, bushes, flowers. Tomatoes if you planted them in January. Cilantro and mint any time of year at all. A place where the soil pushed and the sun pulled life up, up, up.

After the engineers came, Bangalore grew other things. Buildings, overpasses, toll roads.

And walls. Lots and lots of walls.

Brown concrete fortresses around the brand-new flats and offices and shopping malls that would never let us inside. Bracing themselves against the noise of the traffic, the smell of the cars. Against the rattle and clatter of girls like us. Girls who make all the noise that is supposed to be made by boys.

We didn't think much about the walls at first. Forgot that they were there.

Until Janaki Ma'am told us we should scale them.

Because eighth standard wasn't just the year of the engineers. It was also the year of Janaki Ma'am. Specifically, it was the year Janaki Ma'am started finding excuses to teach us, lecture us, push us. Made us believe that we could be more than what everyone else thought we could be. What we thought we could be.

"If you're all going to pass your tenth-standard boards, we have to start now," Janaki Ma'am said. "That's right, two years ahead. I know to you lot that seems like an eternity, but believe me. It's going to go by in a flash. A blink of an eye, I tell you."

"Who says we're *all* going to pass?" Rukshana asked.

"Who says we all *want* to pass?" Vihaan asked.

"Of course you want to," Janaki Ma'am said. Used her sari to wipe sweat from where it pooled in the valleys along the edges of her hair. "Look around you. Call centers, IT companies, multinationals. The Indian space program is just down the street. We just sent some contraption to Mars for heaven's sake. *Mars.* How are you going to work in any of these places if you don't even have a tenth-class pass?"

"You really think we could work at ISRO?" Padma asked timidly.

"Of course you can!" Janaki Ma'am said, pulling out the English language newspaper from her purse to show us a photo of a group of chubby aunties giggling, hugging, taking selfies with their fancy phones. They wore saris and bindis, long strands of jasmine in their hair. It looked like they were on the set of an action film. "See this? These are the Mars scientists. The ones who launched that—that—well, that something or other. All Indian. Mostly *south* Indian. Just like you."

"They're *nothing* like us," Rukshana said.

But not loud enough for Janaki Ma'am to hear. We liked her too much for that.

* * *

Eighth standard was the year of Janaki Ma'am, of the Mars rover, of the engineers. But it was also the year of Kalla.

That same year, a few days before the skies thickened and burst with pre-monsoon rain, words thickened and burst onto the city's walls.

Specifically, the words

KALLA WAS HERE

The wall outside the BSNL office, which used to be the telephone exchange. The wall outside the glass-walled flats, which used to be an empty lot. The wall outside the shopping mall, which used to be a slum like ours. The wall outside the five-star hotel, which was always there but never used to be this full.

"*Kalla*? What does that even mean?" Rukshana asked when we stopped to look at it. Partly because we wanted to, and partly because the longer we took to get home, the longer we didn't have to do our chores.

"It's Kannada for thief," Padma said. She grew up in the country so she knows these things.

"Thief," Rukshana repeated. "Is that supposed to be tough or something?"

"What's tough about a bunch of letters on a bunch of walls?" Joy asked.

Two days later, the murals started. Sprouted and bloomed and spread like pumpkin vines. Spray-painted portraits of women in nighties getting water from a pump. Of auto-rickshaw drivers with chubby mustaches and skinny arms. Of children with sand-colored hair selling plastic pens on street corners.

And always, across the bottom,

KALLA WAS HERE

Letters tall and blue and disciplined. Straight-backed as soldiers. Secret as spies.

* * *

The engineers don't just bring dinner. They also bring the foreign lady.

Eyes as green blue as a parrot's tail. Wrists fair as unboiled milk. Hair as yellow as the pencils our teachers tell us to use when we're drawing sunlight.

The foreign lady's got a camera covered in dials and switches and lights. Every time she takes a picture, she rearranges her whole body, kneeling and crouching and leaning.

We watch her as she frames our lives—or, at least, what's left of them. Vihaan's uncle cycling through the rubble, a handkerchief over his mouth to block out the bursts of gray and brown and red dust that rise up beneath the tires. Yousef's mother rifling through the rubble, wet kohl running down her cheeks, swallowing her sobs with loud, choking gasps. Padma's sleeping brothers curled up like starving kittens in the shade of a coconut tree.

We watch what she doesn't frame too. Fatima Aunty on her cell phone, wagging her finger in the air, barking out demands. Neelamma Aunty telling a dirty joke then throwing her head back and laughing while Selvi Aunty giggles behind her hand. Janaki Ma'am handing out water bottles to the good men, the fathers and brothers and cousins who are back from their shifts at work, ready to listen and help where they can.

"She's getting it all wrong," Joy says.

"She's getting *us* all wrong," Rukshana says.

In Heaven, we are used to treating our girlhood like a territory that must be defended, staving off intruders and fending off disasters with each strategically plotted move.

In our mothers' eyes, in our eyes, it's a war we have a chance of winning. But in the foreign lady's photographs, it's one we've already lost.

* * *

The murals kept appearing, a new one every night. A garden full of birds and trees on the wall in front of the pub that's just come up

on the main road. Young girls selling roses on the wall in front of
the last nut-and-screw warehouse on Mandappam Street. And on
every mural, marching, saluting: KALLA WAS HERE.

Vihaan and Yousef started showing up to school with blue paint
under their fingernails, blue stains on their shirt sleeves.

"Graffiti is a punishable offense," Yousef announced. Stretched
his hands to give us a glimpse of the blue islands on his wrists.

"Where'd *you* learn such big words?" Rukshana asked.

"From the papers," Vihaan said. His uncle owns the used paper
shop, so Vihaan reads the headlines from the day before. "Didn't
you hear? Kalla did a mural *inside* the Royale," Vihaan says.

"What, that fancy hotel where all the foreigners stay?" Joy said,
like she does whenever anyone mentions anything posh. Tore
her eyes away from her own purple finger nails. She said she only
painted her left hand because it's how the film stars do it, but we
were pretty sure she ran out of paint.

"How'd he get inside?" Padma asked.

"No one knows," Yousef said. Shook the article and said, "Here.
Listen. 'While rumors are spreading that Kalla is from the local
slum known as Heaven, authorities are doubtful.'"

"They're not the only ones," Joy said.

"'The quality of the art shows a'—wait, what's this word?" Yousef
leaned over Joy's desk with the paper, but Rukshana snatched it
away.

"'The quality of the art shows a sophistication normally associated with classically trained artists, rather than slum dwellers,'"
Rukshana read. "'The local police chief says, "Whoever he may be
or whatever walk of life he comes from, Kalla is breaking the law.
Make no mistake: when we apprehend him, he will face serious
consequences.""'"

"How do they know it's a he?" Banu asked.

"Although I am glad to see you reading the paper, Kalla or no Kalla, your year-end exams are just a month away," Janaki Ma'am said, sweeping into the room. The air swished with the cotton-silk of her sari, the yellow-edged pages of worksheets in her arms. "Kamala Miss is late today, so I'm taking your social studies class."

We all groaned, but secretly we were pleased. None of us liked Kamala Miss. She smelled like raw onions and bidis. She said the bidi smell was from her useless husband's useless habits, but Joy and Rukshana have both seen her smoking behind the school. ("It's okay if she does it," Joy used to say, "but she shouldn't *lie* about it.")

"Janaki Ma'am," Yousef yelled out, "you think Kalla could be from Heaven?"

"Possibly," she said. Leaned back on the desk like she was really considering the question. Which was something we didn't expect. "Just because something is illegal doesn't always mean it's wrong."

* * *

The morning after Kalla broke into the Royale, the water pump stopped working again. Our mothers crouched along the main road, calculating how many more dishes they could wash, how many more vegetables they could clean, if the water truck didn't show. Wondering if today was the day they'd finally be fired from their jobs for being late again.

So they did what they always did when they got worried: they gossiped.

"Selvi, have you found a girl for that son of yours?" Neelamma Aunty asked. Selvi Aunty had already married off Joy's two oldest brothers. Traditionally, the last brother should wait until Joy's wedding.

But then, Selvi Aunty isn't one for tradition.

"He found someone himself," Selvi Aunty said. An ancient city bus slowed down in front of them and its door folded open. A man with a mustache and skin the color of burnt sugar braced himself against the step and yelled out, "Mainroadmainroadmainroad." Our mothers waved him off.

"You like her?" Fatima Aunty asked.

"She's a nice girl. Wants to go for her graduation in nursing," Selvi Aunty said.

"Same community?" Neelamma Aunty asked. "Known family?"

Selvi Aunty nodded and said, "From our church."

"That's lucky," Fatima Aunty said. Wiped an arm across her forehead. Thought of her daughter Rania, probably, with her Buddhist husband.

"Only problem is this rumor about that graffiti boy. What is his name again? *Kanna*?" Selvi Aunty said.

"Kalla," Neelamma Aunty said. "What rumor?"

"That he's from Heaven," Fatima Aunty said. "I've heard it too. They even wrote about it in the newspaper this morning."

"What, they think your son might be Kalla?" Neelamma Aunty asked. "That dear boy. How could he be doing this painting nonsense when he's always, always studying?"

"That's the problem," Selvi Aunty said. Reached back to adjust the jasmine pinned in her hair. It was a long strand, the ten-rupee kind. One of her older sons must've given her some extra money. "The papers say Kalla's intelligent. My son just finished engineering, came third in his class. Good at drawing too—has to sketch roads and buildings and things for his classes. Doesn't help that he doesn't have a father around."

"Ridiculous," Fatima Aunty said. "Better to have a mother like you than a father like *some* of the fathers I know. My husband, for example. Wherever he is."

"We'll see. Our family is a much better match than what they've already been offered," Selvi Aunty said. "They'll come around."

The water truck pulled up then, smelling like burnt rubber and exhaust. Before the driver even had time to turn off the engine, our mothers surged forward, swinging their sari-covered hips at each other like acrylic maces.

"Took you long enough," Fatima Aunty yelled at the driver.

"If they don't come around, you won't have any problem finding someone else," Neelamma Aunty said to Selvi Aunty. She was the first to put her vessel under the open tap. Water rattled against the side of her drum's fluorescent-yellow sides. Selvi Aunty pressed up against Neelamma Aunty's back, making sure she'd get to the water next.

"None of us had to deal with any of this nonsense," Selvi Aunty said. When she saw Neelamma Aunty's drum was full, she shoved hers under the gushing spout. "Romance, graffiti."

"Can you imagine what our mothers would have said?" Fatima Aunty said, shaking her head. "Mine would've married me off to someone else just to teach me a lesson."

"Banu, darling, why aren't you at school?" Neelamma Aunty said.

Our mothers turned and saw Banu running to the truck, bright orange vessel balanced on her head like a basket of *rangoli* powder. She was already wearing her uniform, backpack, plaits, and semi-shined shoes.

"Give," Selvi Aunty said. Roughly took the drum from Banu's hand and shoved it under the pump after her own. "I'll deliver this to your *ajji*. You go off to school now."

"Yes, Aunty," Banu said. Hitched her bag over her shoulder and ran off. Tripped over a hole in the path and went flying. Caught herself before she landed in a puddle, but not before she splashed mud all over her skirt, her bag, her almost-shined shoes. She looked up at our mothers, eyes widening quicker than the brown stain stretching across her uniform.

"Just go," Fatima Aunty told her. "You're in enough trouble for being late. This much won't do anything."

Banu nodded, turned, and ran again.

"Watch where you're going this time!" Neelamma Aunty said. Even though she knew it was useless.

"At least none of us have to get *that* one married," Selvi Aunty said, shaking her head.

"That one would be lucky to get a boy like this Kalla fellow," Neelamma Aunty said.

"Don't say such things," Fatima Aunty said, finally sticking her pot under the tap. "That poor girl."

"At least Kalla would leave her alone at night," Neelamma Aunty said. Cackled wickedly. "He'll be busy doing other things."

"Neelu!" Selvi Aunty said.

Our mothers' laughter sloshed and gurgled against the sides of the wasted morning.

* * *

"We should stop her," Joy says, staring at the photographer.

"Why? She's not doing any harm," Padma says, shrugging.

Rukshana balls her hands into fists. "She's not even asking permission. It's like she thinks she can do whatever she wants with us. Like we don't even exist."

"Someone's with her," Padma says. "Wait a minute. Is that—"

"It *is*," Joy says. Sucks her teeth and yells, "Banu! What are you bloody doing?"

Banu hovers around the photographer like a minor goddess, the kind they put in Hindu myths to rearrange a crumbling world into something closer to divine. Takes the photographer's hand and leads her through the wreckage. Points out the cracked facade of a framed family photograph, the cracked remains of a ceramic pickle jar. Adjusts a piece of tin so the shadows rearrange themselves into another image. A different kind of light.

"She's going to use her photographs to help us," Banu tells us. Pulls the photographer gently by the elbow, showing her a new frame. "At least, that's what I think she said. She talks funny."

"If she wants to help, then tell her to call the city," Rukshana says. "Tell her to talk to them in that accent and to call off the demolition."

"That's right!" Joy says. When Padma doesn't say anything, Joy turns to her and says, "Come on. Tell your friend, no?"

Padma doesn't answer. Just watches Banu drag the photographer through the ruins.

* * *

A few nights after the newspapers wrote about Kalla, Padma went to Deepa's house for dinner. It's something most of us do at least once a week. Deepa's father only gets back after he drops off the last of the engineers from the restaurants and bars they fill up after work. Puts up with the drunken directions, the whiskey breath, all in hopes that the alcohol will loosen purse strings, that the engineers will hand over too much money and not ask for change. Neelamma Aunty does the stitching for the whole neighborhood, delivering the clothes after seven o'clock, when the posh people get back from their offices. So Deepa's kitchen is always full of food and empty of grownups.

The power was gone again. Without the hum of the ceiling fan to thwart them, Bangalore's night noises crowded into the house, haunted and brash. Crows fought on the rooftops. Bats swooped leathery circles in the sky. Bug-eyed geckos clicked and chirped, their heaving bodies the color of ghosts.

"It's like a spooky movie," Padma said, lighting a stub of candle she brought from her house. The flame dripped a waxy puddle into the humid darkness. "Like the scene just before the hero rescues the lady. And then the item number starts."

Deepa laughed and said, "No heroes coming tonight. This is Heaven, remember?"

"That's okay," Padma said. "Janaki Ma'am gave us too, too many math problems anyway." She tapped the cover of her notebook so Deepa could hear. "No time for romance until after boards."

Just then, the sky turned blue and red and shrill with sirens. A man-shaped shadow flung itself across the doorway. Cotton collared shirt. Short, short hair. Pants gathered up in a funny way, like they were made for someone with an entirely different set of legs.

Padma shrunk into herself. Deepa grabbed the iron roti pan. Wielded it like a weapon. The sirens grew closer, lights flashed quicker. Footsteps and shouts echoed in the allies.

"Please," the shadow said.

Padma lunged like a mother tiger, but Deepa grabbed her ankle, pulled her back.

"Banu?" Deepa asked. "Is that you?"

"Yes," Banu whispered. "It's me."

Banu, our Banu, was dressed like a construction worker. Hair coiled under a cotton towel. Faded men's shirt buttoned over her nightie. Nightie pulled like pajamas between her knees.

Hands covered in blue paint.

Padma broke into a smile. "Kalla?"

Banu nodded. Her cheeks glowed red as AC buses.

"Come," Padma said, dragging Banu out of the candle's thin circle of light, "into the shadows where they can't see you."

"Quickly," Deepa hissed. Pulled Banu down to the floor.

"I'll get the shirt," Padma whispered. "Get the cloth off her head."

Padma undid the buttons on Banu's paint-splattered shirt and threw it in a shadowy corner. Tucked Banu's nightie around her blue-tinged feet, shoved a plate of half-eaten roti into her hand.

Deepa yanked away the towel. Loosened Banu's curls, the length and weave of innocence, the texture of unlit skies. Fingered the ends of Banu's hair and said, "There's paint."

The footsteps grew closer, the men's voices louder. Padma's eyes swept the room. She pulled a comb from beneath a pile of bedsheets and tugged it through Banu's curls. Twisted them into an urgent braid.

"Ow," Banu squealed.

"Quiet," Deepa said, just as Padma said, "It's for your own good."

Outside, men shouted and panted, like they'd smoked too many bidis. Government-issued boots thumped along the dusty path.

"Don't say anything," Deepa told Banu. Which she probably didn't have to do, since Banu never has much to say.

Unless, apparently, she has a bucket of paint and a concrete surface.

The policemen aimed the flashlight into the room, setting the shadows tilting and swaying. Light bounced off the metal pots lined up on the floor, the switch for the fan, the exposed and useless wires.

"Who's there?" the policeman asked menacingly.

"Namaskara," Deepa said, smiling. Talked to the wall even though the men were standing in the doorway. "Would you like some *dosa*, officer?"

"It's roti, darling," Padma said loudly.

"Oh dear," Deepa said. "It's so difficult to be blind."

Banu giggled until she felt Padma violently tug her braid. Pretended to cough so it sounded less like she was laughing and more like she was being choked.

The man grunted and said, "It's just a bunch of useless girls."

"What are you doing alone?" the other officer said. "Don't your parents know that there's a dangerous criminal on the loose?"

"Oh!" Deepa said, clutching her chest. "Is there?"

"Yes," he said. "And he just ran past your house."

"You'll find him, though, won't you, officer?" Padma asked.

"Definitely," the first officer said. Stuck out *his* chest like one of the pigeons that eat the stale roti the temple women put out for good luck. "Our job is to protect you."

"Well, we can't very well do that here," the other officer said.

Backed out of the house, his shadow dark as a buffalo. "Did you see anyone running?"

"Someone went that way," Deepa said. "Under the overpass."

"Yes, yes," Padma said. "I think I saw blue on his hands."

"Come on, then," the officer said. "Let's go."

"Be safe," the other officer said. "If you see anything, call us."

"Of course, sir," Padma said.

Outside Deepa's doorway, the policemen's heavy footsteps, heavy voices, dissolved into the night. Heaven settled back into the lazy lights of blinking fireflies and three-wheeler headlights, the sleepy sounds of pressure cookers hissing and pots banging.

"I knew it couldn't be Yousef," Padma said.

"'A sophistication normally associated with classically trained artists,'" Deepa said, quoting the newspaper. "Of course. It couldn't be anyone but our Banu."

"How do you know?" Padma said. "You can't even see."

"Doesn't matter," Deepa said. "I know our Banu. I know us."

"*Inside* the Royale?" Padma asked Banu. "Really?"

Instead of answering, Banu stuffed a roti in her mouth. Maybe because she was hungry, or maybe because, without a can of spray paint in her hand, she didn't have anything to say.

"If anyone asks," Deepa said, "Kalla *wasn't* here."

* * *

The morning after the police came, Joy sat at her desk and pushed her bangles up and down her wrist. They tossed glassy shadows on the classroom ceiling. Red, purple, green, blue. Anxious tinkling rainbows.

"Stop," Rukshana said, putting her hand on Joy's. "You're going to break one and cut yourself. No one wants to see your blood."

"What do you know?" Joy said gruffly. Tilted her chin at Rukshana's bare wrists.

Normally when Joy talked to her like that, Rukshana would've given it back. This time, though, she squeezed her friend's hand.

"You know the police come and take the boys whenever they need a culprit," Joy said. "Muslims, Dalits. It never matters if they did it or not. It's all the same to the government."

"If anyone had been arrested, we would've heard about it," Padma said from across the room. But she didn't tell Joy she's wrong. Didn't sound convinced either.

They sat like that until Vihaan and Yousef walked in, their eyes dark and hollow.

"They didn't arrest you?" Rukshana asked. Didn't bother to hide her relief.

Yousef shook his head, too awestruck to pretend. "The police came to my house. Said a boy with blue on his hands ran right by my door. We stayed up all night waiting to see if he'd come back."

"Really?" Joy leaned forward in her desk, all her anxiety forgotten. "Did you see him?"

"No," Yousef said. "But *they* didn't either. You know the wall behind the water pump? The one right next to the community hall?"

"I saw it," Rukshana said. She lives on that side of Heaven, near Yousef. "It says 'Kalla was here.' It smelled fresh."

"Like he just did it this morning," Yousef said, shaking his head. "What a guy!"

"Maybe we can put some mark on our houses so he knows we'll protect him," Vihaan said. "Just in case he needs somewhere to hide."

"Harboring criminals is not legal, Vihaan. I believe you recently learned this term—what is it now? Oh yes. A *punishable offense*," Janaki Ma'am said. That woman has X-ray ears—can hear right through school walls. "Which is something you will learn if you go to law school. Which is something you will only do if you pass your boards."

"Lawyers don't need math," Rukshana said.

"Everyone needs math," Janaki Ma'am said. "Even artists. Now turn to page 17."

"Did you just call Kalla an artist, ma'am?" Joy asked.

"All I remember saying is to turn to page 17," Janaki Ma'am said. Circled us like one of the *v*-tailed kites nesting in the neem tree on the school compound. Paused for a split second next to Banu's desk.

Banu's desk. Where Banu opened her textbook, leaving soldier-blue smudges on the edge of the page.

"Honestly, Banu. Page 17," Janaki Ma'am said again, flipping through Banu's book for her. Banu looked up, startled, as Janaki Ma'am swept past. Just in time to see the headmistress hide her smile.

Janaki Ma'am stood at the chalkboard, her back to us, and said, "This Kalla character may or may not get caught. But you will *all* pass your exam."

"They'll never catch Kalla," Vihaan said. "He's too clever."

"Or he has clever friends," Padma said.

Banu stuck her spray-paint-blue hands beneath her government-blue skirt.

"Who says it's a he?" she whispered.

10

Half-Wild

"PADMA? PADMA, WHERE ARE YOU?"

"*Amma*?" Padma springs up from where she's sitting with the rest of us, crouched in front of steaming plates of biryani.

"Where is everyone?" Gita Aunty asks. "Why isn't anyone home?"

"We're all out here, *Amma*," Padma says. "There's been some trouble."

"Trouble?" Gita Aunty says. Rubs her eyes with the back of her hand. "What trouble?"

"First, eat," Padma says. "Then I'll tell you."

Our mothers are brassy and cheerful, larger than life. Fill up space with their bodies, their orders. Their noise. Padma's mother, though? She doesn't take up any space at all. Floats through Heaven like a silhouette. An outline of someone who once was, a charcoal pencil sketch smudged around the edges.

Padma's mother is nothing like our mothers. But Padma says she used to be.

"Did you feed the crows?" Gita Aunty asks. "They'll be hungry."

"I will, *Amma*. Right now it's dinnertime, okay?" Padma says.

Steers Gita Aunty around the bulldozers, away from the line of engineers loading up the bus. Settles her mother on the ground, pours water over her hands to wash off the dirt. The way our teachers did when we were in preschool. Before we knew how to take care of ourselves.

Banu scurries over with a plate of biryani and a water bottle. Hands them to Padma, who hands them to her mother.

"Eat, *Amma*," Padma says. "You need your strength."

Beneath the glow of the rising moon, streetlamps flicker and headlights glimmer, fireflies twinkle and cell phones gleam. The foreign lady's camera flashes, illuminating Padma stroking her mother's back, Banu curling her shoeless toes. Gita Aunty hunching over her meal, next to the space where Banu's *ajji* would be if she wasn't too sick to eat.

Heaven may be striped with all kinds of light tonight. But it's the line between the mothered and the unmothered that always glows the brightest.

* * *

After she gives birth to Padma's youngest brother, Gita Aunty can't stop crying. She cries when she hangs the laundry on the clothesline strung between the roofs of Heaven's houses. When she pours the *dosa* for breakfast, packs the rice for tiffin. Even cries when she sees Padma, even though Padma is the only one who makes her happy.

"Why's your *amma* so sad?" Rukshana asks.

"She misses the village," Padma tells us.

"What's there to miss in the village?" Joy asks. The way she says it, you can tell she doesn't want an answer.

"The colors," Padma says. "Especially the blues and greens."

"There's blue here. Green too," Joy says, pointing to the blue-and-white city bus rumbling by, the peeling green paint on the Dumpsters they installed behind the school.

"Those aren't the greens and blues she misses," Padma says. "She misses other colors. Not those."

"What nonsense," Rukshana says. "Green is green and blue is blue."

Padma shakes her head and says, "There's sky blue, river blue. Peacock-neck blue and God-skin blue. Even sky blue is so many blues. There's a sky blue that smells like rain. There's one that smells like drought. Green is like that too. Rice-paddy green, bitter-gourd green, parrot-tail green. You don't know about them because in Bangalore, you don't have them. Those are the colors my mother misses."

Padma's eyes are full of fear. But they're full of something else too. Something the rest of us wish we had. A memory of air that isn't salty with petrol and construction dust. Of roads lit by stars instead of the headlights of two-wheelers. Of river mud and thunderstorms and beetle wings we'll never feel against our toes, our cheeks. The palms of our hands.

There is city smart and there is country smart. One day, Padma will be both. But we will only ever be one.

Still, Rukshana says, "All that jungly stuff is well and good, but it won't get you anywhere here."

"That jungly stuff is exactly what she misses," Padma says. Like she hasn't heard right. Or like she's heard right, but she's answering wrong. "She misses the birds."

* * *

Before we met Padma, we always took the short way home. Through narrow *gallis* where skinny-shouldered men push wooden carts full of guavas, cucumbers, chili, and salt. Where village women hack open tender coconuts with machetes, sunlight bouncing off of the jewels in their twice-pierced noses. Where city women crouch on straw mats heaped with vegetables, herbs, and fruits, calling out, "Carrots! Bananas! Cilantro! Beans!"

Padma makes us take the long way home. Starts in the alleyway behind the school. Weaves through piles of plastic milk bags and cow dung and rotting vegetables. Opens into the posh neighborhood full of three-story houses with gardens full of roses and carnations, driveways full of cars, entire floors to rent to strangers.

Or, in one house, a veranda just for birds.

There are plenty of birds in Bangalore. Mynahs with feathers the color of mud. Pigeons with necks that pop like rusty bed springs. Kites that carry pieces of rotting flesh in their city-sharpened claws.

These are not those kinds of birds. These birds are the colors of the jewels in the Joyalukka's window. These birds are so posh that if they applied for visas at the American embassy, they would get them on the first try.

When she sees the house, Padma dusts off her skirt, tucks in her shirt. Licks her palm, smooths down her hair. Walks right up to the door and rings the doorbell.

"Madam," she says to the lady who answers. A lady dripping in actual jewels from the actual window of Joyalukka's. "Do you need a maid?"

"In fact, I do," the lady says. Words pleated like she hired the ironwallah to press her tongue. "But you're a bit young, aren't you, darling?"

"Not me, madam," Padma says. "My mother. Her name is Gita."

"Is she neat and clean like you?" the lady asks.

"Yes," Padma says. "And she has impeccable manners."

Where did Padma learn a word like that? We can't help but be impressed. The lady is too, because she says, "Bring your mother tomorrow, darling. She must be a decent woman if she raised a girl like you."

* * *

On the road that wound between Padma's village and Bangalore, golden-green paddy fields gave way to abandoned farms the brown-gray hue of defeat. Stalks of sugar cane and corn slumped against each other like drunks. Every so often green and purple fingers of ragi defiantly pushed their way through the asthmatic earth, the dirt around their roots cracked and brown.

Two hours into the ride, the bus tilted into a ditch. The driver revved the engine, cursed colorfully in Telugu. Passengers covered their heads to protect themselves from the luggage tumbling from the racks above.

Behind Padma, an old woman cackled and slapped her thigh. "My daughter and I dug that ditch. They made us do it for that *sarkari* money."

She was talking about the one hundred days of paid labor the government had started guaranteeing starving farm families, meaningless, measurable tasks, like collecting sticks of wood, digging ditches. At the end of the day, an inspector with sweat-stained armpits would count the sticks, record the depth and width of the pits, determine if the crew had done enough to warrant getting paid. The work was meant for men, but the women were the ones who showed up for it, babies wrapped in their saris, toddlers waddling at their heels.

"We dug and dug so we wouldn't starve to death," the old woman said as the bus tipped and lurched, unable to right itself. "And now, just see. We're going to die anyway."

"I didn't even get paid," Gita Aunty said. "The *sarkari* man promised me, but the money never came."

"None of us were paid, darling," said the old woman. "If we had been, we wouldn't be on this blasted bus, now would we?"

* * *

On her mother's first day of work, Padma wakes her early. Makes her apply the tiniest bit of kohl to hide the dark circles under her eyes, wear the sari Padma has washed and dried and pressed the night before. Holds Gita Aunty's hand as they cross the footbridge, taking a left instead of going straight. As they plunge into the rich neighborhoods, memories of rivers and farms trace watery tributaries on Gita Aunty's cheeks.

Inside the house, the hall hums with whirring ceiling fans, with wind rushing between open windows. The floor is lined with earthen pots full of tall, feathery plants, the walls with tasteful folk art. The air is still buttery with the smell of the *alu* parathas and yogurt the family had for breakfast.

"The work is nothing difficult," the pressed-tongue woman says, gesturing for Padma and Gita Aunty to follow her up the stairs. "We have a girl to do the chopping and cooking. Another girl for the clothes. The *mali* comes for the plants. We'd need you only for some sweeping and dusting and tidying up. And then, of course, we need you to care for the birds."

"The birds?" Gita Aunty whispers.

"I hope you don't mind?" the pressed-tongue woman says, giving the door at the top of the stairs the slightest push. It glides on its hinges, like it's recently been oiled.

Padma and her mother step out onto a veranda wrapped in wooden boards and chicken wire. The air flashes with feathers, beaks, throats, wings. Wooden perches and baskets of seeds hang from the ceiling, swinging back and forth as birds land, pause, take flight. The air smells of ammonia and grain.

"You'll need to clean this and feed them twice a day," the pressed-tongue lady says. "We only get the best organic feed. Oh, and don't forget to make sure they always have water. From the dispenser, not the tap."

Padma bites the inside of her cheek to keep from laughing. No one in Heaven would waste money on a bottle of Bisleri-branded water, let alone a whole twenty-liter can a week just for birds.

"Would you mind, madam," Gita Aunty asks, "if I sing to them?"

Padma tenses. It's over now, she thinks. Her mother has revealed too much, stepped over the line from charmingly naive to downright insane.

But the pressed-tongue woman seems pleased. "That would be wonderful," she says. "I'm sure that would make them happy."

Padma isn't sure then, but she thinks she sees the currents of her mother's waters still.

*　*　*

Padma hears what we say about her, even though she pretends she doesn't. We say that she doesn't know anything—well, okay, she knows *some* things, but nothing useful. That she's from a place that might as well be nowhere.

It doesn't bother her. After all, she knows what nowhere's like.

Nowhere is earth crushed and folded. A place where laughter plows furrows into faces. Makes the green-blue world greener and bluer and greener and bluer. Makes stomachs hurt, throats sore, breath short.

A place where even pain comes from too much joy.

At least, that's how Padma decides to remember it. The way it used to be. Back when her feet were always wet from the mud of rice paddies, her hair was always tangled from too much sun and wind. Back before the world curled up at the edges like a burning photograph held up to a flame.

Whenever they miss nowhere, Padma's father tells them they must be strong. "We didn't come here for the easy life. We came here for more. More jobs, more schools, more money, more chances. So we, ourselves, could become more. More than our village. More than who we are."

But Padma had always thought that they were enough.

* * *

For three months, everything might be better. Gita Aunty sweeps and dusts and tidies up. Brings home rupees folded in the damp end of her sari. Brings the birds their food and water and keeps the veranda clean. Pets them and coos to them in her mother tongue.

The pressed-tongue lady doesn't understand what Gita Aunty is saying but claims that she has never seen the brood so plump and lithe and fluttery.

"These village women just have a way with wildlife," she tells her neighbors. Tilts her pretty pale face for a minute and adds, "I suppose it is because they are, themselves, half-wild."

Gita Aunty still cries rivers of tears. But these days, the waters run with determination, not despair.

"Do you see the city out there?" Gita Aunty whispers to the birds, pointing to the world beyond the veranda. "It is full of rage and fear, but you have courage. You have wings.

"Do you see the buildings?" Gita Aunty chants. "The offices and shopping malls and flats? Between those buildings there are trees. Between those buildings there are homes. All just waiting for us to find them. Just waiting to become ours.

"If you think about it," Padma's mother murmurs, "Bangalore is just another jungle."

Once her mother starts getting better, Padma starts getting better too. Her village accent is disappearing, watering down, getting to be less *ragi mudde* and more *sopu saru*. Every now and then we hear her say a word in English, Tamil, Hindi. When she tells the woman at the vegetable cart how much she is willing to pay for tomatoes or onions or greens, she speaks with a confidence that comes from belonging somewhere, from knowing how things work.

One afternoon, when we're on our way to Vihaan's uncle's used paper shop to watch a brand-new Hindi serial on Heaven's only working TV, Banu says, "Let's bring Padma."

"Ugh, why?" Rukshana asks. "She's so quiet and sad."

"Maybe she's lonely," Banu says. "Or worried about something."

"We're all worried about something," Rukshana says.

"But Padma's worried about her *mother*," Joy says.

We know what she means. Mother-worry is a different kind of worry.

"We might as well get her. I mean, her house is on the way," Rukshana says then. Of course, Heaven is so small that all of our houses are always on the way. But that's not the point.

* * *

When they first arrived at Majestic bus terminal, Padma and her mother stepped onto the jagged pavement, inhaled Bangalore's salty air. Padma carried her brother, and her mother carried the luggage. Her father had mixed up the bus timings and hadn't yet reached the station.

"What now?" Padma asked.

"I don't know," Gita Aunty said. Her voice, usually strong and sure as rushing water, sounded different here. Frail. Timid even. Like she was loosening, slightly, around the edges.

Padma knew then with frightening certainty that whatever her parents sought, it wasn't here, in this granite metropolis that stared at her family with gravel-mottled eyes. Maybe it wasn't anywhere.

* * *

One morning, before she leaves for whatever she does all day, the pressed-tongue lady takes Gita Aunty aside.

"I'm going out," she says, placing the key on the table in the hall. "When you leave, lock the door and tell the watchman."

It is *that* moment. The moment between maid and housewife when trust is bestowed, privilege given. The moment when Gita Aunty knows she is guaranteed a job here, in this house, forever. Here among the jeweled birds and the flame of the forest trees and the tiled floors that someone else is paid to clean.

On the veranda, Padma's mother gazes out the wire-mesh at the pressed-tongue lady gathering up the folds of her *kanjeevaram* sari and stepping into her Mercedes-Benz.

Gita Aunty worries the key in her fingers. Thinks about home. Thinks about trust, family, money. Thinks about birds, trees, farms. Right and wrong. Prisons and freedom.

When the shiny silver car pulls away, Gita Aunty counts to one hundred. Lays the key back down on the table. Reaches into her sari blouse and removes a knife.

Cuts a hole in the wire-mesh window. It is the shape of a summer moon.

Some of the birds leave immediately, but others aren't sure. Gita Aunty cradles the uncertain ones. Sings them village songs, jungle songs. Their claws make crooked tracks on the palms of her hands.

Whispers, "You are strong. You have wings. Use them."

One by one, they go. Padma's mother watches them disappear, fading from the colors of emerald and diamond and sapphire into the colors of leaf and cloud and sky. The hues of their new lives. Or perhaps their old ones.

When they are all gone, she sweeps away the feathers they left behind. Eyes dry, hands steady, she gives the key to the watchman.

Gita Aunty doesn't work at rich people's houses any more. But she doesn't cry anymore either.

11

The Mandap Tree

THE FOREIGN LADY'S LENS FRAMES Heaven at its worst: an apocalyptic wasteland, a ruined landscape interrupted only by inhabitants felled by great struggles, crushing defeats.

With each photo, the camera growls like a bulldozer pushing its way through concrete, rolling over tin. Like one more machine complicit in our destruction.

"Enough," Joy says. Yells across the wreckage, "You, madam! Come."

"You think she speaks Kannada?" Deepa asks.

"She knows what *this* means," Joy says, gesturing to the photographer to come quickly, churning her arm in urgent circles.

"Oy!" Rukshana says. "Over here!"

"Don't scare her," Padma says.

"Oh, for God's sake, Padma. She's a woman, not a squirrel," Rukshana says.

The foreign lady picks her way through the rubble like she's worried about ruining her shoes. When she gets close to us, she says, "Namaste. It is nice to meet you. I am here taking photos."

"What language is that?" Padma whispers.

"I think it might be Hindi," Rukshana says.

"Are you sure?" Joy asks. Because this Hindi is not the Hindi we've pieced together from All India Radio and Bollywood movies, from the sentences we copy out of the workbooks they give us at school. This Hindi is peeled out of the pages of the out-of-date dictionaries our grandmothers used before their brothers burned them all in the name of Kannada pride.

"I am taking photos. I want the people to know what is happening. Now the people do not know what is happening," the photographer says, sounding more and more like the exercises Janaki Ma'am makes us memorize for our tenth-class boards.

"You're saying that you're taking pictures so people know what's happening here?" Joy says.

"Yes, yes," the photographer says, thrilled that we've understood. "The people do not know. I want to make them know."

"You think people don't know what's happening?" Rukshana asks.

"How will they know?" the foreign lady says. Shakes her head and tries again, saying, "*Matlab*, how *would* they be knowing?"

"All they have to do is look around," Padma says. "All they have to do is notice."

"If they know, they would be helping," the photographer says. Points to her camera and shakes it. Like she's trying to shake the right words out of it, the right arguments.

"You think they're going to help? Listen, let me save you some time. Here's what's going to happen," Rukshana says. "The photographs will show up in the newspaper. Rich people will get mad. Lawyers will get involved. A few volunteers will show up and pass out some blankets, maybe, and some food. But the slum will still get destroyed. That's how it happens. Every single time."

"This time will be different," the photographer says. "I will make it different."

Rukshana thinks of all of the slum dwellers she and her mother have stood beside, chanting slogans, raising hell. The hands they've held, the stomachs they've filled. The tears they've dried. All those women, all those girls, and not one of them bothered showing up today.

"It's never different," she says, "and there's nothing any of us can do about it."

* * *

Two years ago, the city destroyed Purvapura, the slum next door. Even though it was nearly a decade old, Purvapura was still just a collection of tents sprouting out of the pavement like blue-tarped weeds, a gaggle of children who hadn't let go of their country accents, country fears. The adults who lived there had jobs collecting garbage, hauling sand. The kind of work our mothers' mothers did so they could earn the money to move to a place like Heaven.

We saw photos of the demolition in all the papers—English, Kannada, Telugu, Tamil, Malayalam. Other people did too. People with money, degrees, power. People who got angry enough to take time off from their corporate jobs to volunteer, protest, file court cases. All that came in the papers too.

It didn't matter, though. The Purvapura families had already lost everything. We could tell from the photos: Shredded straps of school bags, shattered heads of dolls. Twisted wheels of government-issued bicycles, dented pots still sticky with cooking oil. Charred family portraits and god pictures curled up at the edges like clenched fists.

Letters and protests and court cases wouldn't bring any of those things back.

Even though it wasn't our slum, we lost things too. People, mostly. After her house collapsed, Deepa's great-aunt started sleeping in a pipe on the sidewalk. Neelamma Aunty gave her a few hundred rupees and tried to convince her to move in with them. The old lady refused, then she disappeared. They never found out what happened, didn't have the heart to check the local hospitals for a body. Joy's mother's cousin—or maybe cousin's cousin—married a man from that side. Selvi Aunty eventually found out they moved into one of the flats Bangalore builds for the slum dwellers that get removed, a place where Joy says you have to pay two rupees every time you want to use the toilet. Padma's father said one of his fellow night watchmen stopped coming to work, but no one knew whether it was because he was from Purvapura or because he finally got arrested for public urination.

In the end, though, most of us didn't think much about it. We knew the Purvapura people, sure. But we didn't *really* know them, not the way we knew each other. Didn't know their names, their families. What they had for breakfast every morning or what rumors their jealous neighbors were spreading or whether their children were the type to elope.

Except for Rukshana. She knew someone.

Really knew her.

* * *

There's one tree in Heaven that's not like the rest of them. We call it the mandap tree. It's an ancient banyan full of nooks the size of toes, crannies curved in the shape of fingers. Limbs wide and flat like park benches.

Around the middle there's a branch that stretches over a lane full of used-to-be-warehouses. Used to have corrugated walls and cement floors. Used to hold watches and screws and airplane parts and workers hired to box all the things that other people buy, buy, buy.

The people and boxes and bits and pieces disappeared, but the buildings didn't. One by one, the floors became kitchens, stages, changing rooms. Company signs came down and flowery marquees came up. Temples sprung from the pavement like granite lotus blossoms. Bit by bit, piece by piece, the warehouses stopped being warehouses and started being mandapams: wedding halls for the not-so-rich, the never-will-be-famous.

In auspicious months, the street fills up with Hindu brides and grooms and wedding parties. Cars decorated with carnations, brides decorated with gold. Plastic signs draped with garlands reading Ganesh Babu weds Kavita, Kavita weds Suresh, Suresh weds Sujata, Sujata weds Ganesh Babu. Some days, when three Sureshes are wedding three Sujatas, everyone ends up at the wrong wedding. Even the brides and grooms.

The ceremonies lap at the streets like the edge of the ocean, advancing and retreating. Future mothers- and fathers-in-law argue about what the caterers are charging, whether the bride is wearing enough jewelry, why the relatives are acting so local. Children drag their parents to the corner store and ask for paneer soda and vinyl balloons. Guests hitch up their dhotis and saris, fling rice and flower petals at the appropriate times. We can see it all from the mandap tree.

It's like watching our futures unfold.

* * *

Fatima Aunty lets Rukshana wear trousers to school, but she draws the line at formal occasions. So in eighth standard, when we all go to Deepa's uncle's wedding, Fatima Aunty makes Rukshana wear the same clothes as the rest of us: a sequined blouse with snarling clasps that itch her back, catch her hair. A low-waisted skirt that tangles around her kicking knees, flying feet. Silver anklets strung with bells that announce her presence every time she tries to disappear.

While the rest of us eat and laugh and dance and flirt, Rukshana flees. Desperate for a wall to scale, a tree to climb. Some way to heave herself off the ground, untangle herself from the crowd. A place where she can be herself. Alone.

A place like the mandap tree.

Except when she gets to the mandap tree, someone is already there.

* * *

Leela dangles her soft, bare toes over brides decked in pounds of jewelry, yards of silk. Strains her swan-long neck over grooms worrying the ends of their dhotis, facing down the beginnings of the rest of their lives. Holds her body tense as a wound-up top. Like she's waiting for someone else's hands to spin her into motion around the marriage fire. To snap her into a dizzying future.

"Hey, you," Rukshana yells through the branches. "Who said you could be up there?"

"It's a tree," Leela says. When she flicks her eyes at Rukshana, they flash a brown so bright it's almost green. "You don't need permission to climb a tree."

"Maybe not in Purvapura," Rukshana says, "but here in Heaven, you do."

"I'm not asking for permission from a girl who always dresses like a boy," Leela says.

"I don't dress like a boy. I dress like myself."

"Right."

"Like you should talk," Rukshana says, pointing to Leela's clothes. She's wearing a government-issued school shirt and blouse. "I bet you don't own anything besides that uniform."

Leela doesn't answer. Which might as well be a yes.

"That's what I thought," Rukshana says. "I'm coming up."

"Fine. Come up then," Leela says. "I'm not moving."

"Fine. Scoot over," Rukshana says. Scales the tree with village-sure feet. Stops only for a split second when a piece of her blouse catches on a twig. Swears under her breath as she pulls herself up, hears the tear, imagines what her mother will say.

"That was quick," Leela says, making room for Rukshana on the limb where she perches like a starving pigeon.

"City girls can climb trees too, you know," Rukshana says.

Below them, drums thud and horns shriek, a choreographed chaos, brassy and bronze.

"Oh, the men are leaving for Kashi!" Leela says. "This is my favorite part."

Sure enough, a dozen grooms leave the marriage halls, pretending they've changed their mind about getting married, pretending they're on their way to the mountains to become ascetics, men of God. A dozen bridal families follow, pretending to beg the men to stay, to take care of their daughters, to remain in the material world. One family hands their groom a plastic umbrella. When he opens it, rose petals rain around his shoulders, form pastel puddles at his feet.

Leela leans back and sighs.

"Your favorite part is when the groom runs away?" Rukshana asks.

"My favorite part is when he comes back," Leela says. "He decides his wife is more important than his own dreams. More important than God, even. It's so romantic."

On the branch, there's barely enough room for the two of them. They are thigh to thigh, elbow to elbow, knee to knee. The wind picks up, fills the air with Leela's aroma, a mixture of perspiration and jasmine. She smells pure and determined. Nervous and sweet.

"Want me to fix this?" Leela asks, pointing at the fresh rip in Rukshana blouse.

"How?" Rukshana asks. "You carry around a Singer?"

"Something like that," Leela says. Pulls a pouch from the waistband of her skirt. It looks like it's made out of a torn piece of sari that used to be purple. Or maybe red. Inside is a needle and thread. "I don't have anywhere to keep my things so I carry them all with me."

Leela leans across Rukshana and starts stitching. Her too-tight school shirt rides up, revealing a patch of Leela's bare stomach, the skin smooth and even and brown as a seashore worn smooth by the ocean.

"There," Leela says. Snaps the thread between her teeth. Admires the line of invisible stiches. "See? You can't even tell it was torn."

"Huh," Rukshana says.

Leela rolls her eyes and turns around. "You're welcome," she says. "You city girls are so rude."

"If you don't like me, then leave," Rukshana says.

"Why should I leave? I was here first."

"Maybe *I'll* leave then. Just to get away from you."

"Not if I go first."

"Go then!"

"Watch me, no?"

They stop arguing. But neither one of them climbs down.

* * *

Hindu weddings always happen in the mornings. Apparently the first hours of the day are the most auspicious.

Leela understands why. In the mornings, the mandap tree's bark is warm and sun dappled, the leaves slick and clean enough to catch and scatter light. Promises feel less fragile. Bodies less bruised.

At night, the world is a vortex of uncertainty, a black hole of pain. At night, Leela's father lurches home reeking of fist fights and chicken sixty-five. Rotten breath, cut-up knuckles. Babbling about the old days when families from his caste got what they wanted. What they deserved. Land, women, servants. Money and respect.

The old days, before this age of cities and cell phones, computers and concrete. Before this age of pollution. Not the pollution the rich people care about—not the kind that comes from the tailpipes of buses, the sewage pipes of factories. The kind that foreigners rate on a meter of red and green.

This is a different kind of pollution. Makeup, loose hair, tight shirts, short skirts. Mutton, chicken, bacon, fish. Cigarettes, alcohol, English cinema. Romance.

"All these modern women going to work in their jeans pants and lipstick," Leela's father says to the men who sit beside him on the side of the road, sharing a bottle of something poisonous brewed out of coconuts and sunlight. "No wonder there are so many rapes. So many murders."

When the other men agree, Leela's father says, "Remember how women used to be? Back home in the village? Eyes down. Mouths closed. Pure, like Sita. See how she waited for Ram in a garden full of demons? That is how a woman ought to be."

Every sip of toddy makes him surer, nobler. Meaner.

"It's our dharma to shelter our women," he says. "Otherwise who knows what will happen to them?"

Leela and her mother are polluted. Every night, Leela's father tells them so. Voice tough and leathery as an old man's knuckles, fists dense and gritty as factory smoke.

Leela's mornings are black eyes and battered limbs, bruised skin and broken bones.

But mornings are also brides and grooms, gold and silk, fire and roses. Escape velocities mapped out like calculations on an astrologer's chart.

And now, more and more often, mornings are also Rukshana.

* * *

"Hey, you there," Rukshana yells through the branches where Leela is sitting. Holds up a plastic bag full of something soft and cottony and purple and green. "This is for you."

"What is it?" Leela asks. She's wearing her same old school uniform. When the wind blows, it pierces the thinning fabric, and she shivers.

Rukshana puts the bundle between her teeth and shimmies up the tree. Leela takes it from her with pale hands that flutter like nervous doves.

"Just an old *salwar kameez*," Rukshana says, shrugging. Watches the weddings so she doesn't have to meet Leela's eyes.

"Oh," Leela says. Undoes the bundle. Pulls out the long-sleeved top, the baggy pants. Puts the cotton dupatta around her shoulders, hugging it close to her chest. The fabric smells like soap and dust. Like Rukshana. "These are nice."

"I've worn them a million times before. Thought you might as well have it," she says. After a second, she adds, "Purple and green are supposed to be good for fair skin, though. Right?"

"Are you asking me?"

"No," Rukshana says. "That's just what people say."

"Since when do you care what looks nice on me?"

"I don't," Rukshana says. "It's just—I owe you for fixing my blouse. Now we're even."

"Fine," Leela says. "We're even."

* * *

On our way to school, Joy greets Rukshana with a giant smack.

"Ow," Rukshana says, holding her arm. "What was that for?"

"Slapping some sense into you," Joy says. "What are you doing with that girl?"

"Leela?"

"I don't know her name," Joy says.

"Yes you do," Padma says. "You stood up for her against Yousef that one time. You acted like you liked her."

"Standing up for her is one thing," Joy says. The rules of the world are boys against girls. For Joy, who has to keep proving that she *is* a girl, the rules are even stricter. "Hanging around in trees with her is different."

"She needed clothes. I took her some," Rukshana says, pushing her fingers through her hair. "It wasn't even my idea. You know how my mother is with her charity nonsense."

"See," Padma says, sniffling. Links her arm with Rukshana's. "Rukshana's being nice."

"*Nice* is handing her the *salwar* on the way to school," Joy says. "Climbing up a tree and making a special delivery? That's too much."

"Why does it even matter?"

"Because that girl will break your heart," Joy says. "Just watch. That family of hers will be here one second and gone the next."

"Actually, they'll probably be here awhile," Banu says. "Leela's dad is working on that mall they're building in the empty lot. That takes time."

"A mall? In the empty lot? That can't be," Padma says. "That lot is way too small. For a mall, they'd need half of the land in Heaven too."

"All the building materials are stamped with this company called Krishna Industries," Banu says. "They only build malls."

"Don't be stupid, Banu," Rukshana says. "You know you can't even read properly."

"Ignore her, Banu. She's just trying to change the subject," Joy says. "Look, Rukshana, I don't trust that girl, and you shouldn't either."

"It's not like I'm going to marry her," Rukshana says. As soon as she does, her cheeks turn red.

* * *

On Friday, Rukshana and Fatima Aunty go to morning prayers at
their mosque. Arabic verses coat Rukshana's tongue with a hon-
eyed hopefulness, thicken her chest with a syrupy peace. After the
service, when she leaves her mother at the bus stop, she's supposed
to meet us at Deepa's house so we can all walk to school together.

But she doesn't go to Deepa's house. She goes to the mandap tree.

"Hey, you," Leela yells. "Rukshana, right?"

Leela's pinned the dupatta Rukshana gave her to the shoulders
of her government-issued school shirt.

"Don't act like you don't know my name," Rukshana says.

"Hurry," Leela says, staring out over the mandap street. "They're
about to leave for Kashi."

Horns trill and drums rat-a-tat-tat. Silence splits into coppery
shards. Grooms pour out of the mandapams, umbrellas in the air.
Rukshana pulls herself up into the branches, feet still chilly from
the mosque's cool marble floor.

"See that boy, down there?" Leela shouts over the clatter and
clang.

"What, the skinny one?"

"No, no, the fat one. See how he wants to come back from Kashi
so badly? He loves his wife."

"So?"

"So. He'll be a good husband."

Rukshana nods. Tilts her head and watches.

"But then that skinny one," Leela says. "The one with the thin
little hips? He's got no spine. His wife will always get her way."

Rukshana considers. This new game, these new rules. Decides
if she's interested in playing.

Finally, slowly, she says, "That one seems like he doesn't drink."

"Definitely," Leela says, giggling. "He loves his mother too, too much."

Above them, parakeets dart in and out of an empty hole in the trunk of a coconut tree. They plunge into the hollow carrying long brown leaves in their sharp orange beaks. When they emerge, their blue and green tail feathers flare, necks glitter like glass bangles.

"That one can't take his eyes off his wife. Sweet, no?" Rukshana says. Makes a face and a sound like she's going to vomit.

"Too, too sweet," Leela says, gagging. When she adjusts her brand-new dupatta, she brushes Rukshana's thigh.

Probably accidentally. But maybe not.

* * *

The government of India announces that our nation is in crisis. Secularism, they say, is destroying the country. Hinduism is in danger.

"That's what I've been saying all along," Leela's father says. "Our way of life is in peril. We must remember who we are, where we came from. Like the prime minister says, '*Gharwapsi.*'" Come home.

Of course, he doesn't mean us girls. There's no coming home when you're not allowed to leave in the first place.

The boys, though? They wear pressed khaki shorts, paint their foreheads with ash. Fumble with strings of bumpy brown beads, chant prayers in a language they don't understand.

One Sunday morning, our brothers and cousins and classmates leave for a meeting. The lanes of Heaven are lined with orange.

Leela is up in the mandap tree. Swings herself out of the

branches, lands on the pavement with a slap of her bare feet, right in front of Joy's door. She's wearing the *salwar* that Rukshana gave her. Pulls the dupatta over her head, across her face. Just in case her father is somewhere in the crowd.

Joy's on the front step now, wiping her floury hands on her green and yellow nightie. "What're they doing?" she asks.

"I don't know," Leela says. "But I don't like it."

Yousef, who has followed the parade on his bicycle, parks next to them. Joins the conversation like he's always been a part of it. Like boys do.

"Vihaan says he's learning about discipline and morals and ethics," Yousef tells us. "He says he's becoming a man."

"At least one of you is," Joy says. Even though she doesn't believe him.

"They got new shirts," Yousef says. "Pencil boxes too." His voice twitches with something—longing? Fear? Loneliness? Something we've felt in our voices before. Something we thought was the property of girls and women.

"What do they need all of that for?" Joy asks.

"For their mission. They're going to make our country stronger," he says. "Vihaan says India needs order and progress. A return to traditional Hindu values."

Leela asks, "You really think a bunch of men in orange are going to make India better?"

"For Brahmins, maybe, but not for the rest of us," Joy says. Glances at Leela, with her high-caste skin, her Brahmin name. Notices a bruise on Leela's sloping neck, purple and black and winged, the size and shape of a crushed moth. Dark enough to show through the green webbing of the dupatta's borders.

Leela sucks her teeth. "Not for Muslims either. Remember partition?"

"What's partition?" Joy asks.

"People died," Leela says.

"They did?" Yousef asks. Rubs the back of his neck like he does when he's nervous.

"Since when do you care about Muslims anyway?" Joy asks Leela.

"I don't," Leela says. But Joy knows she's lying.

* * *

Under Leela's father's fists, Leela's mother wilts, petal by petal. Wrinkles around the edges. Takes any job she can at any house she can—even if it's just doing dishes, mopping floors. Hands her wages to her husband without trying to save any for herself.

Leela's mother shrinks, but Leela expands. Throws books at the boys, pinches blue bruises onto the arms of the girls. Dares us with her wild and brutal eyes, with looks so sharp we feel like we've been pierced all the way through.

"Leela!" Janaki Ma'am yells over and over and over. "Go to my office. *Again*."

"You see?" Joy spins around in her desk and leans across Rukshana. "I'm telling you she's no good."

"She *is* good," Rukshana says. "She's just got too much inside her. She's got to let it out somehow."

"So let her pray," Joy says. "That's what the rest of us do."

"She does pray," Rukshana says. "But it's not enough."

Every Tuesday before school, Leela goes to the Hanuman temple on the main road. Closes her eyes, moves her lips. Presses her forehead to the ground. When she stands up, she looks like the candles they give out at Joy's church. Pale as unmade wishes, solemn as unlit flames.

Temple goers point to her and say, "See that one, the fair one. So serious, so devoted. So pure. We should all be more like her."

But Leela's prayers are anything but pure. They snarl with poisonous plants, with sharpened blades. Writhe with lizards dropped into pots of chai, snakes hidden between bedsheets. Squirm with cinema-inspired visions of villains falling off of cliffs and out of planes. Of bad men vanishing and fading into the ending credits of a pure, black screen.

Leela thinks heaven—real heaven, where God lives—is probably a distracting place. Someone's got to take care of what's happening here on the ground.

* * *

Leela says to Rukshana, "Look at that one, dressed in pink and green. Wild, like a jungle."

"You like that sari?" Rukshana asks.

"No," Leela says. Then, after a minute, adds, "I like the one wearing it."

The silence between them buzzes louder than a wedding parade.

"That one, there—the one who won't look down, won't cover her face when she's praying. She's got strength," Rukshana says.

"That one has nice hips. She'll know how to dance."

"I like that one with the purple and green sari. See how long her neck is? She looks like a swan," Rukshana says. Winds her fingers through Leela's and adds, "She looks like you."

Leela shifts closer, closer. Rukshana looks down through the tree's sturdy arms. Arms that balance them above the world, press them against the sky. Arms strong enough to catch them if they jump. If they fall.

"I like that one. See? With the fish eyes and bony cheeks?" Leela asks.

Leaves and vines rattle and whisper secrets. Secrets that are becoming almost-secrets. Secrets that might not have to be secrets anymore.

"Why him?" Rukshana asks.

After all the shifting and shuffling and advancing and retreating, finally, they are nose to nose. Forehead to forehead. Hands twined like the branches of the mandap tree.

"He looks like you," Leela says.

Just one more turn, and their lips will be twisted too.

"Leela! Leela, where are you?"

Leela's mother's voice cuts through the air with the sharpness of brass horns, the urgency of beating drums. Rukshana hears the leaves and the vines go silent. Feels herself untwist, untwine.

"Leela! Come quickly, Leela. Your papa woke up and he's asking for you."

Leela slides down the tree fast as a squirrel. Runs away, her fair feet flying.

"Where is your dupatta?" her mother asks.

"Oh," Leela says, hand fluttering to her neck. In the dawn, her bruised skin glows like a cratered moon.

"Never mind. Just leave it," her mother says. "Come now. Quickly, quickly, before he gets even angrier."

In the branches of the mandap tree, Rukshana clutches the dupatta. Twists it, untwists it. Twines it, untwines it. Wraps it around herself like a promise.

* * *

"Hey, Rukshana. Where's that girlfriend of yours?" Joy asks. Gestures at the empty wooden desk where Leela usually sits, dupatta wound strategically around her scars.

"Her mother came and got her," Rukshana says. Too late, she adds, "She's not my girlfriend!"

Joy doesn't say anything. Just rolls her eyes.

"She's not!" Rukshana says. "She's my friend. It's not like I'm in *love* with her."

"Yes you are. Even I can see it," Banu says. Which is really saying something.

"She loves you back you know," Padma says.

"Shut up," Rukshana says. Her cheeks flush.

"Rukshana, watch your language," Janaki Ma'am says, bustling into the room. "Get out your notebooks. Kannada lessons today, and that teacher of yours hasn't bothered to show up."

* * *

In the evening, Rukshana cuts herself peeling carrots. Forgets to go to the water pump, spills flour all over the floor. Leaves the iron on her trousers so long it starts to smoke.

"*Chee*, what is wrong with you?" Fatima Aunty says. She snatches away the iron and starts pressing the pants herself. "Are you trying to burn this place down?"

"Sorry, Ma," Rukshana says. "I forgot to bring home an assignment. Janaki Ma'am will kill me if I don't bring it in tomorrow. Can I go to Padma's and get it?"

Fatima Aunty's face relaxes. "Is that what it is? Yes, yes, go. Just come straight home. I have my union meeting tonight, so let yourself in."

"Yes, Ma," Rukshana says.

But she doesn't go to Padma's house. She goes to Leela's.

* * *

Leela's father's eyes are bleary and he sways from side to side. Squints and burps and mumbles. Lurches like the devil they talk about at Rukshana's mosque.

"Go away," Rukshana says. Voice deep and growling, shoulders tough and square. Hips hidden in the waist of her dead brother's worn out trousers, breasts secreted behind the buttons of her no-good father's tossed-out shirt.

"Thisismyhome," Leela's father slurs. "Youcan'tkeepmeout."

"Yes I can," Rukshana says, although she's not sure if it's true.

Leela's father squints at Rukshana's silhouette, crouched between the strips of light streaming from the worn-out bulbs of streetlamps. With her short hair, with her boy's clothes, he doesn't know what he is seeing. The liquor churns his vision, liquefies his brain.

"Are you a man?" Leela's father asks. "No, no, you're not. You're not a man."

"No, I'm not," Rukshana says. "Thank God for that."

"What are you then? A god? A demon?"

"More like a demon," Rukshana says. Thinks of all the names her mother has called her over the years. Chokes back a laugh. Behind her hands, it sounds unearthly. Like a strangled growl.

Leela's father stumbles, turns. Staggers back to the sidewalk toddy shop, yelling,

"Rakshasa! Demon! There is a demon at my house!"

After the sharp knife of darkness whittles away the edges

of Leela's father's body, after the sharp buzz of traffic cuts through the rusted metal of his voice. After the night flowers open their throats and swallow the brittle edges of his sharp whisky smell. After all of that, Rukshana says, "It's safe now. He's gone."

Leela peeks her head around the doorway like a frightened rabbit. Paws her way to where Rukshana leans against the side of their hut, posing like a stone *apsara* carved onto a temple door.

"Someday I'll escape all this," Leela says. Nestles her head on Rukshana's shoulder. Plays with the fraying cuff of Rukshana's sleeve. "I'll go somewhere where there are no fathers. No toddy shops either."

"A place where girls get jobs and boys make sambar," Rukshana says.

"A place with a garden that someone else takes care of," Leela says.

"A place with an orchard full of banyan trees and a closet full of cricket bats."

Rukshana takes Leela's hand. Together, they watch the stars gather in the cracks of sky between the buildings, between the clouds.

"Someday I'll take you to a place like that," Rukshana says.

"We'll go together?"

"Yes," Rukshana says. "Yes."

* * *

In the morning, after she finishes her chores, Rukshana sits in the doorway and curls Leela's dupatta in her hands. Twists, untwists. Twines, untwines. This, she thinks, is proof. Of something.

When Rukshana hears the knock on the door, she thinks it must be one of us, coming to get her to go to school. Or maybe Yousef asking for breakfast, or Vihaan looking for Yousef.

Instead, it's Leela. And she is smiling.

Rukshana smiles too.

"Hi," Rukshana says.

"Hi," Leela says.

Rukshana looks down at her feet and blushes. Feels words clogging the bottom of her throat, feels her blood quickening. This, she knows, is the time to say something. Something that will turn their almosts into something new. Into everything.

Except Leela is the one who breaks the silence.

"We're leaving," she says.

"What?" Rukshana says. "What do you mean?"

"We're leaving! Not my father. Just me and my mother," Leela says, still smiling.

Rukshana stares at her, speechless.

"What you did for us," Leela says, choking. Clears her throat, and says, "My mother decided she couldn't take it anymore. Or, actually, that she doesn't *have* to take it anymore. So we're going back to the village."

"When?" Rukshana says.

"This morning," Leela says. "We're going to Majestic now."

Rukshana stares at her. Balls up her fingers to press back tears. When she closes them, she realizes that the dupatta is still in her hand. Dumbly, she hands it to Leela.

"No, keep it," Leela says. She leans forward and kisses Rukshana's cheek. Runs away, the bottoms of her feet flashing in the light of the barely risen sun.

* * *

Three days later, at school, a ball of paper flies across the room. Yousef aims it at Joy, but it hits Rukshana in the back of the head instead.

"Sorry, sorry!" Yousef says. Backs away with his hands in the air.

The last time Yousef hit her with a piece of trash, Rukshana gave him an almost-broken nose and a fully blackened eye. This time, though, she just shrugs. Worries a hole in her desk with a pair of half-sharpened scissors.

"What's wrong with her?" Joy asks, shooting Yousef a dirty look.

"Didn't you hear?" Padma whispers back. "The city demolished Purvapura. I saw it when I was reading the paper to Deepa this morning."

"Oh, *Bhagwan*," says Joy, who sometimes still forgets that she's Christian. "Is Leela all right?"

"I don't know."

"She's fine," Rukshana says. When we don't say anything, she says, "I'm sad, not deaf."

"Who knew Rukshana could get her heart broken?" Padma whispers.

"Who knew Rukshana even had a heart to begin with," Joy whispers back. But none of us feels like laughing.

* * *

"Come, come," Fatima Aunty says when Rukshana gets home. "Wash your face and comb your hair. We're going to Purvapura."

"What?" Rukshana says. "Why?"

Fatima Aunty raises her eyebrows. It's the biggest response she's gotten out of her daughter since the night of her union meeting, the night when they planned the protest that was supposed to stop the Purvapura demolition from happening. Except the city showed up a day early, so no one was there to hold up signs, to make a human chain. The bulldozers rolled right through.

"These people have nothing left," Fatima Aunty says. Shoves a stack of chapatis into a plastic bag. Holds it up and says, "The least we can do is bring them something to eat."

Purvapura was never anything special. But tonight, it's even worse: it's nothing more than a handful of families huddled around fires lit from the wooden frames of collapsed tents, demolished shacks. Fatima Aunty drags her daughter through the ruins, telling Rukshana to lift her feet to avoid the broken glass, broken lives. Rukshana lifts her feet so high she feels like she's floating. As though the city has broken all the laws governing human existence. Even the law of gravity.

"Wait here," Fatima Aunty says. "I'll pass out the food and then I'll come get you."

Rukshana sits on what remains of an orange sofa, listens to the metallic crash of families pushing aside walls and doors and roofs to recover photographs, clothing, cooking pots, bedding. To the rush of traffic on the main road, fully visible now that all the houses have been cleared away. Black smoke and gray dust swirl up from the cratered ground, catching in Rukshana's hair, her throat. The air smells charred. Crushed. Exhausted.

"I told you that girl was trouble," Joy says, coming up behind her. Puts her hand on Rukshana's shoulder and squeezes.

"What are you doing here?"

"My mother's aunt," Joy says. "Or cousin? I'm not sure. My mother said we had to come see about them. What about you?"

"Union," Rukshana says.

"Of course," Joy says. Sits down next to Rukshana on the sofa. "Did you see Leela and her mother?"

"They left the night before the demolition," Rukshana says.

"Well that's lucky."

"I stood up to her father. Leela says that's why they left. She says I gave them the courage to run." Rukshana's words sound like the wreckage around them. "She told me I saved them."

"She was right," Joy says. "Look around. They almost got caught up in all this, didn't they?"

Rukshana shrugs. Stares at her feet and thinks, The world is full of almosts. Almost living, almost dying. Almost husbands, almost wives. Almost together. Almost apart.

Almosts that taste like rust and rain. Almosts that empty you, that leave you clinging to nothingness, trying to find a foothold. Trying to survive.

"She wasn't worth it, you know," Joy says softly. "If you love someone, you don't leave. You stay."

"She wasn't safe here."

"You think any of us are safe here?" Joy asks. "Please."

Rukshana squeezes her eyes shut. Color bursts in the darkness between her pupils and her eyelids. She feels Joy's arm tight around her shoulder, pulling her close. Smells Joy's familiar mix of coconut oil and wet lipstick and something else none of us can describe. Something like loyalty.

"Love isn't running away to save yourself," Joy says. "Love is staying together to survive."

Rukshana doesn't answer. Opens her eyes and stares at her hands, her arms. Studies her chipped thumbnail, her calloused fingers. A scar is forming by her elbow, where she cut herself climbing the mandap tree. She touches the tough crescent moon growing over the place where her skin was ripped and torn. The place where she bled.

Examines the injuries she can see. But only because it's easier than considering the ones that she can't.

12

Playing Metro

CITY LIGHTS CHURN THE BANGALORE SKY into an electric orange pink. Night jasmine spread their pointed petals, exhale a fragrance sweet as starlight. Packs of stray dogs pace the streets, weave in and out of traffic. Their voices dissolve into a velvet symphony of howls.

Downtown, the honeycombed windows of government buildings darken, the ceiling fans purr into silence. Employees in offices lined with files pack up tiffin boxes that smell like masalas ground in the towns and villages where they were born. Tuck rubber stamps and signing-in-triplicate pens into crooked metal drawers.

Pens that, earlier today, may have filled out a form allowing water trucks to service our pump, allowing health workers to ration oil and salt and palm sugar to our kitchens. Stamps that may have officially cut off water or kept it going, called for a garbage pickup or a discontinuation of service. Declared Heaven a blank space, a land without history or people, without claimants.

Our mothers tell us if we work hard enough, we can grow up and get government jobs with stable salaries, paid vacations, guaranteed pensions. And, of course, the power to declare who exists and who doesn't. All with the thump of a rubber stamp.

* * *

Before she leaves, the foreign lady says, "I will see you tomorrow. I will come. I will take more photographs." Taps her camera and smiles. Teeth clean and straight and square as the shined-up shop windows along 100 Feet Road.

"*Chee*! She'll sell those photos to a paper and then we'll never see her again," Fatima Aunty says, watching the woman climb onto the bus with the engineers.

When the bus pulls away, our mothers go about the business of managing a crisis. Gather blankets and soap and changes of clothes. Take turns using each other's phones to tell their employers that they won't be in tomorrow. Probably not the next day either. After that, it's anyone's guess. They are bustling and efficient, moving with a surety that surprises us.

"How do you know what needs to be done?" Joy asks her mother. "Have you dealt with this kind of thing before?"

"What kind of thing?" Selvi Aunty asks.

"A demolition."

"I myself haven't dealt with this *exactly*," Selvi Aunty says. "But close enough. There's always something like this going on, isn't it?"

Selvi Aunty's right. Heaven is nothing if not a series of crises. Men lurching home after midnight, collars and shirtsleeves blotted with blood. Women rushing to the police station to post bail for a son wrongfully incarcerated, a husband rightfully restrained. Children stumbling out of tin-roofed huts where their mother has died giving birth, cradling babies swaddled in torn-up saris, blinking their newly orphaned eyes.

No two tragedies are the same. But human needs are never different.

"Luckily, you and I don't have to live like this for much longer," Selvi Aunty says.

"Meaning?"

"Your older brothers are doing well. They send me money every month. Soon we'll have enough to move into a flat."

"You mean move out of Heaven?"

"You don't see any flats here, do you?"

"The government promised to build us some. Fatima Aunty said so."

"*Chee*! Like a government promise means anything," Selvi Aunty says. "How many years have they been saying that? They're too busy building malls to worry about homes for people like us."

Selvi Aunty rests her hand on her daughter's shoulder and squeezes. Joy feels the ridges and plains of her mother's calloused fingertips, a rough landscape of survival.

"Better we find our own place, *kanna*. On our own terms."

Joy knew this was coming. It's what Selvi Aunty always planned. What all of our mothers have always planned, but no one actually did: Move out. Move forward.

"Just imagine. Piped water. Regular power. A real roof, real floors. Doesn't that sound nice?" Selvi Aunty turns her face up to the sky, as though their new home can be plucked from the craters of the moon, the space between the stars.

Joy looks up too. But all she sees is darkness.

* * *

Sometimes we play Metro. Stuff soggy bills and shined-up coins through the plate-glass ticket window, ask for a roundtrip fare to Mahatma Gandhi Road. Wait for the woman with the beeping black wand to scan us for items we cannot afford.

"I hope my jewelry won't set off the detector this time," Joy says.

"Not to mention all my mobile phones," Deepa adds. "You know I like to have a backup in case the network goes down."

"Don't worry, no metal here," Banu says. She never gets it.

On the platform, digital clocks with lime green numbers count down the minutes until the next train arrives.

Seven minutes.

Six.

Five.

We are impatient with the cautionary signs, the razor-sharp lines. The khaki-clad conductors who blow their whistles when we curl our toes over the edge, daring each other to jump into the narrow metallic corridor of safety between the electrified tracks.

Four minutes.

Three.

We don't want the platform. We want the cars with their double-plated windows, their mopped-floor smell. Their machine-cooled air that tastes like steel and money and promise.

We want the lives the cars carry. Their motion. Their purpose. Their speed.

Two minutes.

One.

"Your train is now arriving."

* * *

"Bangalore," our grandmothers tell us, "is a city of befores. Most people, though? They only see the afters."

By the afters, they mean the flyovers choked with Volvo buses and Audis. The women in blue jeans barking instructions to their maids into their company-issued mobile phones, the men in foreign sneakers tapping code into their company-issued computers. The flats sparkling with imported furniture and tinted liquor bottles, the office buildings vibrating with requests for technical help from around the world.

"Before," our grandmothers say, "no one owned air conditioners. No one needed them, what with all the breezes coming off the lakes."

"Before, you could cycle all the way to Commercial Street in the middle of the afternoon without passing a single car."

Before. Before we are old enough to tie our younger sister's plaits, to wish for closed-toe shoes, we sit cross-legged in the shade, listening to our grandmothers coax memories from their hiding places: Braided into the vines of banyan trees, stirred into the mortar between the bricks of school buildings, baked into the egg puffs at the bakery behind the telephone exchange. Mixed into the glue on the backs of government-issued notices warning that this slum will be demolished on this date to make way for this new road or that new building.

"You hear that rushing, that whooshing?" newcomers ask. Eyes shiny, smiles full, ready to start their jobs inventing this and coding that. "It's the swoosh of twelve million dreams coming true."

"What, *that* noise?" our grandmothers say, sucking their teeth. "Don't be stupid. That's just the sound of the traffic at Silk Board Junction."

* * *

On the elevated rails of the Metro, we become our own afters. We are bankers going to our offices at Trinity Circle. We are fancy housewives shopping for four-thousand-rupee handbags on 100 Feet Road. We are film stars on our way to cocktails at the Bangalore Club.

Suspended between the orange and pink rooftops and the white and blue sky, the air is too thin for other people's doubts: there is only enough oxygen for our dreams.

"I hope my lover isn't late this time," Banu says. Today, we are playing film stars. Everyone knows film stars have the most lovers. "I'm supposed to meet him at Koshy's."

"Don't be ridiculous," Joy says. "If you were a film star, you'd never go to Koshy's."

"And *you* would be the late one," Deepa says. "Not your lover."

Deepa and Joy are the best at playing Metro. Probably because they are the smartest. And the bravest. Which in Heaven, is almost the same thing.

"Are you still seeing Sal-*maan*?" film star Joy asks film star Deepa. Yawns delicately, studies her nails.

"Not since he became such a bore," film star Deepa tells film star Joy. "Ranbir is so much more fun."

"All those Khans get old after a while," Joy says. "Although Imran is still delightful."

"That one writes the best poems," Deepa says.

"Why are you always taking Hindi lovers?" Padma says. "What about the Kannada ones?"

"*Chee!*" Joy says, rolling her eyes. "Everyone knows that the Hindi film stars are the best ones."

"If *I* took a lover, I'd want him to know my mother tongue," Padma grumbles.

"Language is the last thing I care about in *my* lovers' tongues," Joy says. Rukshana starts giggling, which makes the rest of us start too. We collapse against each other, a squirming mass of girlish joy.

Until we hear him.

"Is that right?"

Usually, no one notices us. But today is Saturday, and the train is full of boys. Hair sticky with coconut oil. Bits and pieces of mustaches spiking above their lips. Bodies bursting with needs we don't understand.

We girls don't need much. We've taught ourselves not to. We have each other, our mothers, our grandmothers. Our train in the sky. For us, that's enough.

But this boy needs something. Something from *us*. Something we don't want to give him.

"My tongue is quite experienced. All my other parts too," he says. Reeks of *kirana*-cheap deodorant and sidewalk-vendor cologne. Of half-smoked bidis and fake leather shoes left out in the rain. He is all the smells we expect on the skin of the men we will be forced to marry. Smells we will wake up to for the rest of our lives.

Confronted with this boy, this reminder of who we are, and who we will be, the rest of us wilt like carnations. But Joy and Deepa stiffen like weeds.

"Don't tell me about your other parts," Joy says. "That's not how you speak to a lady."

"But you're not a lady. Are you?" the man-boy says, grinning like a dragon.

Reaches out and strokes Joy's neck with a scaly claw.

None of us saw it before. But there it is, an Adam's apple. The brand-new curve we never notice on Joy because we were so busy noticing our own. Curves that are just as unexpected as Joy's. But different.

"Don't touch her," Deepa says. Springs like a cat, strikes the boy across his face. Knocks the dragon breath right out of him. Lands the slap so squarely and surely that for a minute we forget that she cannot see.

The boy lunges, but his friends hold him back. His muscles are taut beneath his shirt.

Just in time, the tinny robot voice announces in Kannada, "This is Trinity Circle."

We are not housewives or bankers or movie stars. We are not even women. We are just girls riding the train. We are just like everybody else. The rest of us rush onto the platform, Rukshana hauling Banu by the elbow, Padma with her arms around Deepa like a straitjacket.

Joy goes last of all. Calm and regal and silent. A queen until the end.

*   *   *

If you're a girl in Heaven, you don't get out much. Too many pots to clean and meals to cook. Too many eyes watching you. When we leave, it's to go to the post office to fill out the deposit forms for our mothers' government-scheme bank accounts, or to the market where we've been sent for onions or tomatoes.

Makes it hard to remember that there is a world out there that is not the same as ours.

Joy goes out even less than the rest of us. When she leaves the muddy paths of Heaven, she leaves more than just tin roofs and hospital sludge. She leaves a fortress, a kingdom she built herself. Subject by subject, brick by brick.

At the post office, the tellers ignore Joy, or ask her to do disgusting things when they think no one's listening. Only one vendor at the market sells her vegetables, and that too, at twice the cost. On the bus, women push her to the back, near the men's section. The section that's all perilous murmurs, malicious grasps and gropes.

Last year, when the health worker put Joy on the scale and told her she was underweight (just like the rest of us), Selvi Aunty took her to the hospital to get the iron pills the government is distributing to adolescent girls.

(Neelamma Aunty said they were only doing it for the elections. Fatima Aunty said who cares why they were doing it as long as they were giving something out for free.)

When the nurse asked for Joy's paperwork, Selvi Aunty handed over her birth certificate.

"*Beti*, I think you brought the wrong one," the nurse said. Purple lab coat over a red-checkered sari. North Indian convent-school voice coated with the congratulations she must get for helping backward women, starving girls. "This looks like it's for your son. Do you have a child named Anand?"

"That's right," Selvi Aunty said. Joy sat straight backed and stone faced, a granite statuette. "This is Anand. He's Joy now."

"*This* is Anand?" the nurse asked. Adjusted her pink-rimmed spectacles.

"Yes," Selvi Aunty said. "We were reborn. As Christians. Anand has become Joy."

"Really, you people will stop at nothing for government hand-outs," the nurse said. Her fair, fair face turned red up to the roots of her salon-cut hair.

"What do you mean?" Selvi Aunty asked. Joy, though, pressed the balls of her feet into the ground, readying herself to leave.

"Like you don't know," the nurse said. "This scheme is for girls! The lengths you'll go to for some extra rations. Really. Get a job."

"I *have* a job," Selvi Aunty said. "Four jobs at four different houses. And Joy *is* a girl. But anyway, what does it matter? She's underweight. The health worker said so. What's that word? *Malnourished.*"

"I can't help you," the nurse said, waving her off. "Take your son elsewhere. And put some proper clothes on him."

Joy stood up then. Regally declared, "Come on, *Amma*. Don't bother with this woman."

But Selvi Aunty wasn't done yet. (Joy learned it from somewhere, didn't she?) She leaned across the table and stared into the nurse's eyes like a cobra hypnotizing its prey.

"Not my *son*," she said quietly. "My *daughter*. Who is ten times the woman you will ever be."

We love Joy. So do our mothers. But outside the borders of Heaven, love just isn't enough.

* * *

When the train pulls away, Padma exhales.

"What were you thinking?" she yells. Maybe at Deepa. Maybe at Joy. Maybe at all of us.

"He can't treat Joy like that," Deepa says. "He can't treat *women* like that."

"He's going to treat women like that for the rest of his life," Rukshana says. "Slapping him once isn't going to change anything."

"At least today, he didn't get away with it," Deepa says. "That's a change."

Padma puts her arm around Deepa. The rest of us don't say a thing.

* * *

Sometimes, after school, Joy walks to the bus stop at the shopping complex across from the water tank. Sits on the corner of the bench like she's waiting for a transfer. Doesn't catch the next bus. Doesn't go shopping either. Just sits. And watches.

This road? It's where the hijras work. Square jaws, Adam's apples, swinging hips. Hair like crows' wings, eyes like temple stones. Our teachers say they are men who dress like women. We think they might be more like Joy—women who are shaped like men.

We believe what our mothers believe: that hijras are magical. Just see how the auto drivers bow their heads when they hand over their coins. How they close their eyes and move their lips when they receive the hijra's blessings.

But Joy? She watches and watches and watches until she sees past the magic, past the superstition. Sees how the hijras count their change before buying something to eat. How they keep wearing their rubber slippers even after they have snapped or torn. How they pretend to ignore the innuendos that rattle like gravel from the tongues of dragon-mouthed men. Hot and rough and smoldering.

Is this my future? Joy wonders.

One July afternoon rain falls in a light mist. The sun moves out from behind a cloud, tossing rainbows across the gray sky.

"It's something to see, isn't it, sister?"

Joy looks up from her bench. A hijra leans against the side of the bus station shelter, looking up at the sky. Poses like she's an item girl, waiting for her sari to get wet enough for her to burst into song.

"This never used to happen in my village," she says. Black-brown eyes lined with kohl. Henna-streaked hair pulled into a loose and windy bun. Creviced cheekbones pink with blush. "Where I'm from, sun is sun and rain is rain. The two don't mix. But here in Bangalore, it's different. And why not? Why should the weather have to follow such meaningless rules?"

She turns then and looks at Joy. "I'm Bhagya," she says. Gives Joy her hand like she's expecting a kiss from a prince. Nails polished black. Fingers rough and calloused. She is royal but faded, like the palaces we see on school trips. But also, somehow, sturdy. "You're one of us. Aren't you, sister?"

Joy chews the inside of her cheek, afraid to answer.

"You must be, what? Thirteen? Fourteen? Not so young. Old enough to start thinking about your future," Bhagya says.

"I'm taking my exams soon," Joy says.

"You're studying. That's good," Bhagya says. "I never made it through school."

"I'm going to college."

"Are you now?"

"They admitted a transgender student into college in Chennai. It came in the papers," Joy says. Leaves out the fact that the girl is Dalit, just like Joy. That's none of Bhagya's business.

"That's wonderful. But tell me, little one. After you study, you get your college degree. Then what?"

Joy presses her lips together tightly. To make sure her doubts don't escape through her mouth.

Right now, Joy is one of us. Our queen. But what about after Heaven?

In Heaven, she is just like the rest of us. But out here, in the real world, she's an unknown, an in between. No one is going to want her to marry their son, to mother their grandchildren. No one will hire her to be a bank teller or a call center operator or an engineer.

"You should join us," Bhagya says. "I'll be your teacher. Live with me. I'll take care of you. Find you work."

What kind of work? Joy wants to ask. What kind of care? But if she asks, then Bhagya may answer. And Joy doesn't really want to know.

"Whenever you're ready," Bhagya says, "I'll be here."

Joy keeps her back straight, her eyes forward. Won't let Bhagya see her be anything less than a queen. Won't let her notice how she digs her toes into the cracks in the pavement. How she feels the rough edges where the tar hasn't properly dried.

This traffic, these buses, this bench—how different it all is from trains in the sky.

So many ways to hurtle through space, to rush through time.

* * *

This isn't the Joy we see, though. The Joy we see is confident, sure. Zooming forward, throwing herself toward the future. Toward love.

It's Deepa's father's second cousin's sister-in-law's niece's wedding, and we're all invited. When Joy shows us the sari—her *first* sari, the first sari *any* of us has *ever* gotten—we tell her it's a waste of money. Spangles sewn so loose that the slightest touch makes them fall like sparkling rain. Sleeveless blouse so thin it'll surely tear with the first wash. Even the bag is cheap, folded out of what used to be the *Deccan Herald*.

"Not even cotton," says Deepa, the seamstress's daughter. Runs the fabric through her fingers so it swishes like rain.

"You could've just taken scissors and cut up some curtains," Rukshana says. "Would've been the same thing."

"No, it wouldn't," Joy says. Smiles. "You'll see."

When she wears the sari, we understand.

The whole world smells like fresh sambar and stale nerves. The bride looks nice enough—wearing red or something—but no one notices her. Not after they see Joy.

In she walks, our Joy of joys, hips swishing, eyes flashing, neck stretched and jeweled like the Sultan's favorite swan.

Yousef stops midsentence. We all stop midsentence, but Yousef stops most of all.

Yousef stares like he's never seen her before. Her collarbone. Her neck. Her ankle. How the watery fabric flows along her crests and valleys. How it makes her whole body ebb and flow.

Joy is the moon and Yousef is the sea. And in that sari, it is always high tide.

As Yousef approaches her, Joy thinks, *This. This* is what it means to be a woman. This is how I will feel every day for the rest of my life. Or, at least, on wedding days, when I am free to wrap myself in seven yards of ammunition.

Yousef presses his thumb into a dimple where Joy's shoulder meets her back.

"What's this?" he asks.

"I don't know," Joy says.

They both watch how a part of him fits into a part of her that may or may not be strange.

Joy is young, and so are we. Not yet familiar with other people's shapes.

But there is one thing Joy now knows, a thing she will teach us all: that our bodies are unique in small but important ways, ways that will put us in charge of other people's hearts.

That we are, each of us, a collection of secrets waiting to be told.

* * *

The digital clock says two minutes. The announcer is about to tell us to please mind the gap, just like they do on the television shows about Britishers.

Padma asks, "Where's Joy?"

We look around, until Banu says, "There. She's over there!"

Joy is standing between the yellow lines, queuing up to board the train going in the opposite direction. The one that will take us back home, like nothing has happened. Like nothing has changed.

Like we can't tell that her heart is racing and tumbling and breaking. That she's pushing down the ways in which her body will betray her. The ways in which her body already *has* betrayed her, when we weren't there to see it.

"Joy, what are you doing?" Rukshana yells.

"Playing Metro," Joy says.

There is Joy in Heaven and Joy in—well, everywhere else. There is Joy with us and Joy without us.

"Are you sure?" Rukshana asks. "We're close enough to walk home from here. We don't have to get back on."

"Walk? What nonsense. It's at least three stops," Joy says. Not like she means it. But like she's trying to. "Come on, hurry up. Or we won't get seats."

"But what if the boy is following us?" Padma says. "He's had enough time to get off and come back and find us. It might not be safe."

"Walk, then," Joy says. "I'll go by myself. Your choice."

"What do we do?" Banu asks.

The train rumbles up to the platform. Brakes screech, tires squeak. The air smells like rubber. Like decisions.

Just as Joy elbows her way through the doors, Padma yells, "Joy, we're coming!"

Because when it comes to choices, one thing is clear. We girls will always choose each other.

*   *   *

A few days ago, Selvi Aunty stepped through the door of Janaki Ma'am's flat, inhaling its smells of laundry soap, incense, and morning rain. Breathed in this proof that with enough education, a woman can have property—an entire life even—that is wholly her own.

Even though Janaki Ma'am has a dining room table and chairs, she settled down on the floor. Handed Selvi Aunty a tumbler of coffee and patted the ground next to her. When she shifted her weight, her crinoline sari sizzled and hummed.

"I don't take too much sugar," Janaki Ma'am said. "I hope that's all right."

Selvi Aunty sipped the coffee, tried not to slurp. Tried to equal the elegance of Janaki Ma'am's house. Of Janaki Ma'am herself.

"I like it a little bit bitter," Selvi Aunty said. "You can taste the coffee's flavor then."

"Exactly," Janaki Ma'am said, nodding approvingly. It made Selvi feel sophisticated, perhaps for the first time in her life.

"I'm Joy's mother," Selvi Aunty said. "She's in tenth standard?"

"Of course I know who you are," Janaki Ma'am said. Because Janaki Ma'am knows everything. Can recite all of our birthdays and histories and family trees. Our mothers' birthdays too, if they were in school with her.

Selvi Aunty didn't go to school in Bangalore with Janaki Ma'am. Didn't go to school anywhere else either. Which is exactly why she was here.

"Joy wants to go to college," Selvi Aunty said. Respecting this place where women and girls make decisions for themselves.

"Of course she's going to college," Janaki Ma'am said. "All of the girls in her class are."

There it was again. That idea that Joy is just like the rest of us. An idea thin as a butterfly's wing shedding its scales. Disintegrating.

"But my daughter," Selvi Aunty said carefully. "She's different."

"She's first in her class right now," Janaki Ma'am said. That's another thing she can recite. Our marks sheets. Every subject, every score, all the way back to lower kindergarten.

"So you think she'll do well on her exams?"

"Definitely. I wouldn't be surprised if she's ranked in the state."

"Her name, though. On the exam. It won't be—her real name."

Selvi Aunty meant Joy's chosen name. Not the name on her birth certificate, on her school-leaving certificate. Both of which she will have to present to a registrar.

"Names are easy enough to change," Janaki Ma'am said, standing up and shuffling over to her antique writing desk. "Especially on marks sheets."

She retrieved a notebook from somewhere in the pile of papers on her desk. Pushed her spectacles down her nose, looked over the top of them. Tucked her chin and mumbled to herself.

"Yes, yes," she said, "let me just find this chap's number."

"You know someone who can help, ma'am?"

"The benefit of being a headmistress," Janaki Ma'am said, "is that my former students do me favors. I am told that it is difficult to say no to me."

"Thank you, ma'am," Selvi Aunty said. Cleared her throat. Plunged on, for her daughter. "Even with her name changed, though . . ."

"I'll go with the two of you for admissions counseling," Janaki Ma'am said. "We'll fill out the forms together. Nobody is going to turn Joy down because of who she is. I'll make sure of it. Like I said, I have connections."

"You'll use your connections for Joy's—situation?"

"Joy's situation," Janaki Ma'am said, "is exactly what my connections are for."

* * *

We hurtle through the compartment's open doors. The train glides forward. We run backward. We run to Joy.

When we reach her, Joy takes Deepa's hand, and says, "You really gave him a good one."

Deepa squeezes back. Pretends she doesn't notice that Joy is shaking.

"Bet she gave him a black eye," Padma says.

"Where are we going?" Banu asks. Trying to remember the rules. "Koshy's? Or that fancy hotel?"

"Home," Joy says. "We're going home."

"Then who are we pretending to be?" Banu asks.

Joy stares out the window into Bangalore's concrete eyes. Thinks about yesterday evening, when Selvi Aunty came home clutching a manila file.

"What's this?" Joy asked, taking it from her mother.

"Look and tell me," Selvi Aunty said.

"You don't know what it is?"

"I think I do," Selvi Aunty said. "But you know my English isn't very good. Just check for me."

Joy pulled a document out of the file. Traced her finger along the raised contours of a seal pressed onto its edge.

"Well?" Selvi Aunty asked.

"It's a birth certificate," Joy said. Swallowing. "It's *my* birth certificate."

"That I know," Selvi Aunty said. Impatiently. "What does it *say*?"

"It says," Joy told her, "that my name is Joy."

Selvi Aunty smiled then. Kissed her daughter on the forehead and said, "Don't look so surprised. It's your name, isn't it?"

"Yes," Joy said. Staring at the paper like it was about to disappear. Like she was in a dream, and at any second, she might wake up.

"Put it away carefully," Selvi Aunty said. "I'll take it and get all the other documents you need to register for college. Janaki Ma'am gave me a list."

"College?" Joy asked. "We have the money for college?"

"Janaki Ma'am promised to help us," Selvi Aunty said. Which in Heaven, is the highest guarantee.

Joy loves Janaki Ma'am's promises. We all do. But for the first time, Joy wonders if this is a promise that Janaki Ma'am can keep.

* * *

As though it's reading her thoughts, the train passes a women's college. Joy looks down at the crowd of girls with dupattas across their shoulders, hair pinned into half ponytails, full braids. She pictures going to class every day with these girls. Without us. Without Janaki Ma'am.

So I graduate, she thinks, then what? How will I interview for jobs? Rent an apartment? Find a husband?

Is this better than what I was offered at the bus stop? Maybe, she thinks, I should go back there. Fall into the life that's expected of me. Maybe the predictable life is predictable simply because it is the life that hurts the least.

But then. There was that feeling of the raised seal on her fingertips. The way her mother said *daughter*, the word circling and settling like a winged creature somewhere in her chest, her stomach, her throat. Somewhere deep and hollow and hopeful.

The dragon boy had tried to knock that out of her. But she wouldn't let him.

"We're not pretending to be anything," Joy announces. Turns to Banu and tilts her head like a Bollywood star. Like a banker. Like royalty. "We're just being us."

"But then it's not playing Metro," Banu says. "Is it?"

"Of course it is," Deepa says.

We don't play Metro much anymore. But when we do, Joy makes the rules.

PART THREE

The Modern Era

13

Returned

SUNLIGHT SEEPS THROUGH the cracks in the roofs of Heaven's remaining homes, pushing our eyelids open, dewing our limbs with sweat. We girls drag ourselves awake and clean our teeth with neem sticks, untangle our hair with tortoiseshell combs. Store the bedclothes, fetch the water. Watch the boys act like Holi has already started, even though it's still two days away.

Vihaan and Yousef crouch outside Rukshana's house, filling bowls of colored powder with dirty water scooped out of an abandoned rain barrel. Padma's brothers circle them, their voices shrill and staccato.

"Let's go to the airport slum and get Raghav! He's always teasing me."

"No, no, let's go to the footbridge. Then we can drop balloons on people's *heads*."

"I'm going to drop a balloon on *your* head."

"No, no! You won't catch me!"

"Yousef, stop wasting water," Rukshana yells. Her arms ache from dragging five full vessels from the tap, which, after two weeks

of dryness, suddenly began to gush. Fatima Aunty called it a parting gift from the useless. Rukshana called it a miracle.

"Chill, *yaar*," Yousef says. "This isn't drinkable. Besides, it's
Holi!"

"Since when do you celebrate Holi? You're not even *Hindu*."

"This is a secular nation," Vihaan says, apparently forgetting
his khaki shorts, his Sunday prayer meetings. Mixes red and blue
powder in a cooking pot that Rukshana is sure his mother will
scrub out later. When he adds water, it swirls into a deep purple.

"What are you lot doing up so early?" Joy asks, coming outside
with a towel wrapped around her wet hair.

"It's Holi," Yousef repeats. Holds open the lips of a cheap rubber
balloon. Vihaan carefully tips the colored water into it, tossing
violet shadows onto the pavement.

"They're destroying our home, and you're playing colors,"
Rukshana says.

"They're going to destroy Heaven no matter what we do,"
Vihaan says. Carefully ties the balloon closed and sets it on the
ground. "Might as well enjoy ourselves."

Rukshana throws her hands up and says, "The worst part is
you're not even going to get in trouble. You'll disappear for the
whole day and come back wet and dirty and who knows what
else. They'll still speak to you sweetly and call you their precious
children."

"We *are* their precious children," Vihaan says.

"What about us?" Joy asks.

"You're precious too," Yousef says, darting his eyes at her. "You
just have more rules."

* * *

There aren't so many men in Heaven. Not so many husbands, fathers. Not so many possible-husbands or fathers-to-be. A few wander around drunk in the middle of the day, ask our mothers for lunch, a handful of rupees. (Usually our mothers say no, and then yes.) A few ricochet between jobs, spending their money on "items" our mothers string between curse words. Toddy. Bidis. Ganja. Other women.

Padma's father is not like the other fathers. He's what our mothers call "a good man." Voice doughy as rotis ready for the pan. Eyes creased at the corners. Hair hennaed to hide the grays. When he sees us girls, he gives us candy from the shirt pocket of his blue uniform with the security company logo. Our mothers object, say we are too old for chocolates. But Padma's father says we're still children.

We like the sound of that.

* * *

One day, at the end of eighth standard, Janaki Ma'am glides into the final minutes of our final class, serious as the Saraswati idol she keeps on her desk.

"You there, Padma," she says. "Come."

It's April, a month before pre-monsoon rains scrub summer away. Sky unblocked, sun's brightness turned up high. It's like living in the screens of our mothers' plastic Nokia phones.

Exams are over, and we're supposed to be doing worksheets our teachers Xeroxed from donated puzzle books. Except Janaki Ma'am has us in pre-tenth-standard boot camp.

"Just like the private school students do," she says smugly.

"I'm pretty sure the private school students are at hill stations right now," Rukshana says.

"Or in Europe," Joy says. "And the United States."

(They don't say it loud enough for Janaki Ma'am to hear, though. Even those two aren't *that* brave.)

Janaki Ma'am has only asked Padma to stay. But we stay too.

"Does your mother work?" Ma'am asks, pulling her brown handloom sari around her stomach. Sunlight glances off the diamond in her nose, her burnt umber skin, her neem-tree-bark eyes. Makes her flash like a lighthouse.

"She stays home," Padma says. Looks at her feet. The tops of her too-tight shoes ripple with her wiggling her toes.

"I see," Ma'am says. "You have a father?"

"Yes, ma'am."

"What does he do?"

"He's a night watchman at an office."

"Are your parents home now?"

When Padma doesn't answer, Joy says, "Yes, ma'am. Uncle leaves for his shift at four."

"Fine then," Janaki Ma'am says. "Let's go." As they're leaving, Janaki Ma'am turns to us and says, "Just the two of us, okay, girls?"

When Janaki Ma'am and Padma get farther ahead, Rukshana turns to Joy and snaps, "What's wrong with you?"

None of us would ever dare to speak to Joy that way. But it doesn't seem to make her mad. She just shrugs and asks, "What?"

"Obviously Padma's done something wrong," Rukshana says. "You just sent Janaki Ma'am to her house before Padma can even make a plan. Before she can even *prepare* for whatever is going to happen."

"You think Janaki Ma'am would've stayed here if I hadn't answered her?" Joy snorts. "Ma'am was going to Padma's house no matter what any of us said or didn't say."

She's not wrong. But still.

"No, but if Padma had a second to think, she could've—" Rukshana says.

"Could've what?" Joy asks.

"Could've—I don't know. Something. Now what is she going to do? How's she going to handle whatever trouble's coming?"

"What trouble?" Banu asks. When we stare at her knife sharp, she shrugs and adds, "I'm just saying. Out of all of us, she's the best behaved."

"Banu's right," Joy says. "Padma's not in trouble."

"How do you know?" Rukshana asks.

"Because Janaki Ma'am came to my house last week," Joy says. "She came to see my mother about letting me go to college. She said she was visiting lots of families."

"You mean lots of families with girls," Banu says. "Girls whose parents might not let them study up to twelfth standard."

"Padma's parents might pull her out?" Rukshana asks. Partly to change the subject. Partly because she doesn't know. "I always thought her father was good."

"Maybe they don't have the money," Banu says.

"Or maybe they *do* and want to save it for her brothers," Joy grumbles.

"They wouldn't do that," Rukshana says firmly. "Didn't I tell you? Her father's good."

"But he's a *father*," Joy says. We know what she means.

We wrap ourselves in silence, but Bangalore keeps chattering and jangling and grinding: auto-rickshaws honk, cows moan, street vendors holler.

"*Tamatar*! *Thakali*! Tomato!"

"Good price. Best price."

We're nearly home before Banu says, "I hope she visits my house."

"Me too," Rukshana says.

* * *

Janaki Ma'am leaves her store-bought sandals outside of Padma's door, ducks her head to fit through the entryway. Padma comes in behind her, tries to see her home through Janaki Ma'am's eyes. Broken fairy lights glowing with stolen power, pots dented and sticky with cooking oil, pressure cooker steaming like a cast-iron dragon. A Tamil Nadu government fan gifted from a cousin in Hosur half-heartedly turns the dense air. A chubby politician's face smiles out from the humming plastic center where the blades meet.

Padma's mother is almost like another piece of furniture, her skin glowing blue in the flame from the kerosene stove, fingers picking stones from the dal for tonight's meal.

Padma's father is getting ready for work. Smells like shoe polish and soap. Makes respectful small talk as he settles our headmistress cross-legged on the floor, asks Padma to boil milk for the guest.

"Padma is talented," Janaki Ma'am says. Padma hands her the chai, and when Janaki Ma'am takes a sip, the steam fogs up her spectacles. "She has a good character. Strong. Determined. One of the most promising students in her class."

Padma's father nods, smiling. "She has a way with numbers, you know. Manages all the money here at home."

"She's also quite good in social studies and Kannada," Janaki Ma'am says. Puts the hot steel tumbler on the floor, removes her glasses. Wipes them with the end of her sari, then points them at Padma's father. "All languages, really. Picks them up fast. She would make a great journalist. Or perhaps even a lawyer. God knows Heaven could use someone like her in the courts."

Padma looks down so her parents do not see her smile.

"We are working extra hours to prepare students for their tenth-grade boards," Janaki Ma'am continues, putting her spectacles back on. "Padma will need time to study. So I hope you'll excuse her from some of her chores and allow her to stay after school for lessons. Free, of course. I conduct them myself. At that time we can counsel her to find a pre-university course."

Gita Aunty turns the stove off. Clacks open the pressure cooker, picks it up, crosses the room, ducks out the door. Sings quietly as she puts cooked rice on the roof for the crows with fingers so calloused that they no longer feel any heat.

"Are you saying she's smart enough to go to college?" Padma's father asks.

"Of course. Her intelligence was never in question," Janaki Ma'am says in her Janaki Ma'am way. Like it's obvious. Like the world doesn't work any other way.

Padma's father nods, asks a few more questions. As Janaki Ma'am leaves, Padma sees her rest her hand on Padma's mother's back.

"Save some for your children, Gita," Padma hears her whisper. "Birds aren't the only hungry ones around here."

When the headmistress leaves, Padma's father says, "This is why we came here. Away from the village. So our children would have everything we didn't." Probably to himself, since Gita Aunty is still singing to the crows.

Even though she knows the words weren't for her, Padma says, "We can't afford it."

"We can if your mother goes back to work," Padma's father says. He puts the palm of his hand on Padma's head. Rests it there a second longer than usual.

Long enough for Padma to know that he's proud.

* * *

It's a tricky thing, finding your mother a job. Especially if your mother is Gita Aunty. She can't read or write or count, so you can't put her somewhere safe, like a bank or a store. Can't be around sharp objects or living things, so you can't put her in a house. You have to find a place where she can mop and dust and talk to herself and stay away from everything that reminds her of anything.

For two weeks, Padma paces the jagged Bangalore sidewalks in her school uniform and too-tight shoes, perspiration dripping down her back. Skirts pink-nosed rats retreating through the gaps between the flagstones. Wishes she could join them in their shady underground worlds.

Instead, she keeps walking. Tries used paper shops, warehouses, wedding halls. The hospital, the lobby of the glass-walled flats. Tries and tries and tries. But no one needs a sweeper with eyes that stare at nothing, a throat that hums with loss.

Even the ones who know the family won't take her. Or, maybe, *especially* the ones who know the family won't take her.

When she runs out of options, Padma goes to the posh neighborhood. Tries the new Western bakeries that smell like yeast and chocolate, the new showrooms that smell like plastic hangers and floor cleaner. The NGOs that come to Heaven to hand out brochures about women's empowerment and financial security, where the receptionists seem irritated by Padma's quest for both.

Still, she won't give up. Not with college at her fingertips. Not when she can almost touch it. Crisscrosses the lanes lined with BMWs and neem trees, shoe stores and private schools.

Until she finds the post office. A building that's all primary colors and right angles. Square walls, square roof, square sign. A cubbied, alphabetized place with no space for chaos.

Outside, a mustachioed man drinks chicory-heavy coffee from a wax cup. Smokes a slim, fragrant cigarette, the kind that comes in packets with English letters on them, that stains collars yellow and molars brown.

"Excuse me, Uncle," Padma asks. "Do you work here?"

When he turns to Padma, she sees the letters embroidered on his shirt pocket. Manager. India Post. Embroidered in Kannada and English.

"Pardon me, Manager Sir. I was just wondering. Do you have someone to tidy up? Things must get dirty with all, the, um—" What did they have at post offices anyway? Stamps? Letters? Nothing sharp or living, that's for sure. "Paper," Padma finishes uncertainly.

"Law says you have to be fourteen to work," he says. Takes a long drag.

"It's not for me," she says. "It's for my mother. We're a good family." She shuffles her feet to cover the stains on her socks, the dirt on her shoes, the scabs on her knees. "Honest. Hardworking. Clean."

The man sips his coffee. Exhales smoke into the salty air.

"If we did have an opening," he says, "when could she start?"

"Tomorrow," Padma says. "Today even. I could go get her now."

He inhales again. Holds the smoke in his mouth. Exhales.

"Five thousand a month, and she comes in weekends. But only after I meet her."

"Six thousand and she gets Saturdays and Sundays off."

"Five thousand five hundred, and Sundays off." Tosses his empty paper cup onto the road. Drops his cigarette butt too. Grinds out the red-orange ash with the toe of his polished leather shoe.

"Fine," Padma says.

"Fine," he repeats. "We'll try her for a month. Come at four o'clock sharp so she can mop after the afternoon shift. Not a second later."

Padma says, "She'll be here, sir. We both will."

* * *

When your mother is like Padma's mother—or, at least, the city version of Padma's mother—you can't just tell her about a new job and expect her to figure it out. You have to take her there, watch her. Sort of like she's the daughter and you're the mother. Like childhood can be passed between generations, can be shaken loose from time.

Every afternoon, Padma leaves her brothers at Deepa's house. Then she goes to her house, collects her mother, and takes her to the post office. They arrive when the workers are leaving, filling their bags with their bus tickets and tiffin boxes, piling the day's completed paperwork on plastic trays. The place smells like fresh stationery and stamp glue and bureaucracy. Like the absence of history.

Well now, Padma thinks. This might work out just fine.

Gita Aunty runs a wet cloth over precarious metal shelves, pushes a mop across the warped tiled floor. Padma follows her from room to room, watching. Does her maths at one desk, her Kannada at another. Monitors her mother's murmuring. Making sure it stays just below the surface.

* * *

The afternoons settle into a rhythm. Dust, dust, mop, mop. Exhale, inhale, hum, sing. A month passes. Two months. Manager Sir hands over the salary, in cash, as promised. The place smells a little less like neglect. A little more like Lysol.

Padma starts to relax. To look around.

That's when she notices that this India Post building is not like other India Post buildings. But it might be a little bit like Heaven.

In this particular India Post office, each desk is covered in letters written in a different alphabet. Envelopes split open, paper creased and soggy. Like they've been folded and unfolded and refolded multiple times. It makes the letters look bewildered, like no one knows what to do with them. Like they don't know what to do with themselves.

The desk where Padma does her maths is the Hindi desk. The one where she does her social studies looks like Hindi but isn't. She can sound it out but doesn't know what it means. Must be Marathi, she thinks, remembering the women in her village who used to pin their saris to their heads. Traces the soldier-straight letters tied together at the top.

Next to that is either Tamil or Malayalam, or maybe both. The desk near the back door is almost Kannada, which means it must be Telugu, like the sign outside Joy's church. The desk near the canteen is English—and although Padma can recite each letter, when they are lined up together, she is never completely sure what they mean.

The last desk in Padma's rotation is the one reserved for Kannada. Stacks of letters twice as high as any other desk, crouching in puddles of gray-yellow sunlight that drip through the building's only window. Maybe that's what makes it feel cozy, snug—or maybe it's the Kannada letters that twine together like the fingers of friends.

She takes the top letter off of the pile.

It's pockmarked with spots shaped like tears. Smells sodden and regretful, like lightning-soaked rain. It says,

Dearest,

You must be very busy in Bangalore building a life for us. Every day I feel lucky for what you are doing for me and our future children. I hope you are taking care of your health. Who is cooking for you? What are you eating?

I know that you are probably tired of my questions. But I haven't heard from you. Please come back. Let us get married so I can take care of you. I can even work beside you. You know I am strong.

Or you can come here and work. We don't need much to be happy. Remember? We only need each other. You told me that.

I do not need an elaborate wedding. I am a very simple person. Even registered marriage is okay.

Counting the days until I am your bride.

All My Love,
Kavya

After school the next day, Padma hurries Gita Aunty to work early. Gets to the office just as Manager Sir lights his last cigarette of the day.

While Gita Aunty fills the mopping bucket with water from the bathroom tap, Padma asks the manager, "Sir? What is this place?"

"A post office," he says. Strikes a match with a yellow flame.

Last year, Padma would have lowered her eyes. Walked away. But nowadays, she sees herself like Janaki Ma'am sees her: Determined. Strong. A future journalist. Or a lawyer. Someone with a degree fancy enough to not back down.

"What *kind* of post office?" she asks.

"What?"

"All the mail is open," Padma says. "They don't do that at normal India Posts."

"Ah, like that," Manager Sir says. But he takes another drag before answering. Inhale, exhale. Pause. "This is a Returned Letter Office."

"Returned Letter Office," Padma repeats. "What does that mean?"

"The other India Posts send us the letters that aren't delivered."

"Why aren't they delivered?"

"Many reasons," Manager Sir says. He speaks deliberately. Like he's enjoying answering Padma's questions. "Maybe the addresses are wrong, or the people have moved. Maybe the handwriting is too sloppy to read, or it's in a language the carriers don't understand."

Padma feels her heart—well, it doesn't break, exactly. But it splinters a little. Cracks.

"But that's terrible," she says. "Do you help them?"

"We try. We certainly try," Manager Sir says. Padma's not sure, but she thinks she hears a little bit of something in his voice. Pride, maybe. Like he actually cares.

"How?"

"We try to send them where they belong. See if we can understand the handwriting. Look at maps of old neighborhoods, check forwarding addresses. We open them and read them. Look for clues." He stares out into the distance, his eyes full of other people's words. Other people's lives. Padma wonders if he has any room left for his own.

"What if you can't figure it out?" she asks.

"We file them away in registers. Wait and see if someone claims them."

"Do people do that?" Padma asks. "Claim them?"

"Sometimes. Sometimes we can read the return addresses, and we send them back. Sometimes they sit there for decades."

"But what about the people who are supposed to get *those* letters? The ones you can't place?" Padma asks. Thinks of all the unanswered questions. The hopes. Regrets. Doubts. "What happens to them?"

"What to do?" the manager says. Drops the end of his cigarette. Grinds the ash into the sidewalk with his toe. "You can't help everyone."

Which is the wrong thing to say to a girl from Heaven.

* * *

Padma tries to do her sums and English sentences. To color her maps of the common crops of Karnataka, balance her chemical equations.

Really tries. But it's no use.

Those silent, still stacks of letters? They've burst into motion. Into sound. Wailing. Sobbing. Screaming. Stories tucked into those letters strain across miles of rivers and mountains and deserts, of days and weeks and years, of farms and cities and empty roads. Claw at Padma with frantic fingers.

Take the love letter Padma wasn't supposed to read. What if the girl who wrote it is waiting by a window, restless in her own puddle of gray-yellow sunlight? What if she is about to lose her only chance at—what? Love? Freedom? At something.

The letter remains at the top of the pile. Handwriting looped and—she can see now—desperate. Beseeching.

Padma takes her eyes off of Gita Aunty long enough to read the letter again. Not just the lines, but between them too. Declarations of love. Of intended marriage. Hope of more than just a lifetime of happiness. Hope of escape.

The return address is clear. From a village smack in the middle of the state. Nowhere near the ocean, or the mountains, or anything glamorous or impressive. It's not far from Padma's native place, actually. Which only makes things worse.

Padma knows the escape routes from a place like that. Especially for a girl.

There aren't many.

Padma recognizes the address. House number two, Shastrinagar Colony, behind the old airport. Street three. It's the address of a slum. Or, at least, it used to be a slum. Before the airport moved.

Now, it's a parking lot. For a shopping mall.

Without a house to go to, this letter will be returned. Padma imagines it in the hands of a girl with arms as knotted and muscled as tamarind pods, skin brown and dry as thirsty cornstalks. Pictures the girl reading it in the dim light of a cowshed reeking of manure and fresh milk. Or worse, being unable to read it, asking her little brother for help. Pictures her doubling over from the pain of the worst kind of heartbreak.

"Just because you can't help *everyone*," Padma says to herself, "doesn't mean you can't help *anyone*."

Padma tears a page from her school notebook. Finds a blunt pencil in the back of a squeaky drawer, a roll of stamps behind the cash counter. Digs a soft, graying eraser from the bottom of her bag.

Writes:

Dearest,

You cannot imagine how it felt to hold your letter in my hands. It was almost as wonderful as holding you. It made me understand how important it is for us to be together.

But, alas. My parents are arranging my marriage. There is nothing to be done. If only—

But wait. In a true romance, wouldn't the boy fight?

This was not a happy ending. It was just another kind of tragedy.

Perhaps it would be better from a family member?

Padma tears out a new page. The ripping sound echoes off the empty walls.

Dearest,

You cannot imagine how it felt to see your letter delivered to our door. Almost as happy as it would've made me to see you marry my brother.

"Unless he doesn't *have* any siblings," Padma mumbles. "Then the whole thing falls apart."

Dearest,

You cannot imagine how it felt to see your letter. Almost as happy as it would've made me to see you marry my son. But sadly, he is no more. He got dengue last summer after all the rain. Before he died he told me to write to you.

This family loves you. We accept you, even if you will never be our daughter-in-law.

Be well and fall in love again and marry someone else. Our son would have been happy with that. Don't waste your life.

Also, after it rains, make sure you don't get any mosquito bites. You never know.

Sincerely Yours,
Your loving
almost parent

"Perfect," Padma says. Shakes her water bottle above it to make a few teardrops. "She thinks he loved her till the end." Folds it carefully, truthfully. The way someone grieving maybe possibly would.

"She thinks his family approved of her." Writes the address, fixes the stamp, drops it in the next day's mail. "No ruined reputation, not a fully broken heart. Now she can meet the man she's *supposed* to marry."

Chucks the returned letter into the rubbish that her mother will soon bundle and destroy.

* * *

Padma never saw her father much. Now she sees him even less. If she and her mother get home early and he leaves for his shift late, they might cross paths with each other on the road, or at the door. Those times, he'll cup his hand around Padma's cheek and smile.

He leaves her envelopes of cash around the house. Padma knows how much is supposed to come in each week. If it's not all there, he's usually left a bag of vegetables, or fabric for new uniforms for her brothers. A reminder that whatever he spends, he does it for the family.

When they're home together, on Sundays, she shows him the bank book from the account Padma opened in her mother's name.

"I was thinking," Padma says, "maybe we should use Ma's salary this month to pay the rent. Just this once—"

"No," Padma's father says firmly. "That's your money for college. We won't touch it."

"Yes, Papa," Padma says.

"How much does college cost?" he asks her, knitting his brows.

"I'll get a scholarship," Padma says. Which doesn't answer the question. But close enough. "Janaki Ma'am says she'll help me."

"Your brothers are keeping up in school?"

"Neelamma Aunty checks their homework every night," Padma says. "She's very smart. I think she wishes she could've gone to college."

"She isn't the only one. Your mother and I wish we had gone too," Padma's father says. Pinches her cheek. Like he hasn't since she was a little girl. "Now you'll go for all of us, darling. You'll set a good example for your brothers. For this whole area."

Padma looks down and blushes.

"Don't make your children go through this," Padma's father says. "If I had gotten an education, I could've given you a better life. I could've—"

"Don't say that, Papa," Padma says. "We have a good life. We have everything we need."

It's not a lie, exactly. More like a story. The kind of story you tell the ones you love.

* * *

Once Padma starts, she can't stop. Every day she sits at the Telugu desk solving maths problems and memorizing poems. Moves to the Marathi desk, telling herself she's there at the post office to make sure her mother stays happy, stable.

But really, all Padma is doing is biding her time until she gets to the Kannada desk, where she can answer the letters of the lost.

Maybe, Padma thinks, it isn't only the future that can be shaped. Maybe you can also shape the past.

* * *

Padma is at the Kannada desk, writing letters she thinks people want to receive.

To children who have written to their parents after being disowned:

Dear Child,

I love you very much and always have. I am very proud of you. I accept everything that you are and who you married and who you love. I trust you.

This is the only letter I can send to you because since you left I have become a spy. If I send you letters they will know I am your family and then you will be in mortal danger. So that's why I don't write you. But I will always be your father so you should not think about whether I love you or not. I do.

Sincerely,
Daddyji

To old friends trying to make amends:

Dear Satyam,

Your apology is sincere. I forgive you. I hope you stop having nightmares about what you did to me because I am very happy and rich and I have married a beautiful woman who is also very kind. We are going to have lots of children together and she makes delicious food. So you don't have to feel guilty any more.

I run a big company now and have lots of duties. Because I became rich lots of people got jealous. So I left home and am hiding somewhere that my enemies can't find me. Also because then they will leave my family alone.

It is very pretty here but I don't answer letters very often. So don't worry if I do not write back. I still accept your apology.

> Wish You All
> the Best for
> a Happy Life,
> Your old friend

And, most often, between lovers who quarreled or split or just got tired of each other:

Dearest,

I never stopped loving you. But I am going to have a really risky surgery and might not survive. You should move on and love someone else. Don't worry, that will make me happy. If I die—which I probably will—then you should know that I loved you and only you and you are in my heart forever.

> Love,
> Your dearest

In the letters Padma writes, people die. Vanish. Waste away. Flee. But they also forgive. Accept. Love. Trust.

With her words, Padma makes the world into the place that it ought to be. A place too dangerous to forget how to love.

* * *

There are signs, of course.

How Padma suddenly starts watching serials with Joy right before dinner, starts listening to the radio plays with Deepa after. How she pays attention when Joy makes Rukshana help her act out dramatic scenes from the latest *filmi* flops. How she listens when any of our mothers wish out loud for a different life.

Sure, it's obvious when it's all laid out. But not to us. Not then. We just didn't see it.

Same way Padma didn't see the big letters "RLO" in the window of the office where she got her mother a job.

When you're hungry for something, it's easy to ignore what is right in front of your eyes.

* * *

One day, Padma pulls out a letter with handwriting that looks a little bit familiar. The slanted sentences, the country slang. Even the envelope smells familiar, like a certain kind of sunlight. A certain kind of rain.

But then, she's probably just imagining it.

She eases open the flap, pulls out the letter. Reads:

Dear Brother-in-Law,

How many years has it been now? Fourteen? Fifteen? Long enough that everyone says it is useless to keep writing. But I don't believe that you are gone.

You are a good man. You wouldn't do this to my sister and your daughter, who is twenty years old today.

Your daughter is getting married. Did you know? She has made a good match. But now my sister needs money for the dowry. She needs you to come to the wedding so she can hold her head up with pride.

I know you took up with Gita because after six years of marriage, my sister still couldn't give you a son. I've heard Gita

has given you one girl, but also two boys, like you wanted.
I accept that. But when you moved to Bangalore to help your
new family, you promised you wouldn't forget my sister. I
know you made good on your promise for years. Believe me,
we saved all the money that you sent. But it's been five years
now since we've heard from you, and there is nothing left.

I think your oldest daughter—the one Gita gave you—is
fifteen now. What would you want for her? Is she so much
more important than your very first daughter?

It is time to accept your responsibility. My sister does
not know I am writing. She would be furious if she knew.
But what you are doing is not right so I cannot be quiet any
longer.

Come back. Pay for your first child's wedding. Stand by
your wife's side at the ceremony so she is not humiliated.
She is your first wife. You have a duty.

You used to be a good man. Be one now.

Sincerely,
Raghav

"No no no no no," Padma whispers. Murmurs and hums like her
mother. Feels herself crumple and fold like paper under teardrops.
"It can't be. It can't."

But it can. It is.

It always is.

Just look at the return address: a place way up north of nowhere.
Rice paddies watered by rivers the color of the afternoon sky.
Yellow trucks scraping sand. Sisters walking barefoot to school
along sandy half-made roads.

Just look at the mailing address: Swargahalli. Behind Vidyalakshmi Hospital. House 3.

Padma's address.

* * *

Padma knows about second families. We all do.

How mothers warn their daughters to keep their husbands away from women with fertile wombs and hungry eyes. How second families hide in places where they cannot be found by first families.

Places like Heaven.

How some fathers—some of *our* fathers—start other families. How our mothers break coconuts and shave their heads and strike all kinds of bargains with God to send their men back. How our mothers blame themselves. Doesn't matter how much he drank or hit or lied. Doesn't matter how much money he gambled away.

Not that Padma's father does any of those things. He's a good man. The letter even says so. All of us say so.

Padma reads the letter and rereads it and then reads it again. Feels her heart, her lungs, her guts, twist into new shapes.

History's shape, though? That stays the same.

Padma and Padma's mother and Padma's brothers are all a second family. Another woman's nightmare. And now, if Padma's father gets this letter, he might want to do the right thing. Not might. He will.

After all, Padma's father is a good man.

If Padma's father *does* do the right thing, he will go back to the village. He will pay for this daughter's wedding. He will face the family he left. The life he could have had.

What if he never comes back? Or what if he does?

How will Padma, the one who has saved her mother and her brothers and all the rest of us from so many disasters, spend her life knowing that she is the cause of someone else's pain?

What kind of future is that?

* * *

It is one thing to write stories to save others. It is another to write a story to save yourself.

Padma knows it's risky, but she takes the letter with her. Tucks it into the waistband of her skirt in the morning when she's getting dressed for school. At lunch, she doesn't sit with us. Instead, she climbs the banyan in the middle of the compound and reads the letter over and over and over. Like she's searching for meanings hidden in the spaces between the words, between the lines. Like if she reads it enough times, its story will make sense. Will change.

But all the reading does is make her tired. Tired of being everything for her mother, her father, her brothers. For strangers who write letters because it is easier to hope than to admit the truth.

Tired of growing into the kind of woman who spends so much time being strong for others that she forgets to be strong for herself.

On the second day that Padma avoids us, Joy calls up through the tree branches, "What's the matter? You sick of us?"

"Something like that," Padma yells down. Really, she aches to be with us. To be folded up in our us-ness, our girl-ness.

But she can't.

Padma's never kept secrets before. But how can she tell us this? After everything she's agreed to—we've all agreed to—about second wives. Second families. Second choices. Promises we've made to one another. That we will not be like our mothers. That when we get married, we won't be the first wife. We'll be the only wife. And that, if we find out we are not the only wife, we will fight. Or walk away. Either way, we will win.

"Whatever it is," Joy says, "you'll get over it."

Padma wonders if that is true. Thinks about the histories she has rewritten for all those returned letters. If this were someone else, Padma thinks, what would I write?

She opens her notebooks and stares at the blank page. Most probably she would kill the father, she realizes. Humanely, though. A heart attack, maybe. Or a coma, like in the serials. Something quick. Without suffering. The news would come from a relative. A mother-in-law, maybe, or an aunt. It would say that the woman, the daughter, may have been abandoned, but that didn't mean that they weren't loved. It would urge the woman to forgive the family, to move on with her life, to find a new kind of happiness.

Love. Trust. Acceptance. Forgiveness.

Just yesterday, they seemed like the truest things Padma knew. Now they feel like the worst kind of fiction.

* * *

Padma sends her brothers to Deepa's house and walks her mother to the India Post. But today, the gray-yellow light is the color of rejections, the crooked metal shelves the shapes of collapsing bodies. Each register of unreturned mail bends beneath the weight of hundreds of hearts as heavy as Padma's. Maybe thousands.

It's a wonder the whole building doesn't sink into the earth.

Padma opens her maths, but the numbers on the page dip and ripple. She blinks rapidly, but it doesn't help. Tears still perch on her eyelids, ready to leave spots on the parentheses and triangles and x's and y's. All the bits and pieces of things that Janaki Ma'am says will help her get to college.

Janaki Ma'am, who is one more person who needs Padma to be strong.

"Ma," Padma finally says. "Is this place okay for you? Is it too sad?"

Gita Aunty smiles her distracted smile. Beneath it, Padma imagines she sees a flicker of the mother she once knew. The mother with black-brown arms and a back knotted and strong from farm labor. The mother whose sari smelled like cooked rice and burnt paddy and courage. "I like it here," she says.

"Why?"

"It's quiet," Gita Aunty says. "It's an easy place to forget things."

"Okay," Padma says. "Then I'm going. But you can't lose this job, okay? You have to stay here. No stealing things or running away or anything like that."

"Go," Padma's mother says, humming under her breath. "Don't worry. I'll be fine."

Padma hopes that this time, her mother's words will not be fiction.

* * *

Padma gets home just as her father is about to leave for his shift.

When he sees her, his face lights up. "Padma," he says, "I didn't think I'd see you today!"

"There's something you should know," Padma blurts out.

"Is everything all right? Is it your brothers? Tell me, darling, I'll help."

"It's about your daughter," she says. "Not me. Your other daughter. From your first family."

She pulls the letter from her skirt's waistband and reads it out loud. Anger coats her tongue like lava, turning the words liquid, volcanic. Explosive. When she looks up, her vision is blurred, like she is looking through a cloud of ash.

Her father remains perfectly calm. Asks, "How much money is in your mother's bank account?"

"What?"

"You heard me," he says. "How much money is in your mother's bank account?"

"That's my college money. You said so yourself."

"That's our family's money. *You* said so yourself."

"*Our* family's," Padma says, "or your *other* family's?"

"Padma," her father says, saccharine as honey, viscous as betrayal. "I moved to Bangalore to give you and your brothers comfort and opportunities."

"Me and my brothers," Padma asks, "or just my brothers?"

"Don't be disrespectful. You have a good life."

"I do *not* have a good life," Padma says. "I have to go to Deepa's house if I want to eat properly. I have to babysit my own mother. My mother who stopped being a mother the second you brought us here. I have to manage the finances and speak to the bill collectors and the tellers at the bank, most of whom look at me like I'm scum. *I* don't have a good life."

"Shut your mouth, you ungrateful girl," he says. "Whatever life you have, I've given you. You know how parents drown their daughters when they're babies? Leave them out for tigers? But when you were born, we kept you. *I* kept you. Now you tell me exactly how much money is in that account before you make me regret my decision."

"No."

"What?"

"No," she says. Padma, who knows the bank tellers. Padma, who reads the notices, keeps the books. "I'm not letting you have the money. And there's nothing you can do about it."

"Why you disrespectful little—"

"You can't read. Can't do math, can't fill out a withdrawal slip. You don't even know where I opened the account," Padma says. "You made *me* do it. So *I'm* the only one who knows."

"Padma, I'm warning you," he says. Raises his hand. It's trembling.

"Go ahead," Padma says. "Hit me."

She means it.

"Well?" she says. Waiting.

He keeps his hand raised. But it never falls.

"Didn't think so," she says. "Now, about the money. Go to the wedding if you want. Give your other daughter a dowry. Just don't expect *this* daughter to pay for it."

* * *

At Deepa's house, Padma's brothers are racing around Neelamma Aunty's sewing machine, reciting their times tables. Every once in a while, Deepa's mother looks up from her tailoring and yells at them to pay attention.

"Hey! Four eights is *not* twenty-four," Neelamma Aunty says. "What is it?"

"Four eights is thirty-two," her brothers say.

"Good," Deepa's mother says. Then, "Hello, darling. Here to pick up these rascals?"

"Yes, Aunty," Padma says. Adds, for the thousandth time, "Thank you for watching them while I take my mother to work."

"*Chee*! How many times do I have to tell you not to thank me. Anyway, good you're here. I was just letting out the hem of your uniform skirt," Neelamma Aunty says. The black Singer sewing machine clacks and rattles. "This should last you another month or two, but tell your mother she needs to get you some new uniforms. Janaki Ma'am can arrange for it."

"You don't have to do that, Aunty," Padma says. "I could've done it. Don't you have a lot of other work to do?"

What Padma really means is paid work. Deepa's mother knows better than anyone that Padma's family doesn't have the money for tailoring. Even simple jobs like this.

"Nonsense," Neelamma Aunty says briskly. "Deepa tells me you have studying to do. Didn't I see Janaki Ma'am visit your house the other day?"

"Yes, Aunty," Padma says, blushing.

"Well then. You just worry about studying. You let me worry about my work. Now go inside. Deepa is waiting for you, I'm sure," she says.

Padma steps into the house, as she's told, inhaling its familiar odor of talcum powder and curry leaves. Deepa, who is pounding ragi into soft, doughy balls, says, "Hey, useless! Come here and help me chop some spinach for *sopu saru*."

Padma rolls her eyes, but only because she knows Deepa can't see it.

"You're early," Deepa says, scooting over to make room for Padma beside her on the floor. "Your mother is okay by herself now?"

"Seems like it," Padma says. Takes a straw mat from the corner of the room and sits down on it cross-legged.

"Good," Deepa says. "Now what's wrong with you? I'm blind, and even I can see that something is on your mind."

"Nothing," Padma says, a little too quickly.

"Liar."

"Oh, shut up. Where'd your mother put that washing bowl? This spinach is filthy."

"Check in the corner by the water," Deepa says. Her braid sways slightly as she pounds the ragi, her wrists and fingers fluttering and hopping like babbler birds.

"There *is* something on my mind. But I don't want to talk about it right now," Padma says, tipping water from the drum into the bowl of spinach. Words barely louder than the sloshing of the water.

"Then don't talk about it now," Deepa says. "Or ever, if you don't want to."

Could this be an option, Padma wonders? What if this story, the story of a second family, of one of the most hated things in Heaven, is fully told? What if there are no words to add, no problems to resolve? What if she never has to speak about it, think about it, grapple with it, ever again?

"Whatever it is, I'm glad your mom is settled and you're back to coming here after school. I missed you," Deepa says.

"Of course I'm back," Padma says. "Where would I go?"

"College," Deepa says. "Pre-university. Places I can't go."

"That doesn't matter," Padma says. Even though she knows it does. "You can't get rid of me so easily."

Padma stuffs the spinach in the bowl full of water. Swishes it back and forth, back and forth. Insects float to the top, tiny black corpses with paper-thin wings.

From outside, Deepa's mother yells, "Padma, why are you washing vegetables? Shouldn't you be doing your math problems? Make my lazy daughter do it."

"Don't call me lazy, *Amma*! I'm blind, not deaf."

"I'll just help her and then do my maths, Aunty."

"Fine, fine. But don't try and get out of your homework, young lady. I'm watching you."

"Yes, Aunty."

In Heaven, there are first families and second families. But there are other families too. Families born out of something more than blood. Families that cannot be erased with a new letter, a new story. A new neighborhood, a new wife.

"Wash that well now, Padma," Deepa's mother yells. "Last time that cheat gave me spinach full of tiny, tiny flying ants. Filthy."

"Yes, Aunty, I'm doing it," Padma calls. "But there are still a lot of ants. You should go somewhere else to buy your spinach."

"This is what I keep telling you," Deepa yells.

"Who else is going to give me such a good price? And excuse me, you two boys, just because I'm talking to your sister doesn't mean you stop reciting. What are thirteen twelves? Tell me."

Deepa and Neelamma Aunty argue, and Padma's brothers chant. Padma thinks of the silent post office full of love and loss and tragedy. Of stories begging to be rewritten.

She thought she would miss it. The power, the possibilities. The bending of time. But here, in this chaos of sisters and mothers and brothers, of families lost and found. Here, in this glorious present, she doesn't miss a thing.

14

Lathi Charge

"THE FOREIGNER'S BACK," Neelamma Aunty says. Teeth busy clutching a collection of safety pins, eyes busy glaring at the photographer framing the ruins of our lives. Hands busy wrapping herself in a cotton sari one of her clients gave her for Deepavali. It's airier than her usual polyester blend, better able to weather sunshine and anger, uncertainty and rage. Perfect for a protest.

"What was that?" Deepa whispers, trying not to wake Banu's *ajji*, who is asleep even though it's at least two hours past sunrise.

Neelamma Aunty pulls the remaining pins out of her mouth and whispers, "The photographer woman. She's back. These people, I'm telling you. Always around when we're at our worst. But when we're at our best? Nowhere to be found."

"I know, *Amma*, I know," Deepa says, groaning quietly. "Stop complaining and get ready. Let's go."

"Who says you're coming?"

"Of course I'm coming."

"*Chee*! Absolutely not. Today, you stay here."

"What? Why?"

"It's not safe."

"Not *safe*? But all the other girls are out there. Why should it be different for me?"

"Of course it should be different for you! You're—"

Just then, Banu's *ajji* unleashes a giant, booming snore. Shreds the air into pieces. Sends Deepa and Neelamma Aunty into a fit of giggles.

"She's louder than a bulldozer," Neelamma Aunty whispers.

"Is she all right?" Deepa says, gasping.

"She's fine!" Neelamma Aunty says. "That woman's survived all this before. She'll do it again."

"What do you mean, again? This isn't the first time they've tried to destroy Heaven?"

"No, no. Every few years they try something. The last time was just before you girls were born," Neelamma Aunty says. "Back then, our houses extended up to the main road. The city wanted to widen it from two lanes to eight, but Heaven was in the way."

"So what did you do?"

"The same thing we did yesterday. Got in front of the bulldozers and yelled and screamed and carried on. Not me, though. I was pregnant with you, and I didn't want to take any chances," Neelamma Aunty says. Rests her hand over her womb. A place where so many babies grew, so many died. Sometimes, she still feels them quivering. Still feels like a vessel full of ghosts.

"If you weren't at the protest, then where were you?"

"Inside our house. I forced all the children to come with me. We were there for hours," Neelamma Aunty says, skin prickling with memory. The feeling of her hand pressed against the vibrating walls, her feet pressed against the quaking floor. Of protecting

Deepa, her unborn child. "We came out only after the bulldozers went away. After the lathi charge."

"Lathi charge?" Deepa asked. She's heard the phrase in the newspaper articles we read to her every morning. The words sound venomous, insidious, like the twin tooth marks of a spider bite. "Was it scary?"

"I'm sure it was," Neelamma Aunty says. "I was inside, remember? We heard a lot of yelling and cursing. And then it got quiet, and everything stopped."

"It can't have just stopped. Someone must've done something," Deepa says.

"Someone *did* do something," Neelamma Aunty says. Remembrance seeps into her mind like a puddle under a locked door.

"Who?"

"People said it was Banu's *ajji*," Neelamma Aunty says. "But I don't think anyone knew for sure."

* * *

Banu's *ajji* grew up with six sisters who were said to be the most beautiful girls in the district. Skin fair as clarified butter, eyes light as filter coffee. After every one of their coming-of-age ceremonies—and sometimes before—marriage proposals flowed in, each offer more prestigious than the last. Wealthy suitors and their powerful families made unbelievable promises to waive dowries, to split the costs of weddings. Promises unheard of in a village where women identified only as the wives of their husbands and the mothers of their sons, where the oldest grandmothers couldn't even remember their original names.

Banu's *ajji*'s parents should have been overjoyed. Instead, every potential groom made them more anxious. Because standing before all of this good fortune was an insurmountable obstacle: Banu's *ajji*.

Custom dictated that none of the girls could marry until the oldest was settled. Banu's *ajji* was the oldest. And Banu's *ajji* was not like her sisters.

Skin dark and leathery from years of herding sheep. Hair perpetually matted with dust and grass and sunlight. Second toes longer than the first, which everyone knows is a mark of independence, a warning sign that a wife will be impossible to control.

By the time Banu's *ajji* turned sixteen, she hadn't received a single proposal. Her parents panicked, sure that if they waited any longer, they would have seven old maids on their hands instead of just one. So they called Banu's *ajji*'s mother's third cousin's family. A family with five unmarried sons and no daughters, with plenty of hands for the field but none for the kitchen.

A family that didn't have the money for a servant but certainly had the space for a wife.

"Strong as a buffalo, this one," her mother-in-law said at Banu's *ajji*'s bride viewing, "and doesn't seem like the complaining type. Her horoscope's a good match for my second son. We'll take a dowry, but there's no need for a wedding. Let's register the marriage and spare the expense. What do you say?"

Banu's *ajji*'s parents were delighted. By the end of the week, they obtained an official marriage license through the family court, sent their oldest daughter to her new husband's village, and put out the word that their second daughter was ready for offers.

Banu's *ajji* never saw her parents again.

* * *

The air in Deepa's hut feels heavy, trapped. So does Deepa. She paces the floor like a caged animal, heat and bitterness pressing against her body like iron bars.

She keeps up her restless circles until Banu's *ajji* finally stirs.

"Deepa, darling. Bring me some water, no?" she asks. Her words are raspy, labored, defeated. As though her lungs resent the fact that they are still expected to carry on.

"Here, *Ajji*," Deepa says, handing the old woman a bottle of lukewarm water. "I'm sorry it isn't cold."

"Thank you, child," Banu's *ajji* says. Seeing the clouds pass across the girl's face, she asks, "What's wrong?"

"*Amma* said I couldn't go out there," Deepa says. "It's not fair."

"Don't be so hard on her, darling. She's just trying to protect you."

"I don't *need* protection. I'm not a child."

"I see," Banu's *ajji* says, smiling. But only because she knows Deepa can't see. "You're an adult now, is it?"

"Only when my mother thinks it's convenient," Deepa says, grumbling.

"You girls," Banu's *ajji* says. "So ready to be old."

"It's not like we're *young*," Deepa says. "Not the way the boys are, anyway. Playing and studying and doing whatever they want."

"You're right," Banu's *ajji* says gently. "It's not easy to be a girl. But trust me, my dear. It is much, much harder to be a woman."

* * *

During the first few months in her husband's home, Banu's *ajji* fell into a rhythm of chores punctuated by the thrumming beat of her mother-in-law's constant criticisms.

"Don't skin the vegetables so thickly. Just see how much you're wasting."

"Don't scrub the shirts so hard. Just see the marks you're leaving."

And, sometimes, when her mistakes were worse than usual, "We did you a favor, bringing you into this family. Don't make me regret my generosity."

As for the man she married, Banu's *ajji* rarely saw him. During the day, he worked in the fields with his father and brothers, coming home only long enough for Banu's *ajji* and her mother-in-law to serve them meals. When the sun set, he lay down beside Banu's *ajji* in a room the family had built for the newlyweds with walls made of cow dung and a roof made of straw. After an hour or two, he always left, returning early in the morning smelling like gasoline and cheap foreign cologne—cologne that Banu's *ajji* was sure he didn't own.

Every night he disappeared, and every day Banu's *ajji* said nothing. What good would it do? She wasn't a wife so much as a business arrangement, a stone that felled two mangoes, a solution to the problems of two families burdened with the wrong number of girls. Who was she to fault her husband for seeking love elsewhere, for supplying himself with everything he had been denied?

Besides, her husband fulfilled his one conjugal duty by impregnating her on their wedding night. At least, that's what she assumed he'd done. She didn't actually know how women became pregnant; no one had ever told her. When he mounted her, pressing his rough farmer's hands against the dirt floor instead of her bare skin, she was confused, but circumspect. Observed his movements with a detached curiosity, assessing whether this ritual would become a new inconvenience in her life. So far, it hadn't.

In those first days of her marriage, she was happy only in the mornings, when she rose before the rest of the household, sometimes even before the sun. Then, in the pearled light of the waking world, Banu's *ajji* crouched on her heels outside the hut's door, a mud pot full of rice flour cradled in her arms. Gathering the soft mixture in her fingers, she moved her hands in delicate circles, spinning the powder into flowers, stars, comets, planets. Whole galaxies away from the life she knew.

Her mother-in-law, who woke up soon after, would come outside to examine Banu's *ajji*'s work. Tilting her head and shoving her fists into her hips, she'd say, "Well that's not so bad now, is it?"

It was the closest she ever came to a compliment.

* * *

Our mothers say there are no secrets in Heaven.

They're wrong, of course. There are plenty of secrets in Heaven. Secrets that hide in pots and pans, waiting for an excuse to bang and crash and roll and boil. Secrets that soak in pooled-up sunlight, watching the world with half-moon eyes. Secrets that lunge out of doorways, wind around windowsills, baring their fangs, making sure they are seen. Secrets shaped like the edges of shadows, the bottoms of clouds. Hues and textures that are woven so tightly into our vision that they are easily missed, even when they are right there, right in plain sight.

There are plenty of secrets still left in Heaven. Plenty of hiding places too.

Banu's *ajji*'s past? That's the biggest secret of all.

We don't know where she came from, who her parents were, or who her husband's parents were. How much or how little she studied, and whether she wanted to study more. We don't even know her real name.

Back when she lived with her husband and her son and her son's wife, Banu's *ajji* introduced herself as Kadhir's mother. Now that Kadhir Uncle is dead, she says she's Banu's *ajji*.

"I know that you said that in your village, women don't use their first names," Banu says. "But you live in the city now. Why not tell people what you're really called?"

"The first thing I want people to know about me is that I'm your grandmother," Banu's *ajji* says. "So when I meet them, that's what I tell them."

"But there's nobody left to meet. And everyone you've met already knows," Banu says. She's right—Banu's *ajji*'s universe includes only Heaven and its orbit. Parents, teachers, headmistress. A vegetable vendor here and there, a doctor or nurse who came by with free injections. Migrants who moved in and out, staying for a few months, a few years.

"What's wrong with calling myself your *ajji*?"

"Nothing. It's just that all the other mothers use their proper names. Don't you have a proper name?"

"I do. But like I said, it's not important."

"But it's your *name*," Banu says. "It's who you *are*."

"Who I *am* is your grandmother," Banu's *ajji* says. "There are lots of other parts of me, but you are the most important."

"So is your name a secret?"

"Not a secret, exactly," Banu's *ajji* says thoughtfully. "Just something that the world doesn't need to know."

* * *

Soon after Kadhir Uncle was born, Banu's *ajji* was told she was moving to the city.

"You'll work beside my son as a pressingwallah, ironing the clothes of engineers for money," her mother-in-law said. "My husband's arranged it."

"City?" Banu's *ajji* asked. "What city?"

"What city, she asks? Just see this dimwitted girl," her mother-in-law said, cackling. "Bangalore, of course. What other city do you know?"

Banu's *ajji* blushed, but she didn't say anything. When she was a girl, Bangalore was a scattering of bungalows and ration shops, a single stop on a bus route bumping over dirt paths. Going to Bangalore wasn't going "to the city." It was going "to market" or, maybe, sometimes, "to town."

If Banu's *ajji* could read, she would've known that, just as she was no longer a child, Bangalore was no longer a sleepy hamlet peopled with air force families and retirees. Would've seen the names of new companies hurtling through the newspapers, surging across the want ads like electrons stringing together a new kind of current: Infosys. Texas Instruments. Wipro. Names of places where people made things. Things like computers and calculators, cell phones and semiconductors. Money, money, and more money.

But Banu's *ajji* had never been to school for longer than a week at a time. Which means that when she packed some saris and a bar of soap in a bag sewn out of empty rice sacks, she had no idea where she was going. Or why she was going there.

She boarded the first bus with her luggage in one arm, baby Kadhir Uncle in the other. Then another bus. Then another. On every vehicle, Banu's *ajji*'s husband settled her and their child into a window seat, submitting himself to the rancid crush of passengers packed into the aisle. Each seat was a small kindness, a tiny sacrifice. Banu's *ajji* noticed, and she was grateful.

When they finally reached Bangalore, Banu's *ajji* nursed her son under her sari and pressed her nose against the bus's double-paned glass. Watched the city unfurl like a roll of half-developed film. Cinemas and parks, churches and mosques, offices and petrol pumps. Lake breezes puffing perfumed petals off of the limbs of blooming trees.

They passed a building with tall red letters on the roof. Banu's *ajji* heard the woman sitting behind her ask, "What does that say?"

"Karnataka Slum Clearance Board," the woman's husband said.

"Slum *Clearance* Board? Or just Slum Board?"

"Slum *Clearance* Board."

"So the point is to get rid of slums, or to help them?"

"Get rid of them I guess."

"That doesn't seem fair. If people live in a slum, they probably need help. No one *wants* to live in a slum."

"Hmm, true, true. But maybe that's why these people *want* to clear slums. So no one *has* to live in them."

"If that's it, then that's quite good, isn't it?"

Listening to them, Banu's *ajji* wondered what it would be like to be in a marriage like theirs. To have conversations with whole words and phrases instead of just gestures and grunts. To ask each other questions. To answer.

Twenty minutes later, they disembarked in the middle of a forest so dense that Banu's *ajji* thought her husband had missed their stop. Instead, he pushed through shrubbery and high grass, shoved aside branches, and stepped over tree roots. Brought her and Kadhir to a clearing where a few families had strung plastic tarps between wooden poles sunk into the muddy ground. Where women crouched over smoky cook stoves, washed dishes in barrels of rainwater, sewed patches on the holes in their children's clothes. Where everyone looked exhausted, fragile. Broken.

She wanted to ask her husband how he had found this place, and why he seemed to know it so well. Why he was so happy to trade a farmhouse built on an endless expanse of black earth and green fields for this cramped wasteland with a cut-up sky?

But hers was not a marriage of answers. So all she asked was, "Where are we?"

"Our new home," her husband said.

Left to her own devices, Banu's *ajji* narrowed her questions down to the smallest ones, the ones she could ask wives, mothers, daughters. Women like her, brought to this place with no information, no choice. Questions like, where is the best place to buy cheap vegetables? Where is the right place to hang laundry? Where does the water come, and how often?

Neelamma Aunty's mother was the first to take pity on Banu's *ajji*, offering her a cook stove and a stack of pots and pans.

"I'm sure I'll have more to give you soon. We're moving to government quarters, you see, and planning to start fresh," Neelamma Aunty's mother said. (She didn't mention that she wasn't taking Neelamma Aunty with her—Banu's *ajji* would find out later.)

"Congratulations, Aunty," Banu's *ajji* said, readjusting Kadhir on her hip. "That's wonderful."

"My son found a position with the space program. He's a driver,"

Neelamma Aunty's mother continued. "They gave him a flat and everything. He has an eighth-class pass so they say he may be able to become a supervisor. I suppose your husband hasn't studied that far, has he?"

This kindness, then, was a warning, Banu's *ajji* realized. A caution not to expect much. Still, she was grateful. So grateful, in fact, that she took a bowl of rice flour to Neelamma Aunty's mother's doorstep the next morning at dawn. Crouched in the dirt, she laid out a series of dots, diagonals. Connected them with curves and lines and flourishes. When she finished, she sat back on her heels, admiring her work.

"Who's there?" Neelamma Aunty's mother asked. Her voice trembled, like she'd been woken up this early before. More than once, probably. And probably to receive bad news.

"It's me," Banu's *ajji* said. "Sorry to disturb."

"Ah, yes. The one who took my pots," Neelamma Aunty's mother said. After her eyes focused in the dim light, she said, "This is beautiful. Is this what *you* do for work?"

"For work?"

"Rich people pay for *kolam*. Here they call it *rangoli*, though— some north Indian word. Whatever you call it, they don't know how to do it themselves." Neelamma Aunty's mother knelt down and studied the intricate patterns. "You should get yourself some powders and go make some money."

"Oh no," Banu's *ajji* said, blushing. "I shouldn't work outside of the home."

"Why not?" Neelamma Aunty's mother asked.

Even though Banu's *ajji* mumbled another excuse, she thought to herself, Actually, she's right. Why not?

Here in Bangalore, she was not the illiterate, lazy-eyed shepherdess ruining her sisters' futures. The toiling spouse working off the debt of her family's desperation. The woman whose husband was too disgusted to touch her. Here, she was simply the pressing-wallah's wife. Kadhir's mother. A woman who was good at *kolam*.

Thus far, her life had been a collection of the consequences of other people's choices. But maybe it no longer had to be. Maybe, now, the choices could be her own.

* * *

Deepa rubs orange-yellow oil onto Banu's *ajji*'s shoulders, feet, back. Neelamma Aunty got it from Fatima Aunty who got it from some woman in her village who knows which herbs heal soreness. It smells like a wet jungle. Makes the tips of Deepa's fingers burn.

"Mmm, that's good," Banu's *ajji* says with a sigh.

"*Ajji*," Deepa says, "*Amma* says that they tried destroying Heaven before."

"Yes," Banu's *ajji* says, closing her eyes. "About fifteen, sixteen years ago, I think. Just before you were born."

"*Amma* says you're the one who stopped them."

Deepa feels the old woman's limbs tighten, muscles knot. Underneath Deepa's oily fingers, Banu's *ajji*'s body suddenly feels thick with memories.

"Yes," Banu's *ajji* says, "I was."

"What did you do?"

The hut fills up with city noises. Insects buzz and geckos chirp. Car horns blast and bus brakes screech. Somewhere nearby a cell phone rings. Banu's *ajji*, though, stays quiet.

Just when Deepa thinks the old woman has fallen asleep again, she says, "It doesn't matter what I did. But I can tell you that it won't work now. Otherwise I would've done it already."

"Did you know someone, *ajji*?"

"Not someone, exactly," Banu's *ajji* says. "More like something."

* * *

After Neelamma Aunty's mother suggested she should start a *rangoli* business, Banu's *ajji* saved five annas here, ten paisa there, until she had enough to buy herself a basket of powders. Just four colors to start with: red, yellow, blue, and purple.

Once she had the powders, all she needed was permission. The night her kit was complete, she sat cross-legged on the bare earth in front of their family's tent flap, peering into the night, waiting for her husband to come home from wherever he always went. The ground was cold and dewy beneath her thighs.

There were no streetlights in the neighborhood yet, but that night, the moon was full, turning the world as bright as day. Which is why Banu's *ajji* could clearly see her husband when he emerged from the underbrush, sometime after midnight. Even if it had been pitch black, she would've known him: the way he swung his arms when he walked, dropped his shoulders, bowed his legs. After only a few years, his silhouette was already as familiar to her as her own.

He wasn't alone. A few steps behind him, a moonlit shadow wove between the trunks of trees. Tall and boxy. Close-cropped hair, muscled neck.

A man-shaped shadow that, with whispered urgency, pulled her husband into a passionate kiss.

Banu's *ajji* squeezed her eyes shut. Had she imagined it? But no, when she looked again, there they were, their bodies smashed together, hands searching each other's backs, lips searching each other's mouths. Clinging together like the steely remains of a two-car collision.

She knew that she was supposed to be shocked, indignant. Maybe even distraught. Instead, she was flooded with relief.

Because now, she had answers. She knew where her husband went. Knew why he didn't touch her, speak to her. Knew that his throat was sealed with a potent mixture of shame and guilt and confusion. Knew the real reason he agreed to move to Bangalore. Not for money. For love.

She watched her husband and his lover—because that's what this man was, she realized, her husband's lover—but she didn't say anything, didn't move. After all this time, she could wait. Wait for her husband to see her. Or, more specifically, to see her seeing him. To know that she knew.

Tonight, when she told him that she wanted to work, he would say yes. In fact, from now on, no matter what she asked him, he would always say yes.

* * *

"Do you need anything else, *ajji*?" Deepa asks. Washes *ajji*'s cup in a barrel of water that's been sitting in the sun, just outside the door. It's so hot it feels like Deepa warmed it up on a stove.

"Besides a new set of lungs?" Banu's *ajji* asks. Laughs a laugh like scraping metal.

"What happened to your breathing, *ajji*?"

"All those years of ironing," Banu's *ajji* says. Puts a rough hand on Deepa's hair. "The coal turned my lungs black. Did the same thing to my husband."

"He passed away?"

"Years and years ago. Right before my son, Banu's father, got married. It's a shame Banu never met her grandfather. He was handy, just like she is."

"Do you think that's where she got it from?"

"She didn't get it from her father, that's for sure!" Banu's *ajji* laughs two or three loud, wild guffaws before her joy dissolves into a cough that jangles like rusted tin.

When Banu's *ajji* recovers, Deepa asks, "Do you miss him, *Ajji*? Your husband?"

"Every day, my darling," Banu's *ajji* says. "Every single day."

* * *

Banu's *ajji* loved doing her *rangoli* rounds. Back then, in the mornings, Bangalore's air was still crisp with unfurling leaves and rippling water. Crows cawed and swooped between houses eating the cooked rice and lentils Brahmin women left on windowsills. In the near distance, the *azaan* poured from the tinny speakers of a newly constructed mosque, syllables smooth and shimmering like liquid bronze.

Above it all, her own voice, clear and strong, calling out, "*Rang-o-leeee! Rang-o-leee!*"

She loved the families too, and the houses. Strings of green lime and red chilies swinging from doorframes, warding off the evil eye. Clanking wrought-iron gates, posh housewives in cotton nighties and bare feet, saying, "My grandchildren are coming today. Can you do something special?" Or, "It's my husband's birthday. He likes the color red." Or, her favorite, "I saw what you did at the neighbor's house. Do something like that for me. Something to make them jealous."

While Banu's *ajji* squatted on driveways and doorsteps, coaxing designs out of her ever expanding set of colored powders, her husband would wake their son. Bathe him, feed him, walk him to school. Banu's *ajji* would be home in time for her husband to go collect the clothes that the two of them would spend the day pressing, often knocking on the doors of the same houses Banu's *ajji* had just left, carefully stepping around the patterns drawn an hour before.

"My wife's been here, I see," he'd say with something like pride.

"That's your wife?" the client would say, handing over trousers, dress shirts, saris, *salwars*. Some damp with morning dew, others smelling like yesterday's sunshine. "Such talent. You both are going places, I tell you."

They did the ironing in a three-walled shed, a boxy thing her husband had slapped together using plaster of Paris and bamboo. Together, they watched the children leave for school, the mothers go to work.

When her husband left to do his deliveries, the neighborhood women and girls would stop by to talk, describing the parents that pushed them out of the schools they loved and into the marriages they despised. The toddy-soaked husbands that showed up only long enough to fill their wombs with unwanted children. The employers who left finger-shaped bruises on their arms, turning their skin into tangled blooms of green and black and blue.

Banu's *ajji* helped them as much as she could. Made friends with the local health workers and the school officials. Ferried wives and daughters to the post office when she knew the sympathetic clerk was on duty, the one who was patient enough to open bank accounts for women who pinned dupattas on their heads to hide their torn hair, their black eyes. Became someone reliable, dependable. Useful.

Sometimes, if a neighbor's problem required carpentry—a leaky roof, for instance, or a cracked wall—she'd ask her husband to help. Sometimes, she didn't even have to ask.

"I heard you talking," he'd tell her later. "I thought I'd do it before you started nagging."

It was a joke, Banu's *ajji* knew. She didn't nag him. Barely spoke to him, really. It was too risky, all those words. So much of the truth of their marriage was hidden. These days, neither one of them had the energy to lie.

Once, when they were ironing, her husband said to her, "If you wanted to find someone, I wouldn't mind."

"Find someone?"

"Someone like I have," he said.

"Are you mad?" She laughed. "Why would I need another man in my life? You and your son are more than enough trouble."

"Fine, fine," her husband said, laughing too. "I know my son and I could both do better."

"Oh, you know I'm teasing. You're a good husband and a good father. A good man, really," Banu's *ajji* said. She paused then, digging through the silence for a way to say what she meant. A way to speak the unspeakable. "That's why I'm fine with you. Whatever you want to do, I'm fine."

"All right," he said, clearing his throat. He clapped her awkwardly on the back, as he would a brother or a cousin. A friend. "All right then."

It was the closest he ever came to thanking her.

At night, after they were both sure Kadhir was asleep, she

watched her husband weave through the lopsided tents, sidestepping the sewage running down from the new hospital. Stealing away from this home built on adultery, this marriage built on disappointment. From the cancer that neither one knew was pushing its coal-colored fingers into their lungs.

There, beneath the blinking stars and airplane taillights, Banu's *ajji* breathed in deeply and said to herself, Well now. Just see. After all this, I've ended up happy. We both have.

How strange, she thought. How very, very strange.

* * *

The first time the city tried to demolish Heaven, our mothers' mothers and their husbands streamed out of their houses with rocks and crowbars and broken metal. A few of our mothers did too. Rushed toward the bulldozers like fire from a dragon's mouth. Wedged open the bulldozers' doors and pulled out the drivers.

The police came quickly, so quickly, in fact, that some people thought they must've been crouched in the bushes the whole time, their khaki uniforms the color of the undergrowth. They came screaming out of the foliage, twirling their lathis. The people of Heaven ran right at them, welcoming a new target for their unspent rage.

The police commander stayed out of it, marching coldly around the perimeter, measuring out his officers' madness. When necessary, he pulled them back, yelling, "Just scare them. Don't murder them. We don't need the extra paperwork."

When necessary, he also yelled, "Harder. Faster. Teach these ruffians a lesson."

When the bulldozers came, the first thing Banu's *ajji* did was find Neelamma Aunty and the neighborhood children. Shoved them all into Neelamma Aunty's house and shut the door. At first the smallest ones hurled themselves against the walls, mewling like indignant kittens, insisting they were old enough to help. Banu's *ajji* ignored them, her back against the house, staring into the trees and willing her husband to come home from his deliveries early so he could tell her what to do.

She didn't find her husband. Instead, she found the police commander.

Boxy shoulders. Muscled neck. Close-cropped hair. But more than anything, the smell. That sickly sweet cologne. Banu's *ajji* knew that smell.

Banu's *ajji* adjusted her sari. Dusted off her hands, hitched her petticoat up from where it was peeking out beneath her skirt. Slunk up to the commander, careful as a cat. Surefooted. Calm.

"What do you want, woman?"

"Commander, sir, I think you know my husband," she said, staring at the ground.

"Who is your husband?"

"The pressingwallah," she said. For a second, her eyes flicked up at him, her gaze black with knowledge. "I think you know him quite well, in fact."

The commander didn't say anything. Just tightened his grip on his lathi, tensed the muscles on his neck. They stuck out like rope.

"Call off your men," she said quietly.

"You don't scare me," he said, his voice low and strained. "You have no one to tell. Even if you did, who's going to believe the words of a crazy old *kolam* lady."

So it *is* him, she thought. He knows what I do for a living. My husband has told him. The edges of her advantage felt crisp as a one-thousand-rupee note.

"Your officers may not believe me," she said, "but my husband will."

The man grunted. So she continued.

"He'll believe me if I tell him that you allowed our home to be destroyed," she said. "That you stood by while we lost all of our possessions. Our papers and our savings. Our livelihood. Our reason for being in this city at all, really."

He cleared his throat but still did not speak. She was close enough to see the stubble on his chin, his neck. Some of it, she saw, was speckled white. It reminded her of the rice flour she used to make her first *kolam*s. The ones at her mother-in-law's house.

Banu's *ajji* kept her eyes on the ground, but she was sure she could feel the police commander assessing her. Feel his blood pulsing in his ears, drowning out the noise of people screaming, banging, rioting. Of houses falling to the ground.

"He's not in love with you," the commander said finally.

"I'm not in love with him either," she said. "I'm not in love with anyone, in fact. So if we move back to the village, it's all the same to me."

"He would never move back to the village," the commander said, laughing harshly.

"If we lose our home, we'll have to," Banu's *ajji* said firmly. "We have nowhere else to go."

The air vibrated with pounding footsteps, desperate screams. Unmitigated rage. But Banu's *ajji* felt that she and the commander were somewhere else. Somewhere cold and still and silent. Somewhere between what would happen and what would not.

A place where Banu's *ajji*, and not the policeman, had the power.

"Call off your officers," Banu's *ajji* said quietly, "and then call the city. Tell them to stop all of this. Not just for now, but for good."

In Heaven, the ground quivered, the trees shuddered. Even the wind seemed to tremble. But Banu's *ajji* felt still and sturdy and bright.

After a minute, the police commander yelled, "Officers! Stand down!"

After five minutes, he called his contact in the city, speaking just loudly enough that he knew Banu's *ajji*—but no one else— could hear.

After ten minutes, the bulldozers pulled away.

* * *

"Hello? Deepa, are you in there?"

Banu's *ajji*'s eyes flutter open. She'd fallen into a confusing half sleep, somewhere between dreaming and waking. Now, covered in sweat, in a house that isn't her own, she is sure that the voice is part of a dream, or perhaps a haunting. It sounds like Kadhir, maybe, or her husband. After all, what human male would show up in a slum in the middle of a demolition, when they could be out playing at colors or cards or anything at all besides being a provider?

But when she opens her eyes, it's not a specter speaking, but a boy. A boy who is not like other boys but might be a little bit like Deepa.

"Who's there?" Banu's *ajji* asks sleepily.

"Hello, Aunty," says the boy politely. When he steps through the doorway, Banu's *ajji* sees that he is bent over. At first she thinks he is leaning over to enter the house. Until she realizes that his hunch is not something he's doing, but his actual back.

"What happened to your—"

"Polio, when I was a child," the boy says. Smiles charmingly and adds, "But don't worry, Aunty, my health is just fine. My mind too."

"You! What are you doing here?" Deepa asks. She comes in from around the side of the house, where she's been soaking up the day's pathetic excuse for a breeze.

"Deepa!" the boy says. "I've been so worried. Are you all right? Where's your mother?"

"Yes, yes, I'm fine. Just bored out of my mind," Deepa says. "My mother's outside. Can you take me to her?"

"Of course," the boy says. Reaches for Deepa's elbow like he's done it before. Like it's his right.

"One minute, young lady," Banu's *ajji* says. Fighting to find the strict mother she knows is still inside her, the one that kept Kadhir Uncle and Neelamma Aunty and so many of our mothers out of harm's way for so many years. "Where do you think you're going? Who gave you permission? And who is this boy?"

"This boy," Deepa says, "is my future husband."

* * *

The night she stopped the demolition, Banu's *ajji* heard her husband speaking to the neighbors. Listening, really, and fixing things: the fractured frames of their fallen homes, the rusted remnants of their broken roofs. The neighbor's child stood off to one side, watching and kicking at the dirt with his bare toes.

"They came without warning and they stopped without warning," the neighbor was saying. "It was the strangest thing."

"*Ajji* stopped them," the child said.

"Who? The *kolam* lady?" the neighbor asked. "No, no. That can't be."

"She stopped them," the child said. "She said something to the head police officer and then it stopped."

"She spoke to the commander, is it?" Banu's *ajji*'s husband asked. His voice was strained, but she was sure no one else could tell. No one else had heard him speak enough to notice.

"That can't be right," the neighbor said.

"Why not?" her husband said. "My wife is a resourceful woman. I'm sure she thought of something."

"Well that's true. She's a good woman, Kadhir's mother."

"Yes," her husband said. "She is."

He means it, Banu's *ajji* realized then. He's changed.

But then, Banu's *ajji* had changed too. The way she spoke to the police commander? It was no longer the way she spoke to her husband. Sometime during the decade and a half that they had been married, she had stopped being the unwanted wife. He had stopped being the unwilling husband.

Love had never grown between them. But something else had. Affection, perhaps. Respect. A marriage that, against all odds, had also become a partnership.

"What could she have possibly said? That policewallah doesn't listen to anyone, least of all women," the neighbor was saying.

"Forget the commander. These knots are all wrong," her husband said. "Bring me some rope so I can mend it."

He didn't actually address the question. But Banu's *ajji* knew he knew the answer.

* * *

"Just where do you think you're going? Your mother told you to stay here, so you will stay," Banu's *ajji* says, her throat dry and aching, her voice devoid of its former gravitas.

There was a time, decades ago, when every child in Heaven bent themselves willingly into Banu's *ajji*'s care, obeying her orders, eager to please. Today, though, she is not taking care of Deepa so much as Deepa is taking care of her. And both of them know it.

"I have my husband's permission," Deepa says. "Traditionally, he outranks my mother, doesn't he, *Ajji*?"

Banu's *ajji* raises her eyebrows at this boy Deepa calls her spouse. He shrugs, grimaces, grins. He is young, this one, but he is reliable. Banu's *ajji* has seen enough men to know that much.

"At your own risk then," Banu's *ajji* says.

"The city's not going to hurt me, *Ajji*."

"It's not the city I'm worried about. It's your mother."

"I can handle her," Deepa says, pinning a dupatta to her shoulders. Softly, she adds, "But if you need me, *Ajji*, then I'll stay."

"*Chee*! Don't be silly. Why would I need you?"

"I'll be out there with everyone else. But you'll be here all alone."

"Alone? That's nothing. I'm used to it, aren't I?" Banu's *ajji* says. The words taste corroded, bitter. Like the lies that they are.

It's been fifteen years since Banu's *ajji*'s husband died, a decade since her son and daughter-in-law did too. Almost twenty-four hours since the city leveled the home her husband built, since she lost the place where she raised her child, her grandchild. The spaces between these massive losses were dotted with so many smaller ones: friends, relatives, neighbors. All crushed beneath the wheels of horrors and hardships reserved only for the poor.

After Deepa and her fiancé leave, Banu's *ajji* closes her eyes. Focuses on the air the fan valorously churns into a tepid breeze. Listens to her own frail chest rising, falling, rising, falling, to her lungs crunching like breaking tin, like crumbling bricks.

Destruction, Banu's *ajji* realizes, always sounds the same.

15

Crooked

THE AIR IS AS SOUPY as twice-warmed sambar, as viscous as stale rice porridge. We cluster in the shadow of the bulldozers, shifting every hour, chasing the shade that migrates with the sun. Our mothers spread worn-out bed sheets and dupattas over the dirt, ply us with freshly boiled drinking water and sliced-up cucumbers seasoned with chili and lime. Our neighbors come and go, joining us during the breaks between their jobs washing dishes and mopping floors. We can't blame them—in Bangalore, there's no such thing as demolition leave.

The main road is a symphony of men and boys. Water balloons splash and water guns pump, throats screech and bare feet thump. Rhythms pounded out by people who are expected to protect no one besides themselves.

Halfway through the morning, the bulldozer drivers arrive, loose change and bus tickets crammed into their shirt pockets, bidis and betel nut crammed into their mouths. The one with the tennis shoes has a purple stain on his trousers, like he was hit by a color-filled water balloon and didn't have time to change.

"You're back, is it?" Fatima Aunty asks. She tries to sound

threatening, but her words fall limply in the wilting heat. "Don't even try to start those bloody machines."

"Don't worry. We'll wait for the police to come beat some sense into you first," says the driver with the wart. Spits a wad of betel on the ground, where it hits the dirt with a blood-colored splash.

The driver with the patchy face shrugs and adds, "Demolition or not, we still get paid."

Not long after the drivers find their own shade, the photographer shows up too, full of pride at fulfilling her promise. All morning, she crouches and ducks and leans, dancing her strange dance of pessimism and pain. At first, Banu trails her again. Before long, though, she gets bored of helping the foreigner frame the same pathetic images over and over and over again.

"This is torture," Rukshana says as Banu collapses next to her.

"I wish something would just *happen*," Joy says, sighing in agreement. "Anything at all."

As though she's heard, Neelamma Aunty's voice slices the thick air like a machete through a tender coconut. Sharp and curved and angry.

"Is that my *daughter*?"

"Can't be," Selvi Aunty says. "You told her to stay inside, didn't you?"

"Anyway I can barely make them out," Fatima Aunty says, peering at the two silhouettes that are slowly approaching us, still too far away to be more than outlines of bodies struggling against the glare of the unforgiving sun.

"It's her. I can tell," says Neelamma Aunty, who in the past sixteen years has barely left her daughter's side. Knows Deepa's movements better than she knows her own.

Still, Selvi Aunty says weakly, "Your daughter's a good girl. She would never disobey."

Rukshana guffaws and Joy hits her on the back of her head.

"Which one of you is responsible for this?" Neelamma Aunty says, rounding on us, like she's just remembering we're here. We see her tallying our numbers, making sure we are all present and accounted for, like our teachers do every morning.

There's Banu, sketching a city skyline in the dirt. Padma, doing practice questions from a board-exam preparation book she's borrowed from Janaki Ma'am. Joy, reciting Urdu couplets to Rukshana, who is making faces to cover up how much she's enjoying them.

"I don't think the girls are to blame this time," Selvi Aunty says, squinting into the distance. "Deepa's coming with—someone else."

Fatima Aunty follows Selvi Aunty's gaze and shakes her head. "She's right, Neelu. I'm sorry to say it, but today, you only have yourself to blame."

"What are you talking about?" Neelamma Aunty says.

Until she sees it too.

"*Hai Ram*," Neelamma Aunty says, slapping her forehead like an overwrought mother-in-law in a Kannada-language serial. "Just see. Those two aren't even married yet, and already they've started."

* * *

Last Thursday, we walked to school on a winter morning and left on a summer afternoon. Bangalore's like that: in just a few hours, the city switches its allegiances, trading one season for another. Sunlight blazes and riots, breezes cower and still. Summer soaks the earth, saturates the sky. Seeps into our bones injecting us with restless heat, reckless abandon.

"Let's skip our chores and go to Lal Bagh," Rukshana said. She's loved the botanical garden ever since she figured out how to climb the silk cotton tree without getting caught.

"Too far away," said Padma, who had to pick her mother up from work.

"Fine. Then let's get Bowring *kulfi* at that place by the Metro."

"Too expensive," said Banu, who spent all her money on medications for her *ajji*.

"Let's go to the park," Joy said. Held up a day-old English-language paper her mother rescued from the dustbin of one of the houses she cleans. "The one on the posh side of town."

"The posh park?" Rukshana asked. "Why?"

"Because today it's covered in butterflies," Joy said, flapping the paper open with a flourish that makes its pages rustle like beating wings. Peered at the mess of English letters, traced the smudgy photograph. "It says here that hundreds of butterflies have come to Bangalore from all over the country. They find the leafiest places in the city to lay their eggs."

"They're mothers!" Padma said. "That's beautiful. Then where do they go?"

"Nowhere. After they lay their eggs, they die."

"So they just leave all their children behind?" asked Banu, voice trembling.

Joy swatted her and said, "Don't be so negative. You're the artist, no? You of all people should appreciate it."

"Plus, it's close by, and it's free," Padma said.

"Exactly," Joy said, closing the paper and folding it carefully. "Come, let's get Deepa."

"Deepa?" Rukshana asked. "Why would we take a blind girl to see butterflies?"

"Because she's one of us," Joy said sharply. "Now let's go."

Joy's words launched us like rockets into the brand-new weather. We careened through Heaven, crackling like fireworks, boisterous and bright and bursting.

"Deepa! Let's go!" we yelled. "We're taking you out."

But unlike us, Deepa's house was silent. There was no Neelamma Aunty in her usual place behind her Singer sewing machine. No Deepa on the doorstep chopping beans and tomatoes and onions. No hum and buzz and chatter and sizzle pouring out through the open door, inviting us in with all our chaos and complications and noise.

"They must be inside," Padma said, bounding through the door. But before she fully crossed the threshold, she halted and said, "Oh!" We slammed into her, one by one, flailing like carom pieces. Stopped cold by the scene we had inadvertently disrupted.

Deepa's family sat cross-legged on the ground. Neelamma Aunty worried her sari with her cut-up hands, fingers calloused and scarred from needles aimed the wrong way. Deepa's father bounced his knee up and down, brow taught and wrinkled, weathered from years of driving in the sun and rain. Deepa sat perfectly still, face secreted behind the *pallu* of a purple organza sari, wrists dense with bangles, legs dense with anklets.

They faced a family sitting against the opposite wall. A mother who could've been our mother, a father who could've been our father. And a boy, who could've been our brother—or, actually, our much older cousin.

The boy—who might be a man—did not look right. Spine crooked and bent, shaped like the years before we were born.

Before every child in every slum opened their mouths to receive bitter and lifesaving polio vaccines on their tongues. Before the Rotary Club hung yellow banners on the footbridge declaring India polio free.

And this boy. This crooked boy that none of us would give a second glance?

Deepa was serving him a cup of tea.

"Looks like the butterflies aren't the only ones thinking about reproduction today," Rukshana whispered.

*　*　*

"Good morning, um—Aunty," Deepa's fiancé says. Swallows hard and looks to us for help, but all we can do is shrug. How are we supposed to know what to call your future mother-in-law? Especially when she's staring at you the way Neelamma Aunty is staring at this boy. Like she wants to send him to the mountains of Kashi in the middle of an avalanche.

"What do you two think you're doing?" Neelamma Aunty asks. "Deepa, I specifically told you to stay at home."

"You can't tell me I'm old enough to get married but I'm too young to protest," Deepa says. "It's not fair."

"Of course I can. I'm your mother. I can tell you whatever I want."

"That doesn't make any sense. Am I an adult or not?"

"An adult? Ha! That you're definitely not."

"Well I have permission from my husband to be here, so there's nothing you can say."

"He's not your husband! You're not married yet! You two aren't supposed to be talking, let alone wandering around together."

"Oh, so the fact that my fiancé cared enough to check on me is a bad thing, now? You'd rather pair me off with someone heartless who doesn't care about me and my family?"

"Aunty, I apologize for the impropriety, but—" Deepa's fiancé says.

"Nobody asked you," Deepa and Neelamma Aunty say at the same time.

"Oh. I, um, I mean—"

"Shhh," Joy says, grabbing the boy's arm and pulling him into our quieter, safer fold. "Let them be. They'll burn each other's fuses out, just wait and see."

"Are they always like this?" the boy whispers.

"Worse," Padma says.

"But not as bad as the rest of us," Rukshana says.

Our mothers' tempers are constantly ignited. Selvi Aunty and Fatima Aunty once yelled for two hours about who was entitled to more space on their shared clothesline. Neelamma Aunty stopped speaking to Vihaan's mother because she removed Neelamma Aunty's bucket from the water line. Banu's *ajji* once threw a brick through a window because she was so angry about losing an ironing client to a neighbor.

Deepa's future husband, though, doesn't know this. He's never lived in a place like Heaven, where rage turns the air red and ugly and ripe. Never had to raise daughters after a father abandons them. Never had to learn to mother after being unmothered, how to love after being unloved. In Heaven, anger is not about any one person. It's about the whole world. The people around you are just close enough to take aim.

The foreign woman hears us too. Looks up from where she is

photographing a stray dog and her puppies curled up among the jagged pieces of a broken roof. Scar above her eye, thumping tail broken off in the middle, puppies pulling hungrily at her teats. It makes us feel embarrassed. Like this dog's survival is more photogenic than our own.

It makes our anger flare just as hot and strong as Neelamma Aunty's. Stronger even.

"What are you looking at?" Rukshana yells.

"No, no," Deepa says, turning away from her mother and gesturing at the woman. Uses a voice fit for the starving puppies, for the suckling dog. "Come, come. It's okay."

"What do you think you're doing now, you mad girl?" Neelamma Aunty yells.

"Saving Heaven," Deepa says. "Now stop screaming and help me."

* * *

We all know the rules. Daughters listen to their mothers before their marriage, and to their husbands after. Because all daughters must get married. Or, more specifically, daughters must get married to the highest bidder. And for girls like Deepa—girls like us—bidders aren't guaranteed.

As far as fiancés go, this family was probably the most Deepa's family can hope for. The first time we saw them, we could tell they weren't rich, but they were better off than we were. The boy and the father wore shirts so new that the collars were still crisp. The mother wore gold on her wrists and ears, diamonds in her nose. Neelamma Aunty and Deepa's father mostly stared at the floor, trying to hide the callouses on their toes, the frayed hems of their clothing.

The longer we watched , the more we realized how much was at stake. The less we knew what to do.

Deepa was the first of us to go like this. It did not feel like an auspicious beginning.

"Girls, this is not a good time," Neelamma Aunty said, smiling a smile as thin and false as the fabric hiding Deepa's face.

"Sorry, Aunty," Padma said.

"We were just going to see the butterflies," Banu stammered. "It's supposed to be a once-in-a-lifetime experience."

"Butterflies?" the crooked boy asked.

"There's an unusual number of them at the park right now," Joy said in her most sophisticated voice. "The newspaper is calling it a mass migration."

"You're taking a blind girl to see butterflies?" The boy's father laughed, a noise like falling rocks. The boy's mother covered her smile with her hand, flashing flamingo-pink nails sculpted in a salon.

"Well I think it's a wonderful idea," the crooked boy said.

Something in the air straightened.

"Why don't I escort them?" he said. "We'll get to know each other. Make sure this alliance is correct."

"I'm not sure if that's proper," Neelamma Aunty said, glancing at the boy's parents.

"No, no, no. Don't worry. My son has the right idea," the boy's father said, booming the way big men do. Slapped Deepa's father's shoulder and said, "Have to keep up with these modern times. Let's give them an hour, shall we?"

"An hour is fine," Deepa's father said.

"You'll be careful?" Neelamma Aunty asked.

"Of course, Aunty. Don't worry. I'll take good care of her," the boy promised.

"We all will," Padma said. Shot the crooked boy a look as straight and sharp as a knife.

* * *

"The foreign woman's coming over here?" Deepa asks. "Are you sure?"

"A blind girl, a boy with a crooked spine, and a hijra-in-training? All standing in a pile of rubble?" Joy laughs bitterly. "Of course she's coming."

It's exactly the kind of truth the photographer dreams of capturing on camera. A truth so anemic that it might as well be a lie.

"Excellent. Where are the drivers?"

"Around the other side of the bulldozer," Padma says.

"Just what are you up?" Neelamma Aunty asks her daughter.

Deepa ignores her mother, turns toward the sound of the photographer's footsteps, and says, "Please, ma'am, will you take a photo of me with my would-be?"

"That was perfect. How'd you learn to speak Hindi like that?" Rukshana asks.

"Same way I learn everything," Deepa says. "By paying attention."

The photographer approaches and asks, "'Would-be'? What is 'would-be'?"

"Would-be. The man I'm going to marry."

"He is your husband?"

"Not yet. Soon," the boy says eagerly. Clutches Deepa's hand like he's being photographed on the flower-strewn stage of a wedding reception, not the dust-covered ruins of a half-destroyed slum.

"Your eyes. Are your eyes fine?" the photographer asks, her Hindi dissolving in her excitement. "You. Your back. Your back okay?"

"Don't worry about my back," the boy says. "Just listen to my fiancé."

"Let's go over there," Deepa says. Slowly, clearly. Like she's talking to a child. To Joy she says in Kannada, "Take us over by the drivers. Then make me look as pathetic as possible."

"Are you trying to get yourself killed?" Rukshana asks.

"I'm trying to *prevent* us from being killed," Deepa says.

"Stop arguing, Rukshana," Padma says. "For once in your life, just listen."

Joy leads Deepa and her fiancé to the emaciated strip of shade where the drivers smoke putrid bidis, sip fizzy drinks. Discuss wives, children, threats to their own futures, disasters that loom over their lives that are as cruel as the bulldozers they are paid to drive. In their distraction, they don't notice Deepa, her cheeks radiating heat. Don't see Joy loosening Deepa's hair so it falls tangled and half-plaited down her back. Don't see Deepa clinging to her future husband's arm, body sagging with exhaustion. Don't see Banu taking the photographer by the elbow, the way we do with Deepa when we take her someplace she's never been before.

Which makes sense, really, since the foreign woman suffers from a different kind of blindness.

Don't see Banu kneeling down and showing the photographer a frame she's squared between her fingers. Inside are Deepa, Joy, and Deepa's fiancé. So are the drivers, BBMP vests glittering, lit bidis glowing.

When the clicking starts, when the flash goes off, the bulldozer driver with the wart looks up, drops his jaw. The bidi he's just lit slips out of his mouth. Falls to the ground in a shower of orange sparks, black smoke. Burns itself out in a burst of rotten flame.

* * *

The day we met Deepa's would-be, we walked to the park in a huddle, whispering and worrying and glancing at Deepa and her crooked boy trailing behind us, arm in arm.

"How could Neelamma Aunty allow this?" Padma seethed. "Just because Deepa's blind doesn't mean she deserves to marry someone like—like—*him*."

"His parents are horrible," Rukshana said. "Did you see how his father spoke to us?"

"I bet they think they're doing her a favor," Padma said. "They think she's just a pair of useless eyes and nothing else."

"Exactly," Joy said. "Deepa's blind, but she's the best dancer in Heaven."

"The best storyteller. The best cook too," Padma said.

"The most loyal friend," Banu said, fingering bits of paint hidden inside her curls.

"So what do we *do*?" Joy asked.

Joy was right. It was time to hone a strategy, to prepare for battle. But when we turned to check on Deepa and the boy, what we thought was a war looked a lot more like peace.

"So can you see anything at all?"

"A little," Deepa said. "I'm surprised you asked. Most people think blind people live completely in the dark."

"I'm studying public health and management. When my parents

told me about you, I decided to do some research," the boy said. "Did you know that India has some of the highest rates of childhood blindness in the world?"

"Do you need that for your course? Or just for our marriage?"

"Probably just our marriage. But I like doing research. I like knowing what else is happening in the world."

"Me too. Especially since I don't get to go out in the world very much," Deepa said.

"That's a shame," the boy said, nodding seriously. "We'll have to do something about that when we're married, won't we?"

As they talked, the boy maneuvered Deepa around the jagged edges of the broken sidewalk, the snapped power lines that swung from the poles like electric snakes. Smiled a not-on-purpose smile. Like he was enjoying himself.

"You know how there's more to Deepa than her useless eyes?" Banu asked. "Maybe there's more to this boy than his crooked spine."

* * *

When the drivers finally realize they're being photographed, they fly into a rage. Their voices slap the air, furious and violent.

"What the hell is this?"

"Who are you clicking?"

"Stop right now," the one with the wart says to the foreign lady. Points at her with an index finger bent unnaturally at the top, like he's got arthritis, or an old injury that didn't heal properly. Clenches his jaw so that the muscles pop beneath his black and white stubble.

"Which one of you called her?" asks the driver who is wearing tennis shoes. His words quiver with panic.

"What, you think *we* brought her here?" Selvi Aunty shouts.

"Watch your mouth, woman."

"Don't tell her what to watch and what not to watch. Idiot."

Their noise builds, drowning out the frenzy of the main road, where water balloons burst on vehicles and pavement, autos swerve out of the paths of drunken boys and men. The city is loud, but Heaven is louder.

"You lot will stop at *nothing*," says the driver with a patchy face. Pulls the bidi out of his mouth and throws it on the ground. Grinds it viciously under the sole of his blue plastic sandal.

The driver with a wart pushes his face so close to Deepa's that when he speaks, his sour breath heats her cheeks.

"Make that woman leave. Now," he says.

"What? A little blind girl like me?" Deepa says. "How could I possibly do that?"

The driver swears loudly. Pounds his fist into the side of the bulldozer so hard that he dents the metal. Doubles over in pain, yelping in every language he knows.

The foreign lady clutches her camera so hard that the skin on the top of her knuckles changes color.

Which is funny, because when we close our fists, our skin stays exactly the same. Like our bodies are already the color of crisis.

Banu shakes her head and says, "Keep going. Keep clicking. More pictures."

The photographer gulps. Says in her broken Hindi, "I am here to help."

Even though Deepa is the only one facing down an angry man, she is also the only one who stays calm. Soothingly, she tells the photographer, "Of course, of course."

Under her breath, she adds in Kannada, "You're helping us more than you'll ever know."

* * *

The park was only three streets away, but it looked like a foreign country. Women the color of unlit camphor walked briskly in circles around the edges of the green lawn. Foreign tennis shoes squeaked, handloom dupattas fluttered. The only person who looked like us was a gardener gathering fallen branches, pulling up thorny weeds.

But the humans didn't matter. Because everywhere, everywhere, we saw them: the butterflies.

Migration, as it turns out, isn't always a bunch of straw-haired country kids hauling sand on their heads. Sometimes, migration is the vibration of ten thousand new mothers beating their tiny, spangled wings.

Deepa felt the feathery brush of insect feet, smelled the flowers unfurling their petals to make space for new life. Heard our gasps and sighs and *ooh*s and *ahh*s. But of course, none of that was really the point.

"What is it like?" she asked.

"It's glittery and blue," Padma said. "Like the river in my village."

"It's like the necklace Kaju wore in that item number we all like," Joy said.

Deepa nodded even though she didn't understand. What are glitter and jewelry and item numbers to a girl whose world is webbed and black?

"Oh look!" Banu said. "Deepa, one landed on your hair!"

"Really? What is it like?" Deepa asked eagerly.

"It's bright orange with black bits."

"It looks like a tiger?"

"Or like a fire?"

"It's like warming your hands over the *dosa tava* after the sun goes down," the boy said.

We looked again. Banu nodded and said, "You know, he's right."

"These?" she asked, sweeping her fingers over a blood-colored blossom covered in blue and black wings.

"These are like the wind that blows right before it starts to rain," the boy said.

The boy took Deepa's arm and led her around the garden, guiding her hands toward clusters of wings. Butterflies nudged Deepa's fingers with their honey-hungry noses, dropped their scales like silken rain.

"This one is like the smell of wild mint when it first pushes out of the soil. This one is like dry tree bark scraping against your fingers. This one is like handing out chocolates on your birthday."

"How'd you get so good with words?" Joy asked.

"I like to read," he said. "The college library has a lot of novels. They let you borrow them if you're a student."

"Really?" Joy asked. "English or Kannada?"

"Both," the boy said, nodding seriously. "You can't understand other people's stories if you don't understand your own."

"I wish I could go to college," Deepa said.

"Of course you can," the boy said. "They have correspondence courses now. That's how I got my tenth- and twelfth-class pass."

"Would that be all right?" Deepa asked.

"Why are you asking me?" the boy said, laughing. "If you want to study, of course you'll study. Haven't you heard? Education is a human right. The government says so."

The way he answered, we could tell he knew that Deepa read the papers every day. That he knew a lot about Deepa, in fact. Maybe even a few things that we didn't. Couldn't, because we never thought to ask.

At the end of our hour of freedom, all of us were chattering and giggling as though the boy was one of us. As though his spine was not the shape of a question mark but a full stop. As though he was not the man taking our friend away but a boy bringing us closer together.

* * *

Deepa never learned to write her Kannada letters with an ah-ahhh, oh-ohhh, ee-eeee or her English alphabet with an A, B, C. But she learned other things. How to be angry and demanding, clever and mighty, even when the world tells you to be silent and grateful, weak and small. How to eavesdrop on the right people at the right time. How to turn condescension into an advantage. A weapon, even.

The drivers have all closed in on Deepa now. She can feel the rage rolling off of their bodies, a cocktail of indignities brewed from decades of being told who they can and can't be, what they can and can't do. Rage for their families. For themselves.

She knows that rage. She has it too.

"We didn't invite this woman, but we are friendly with her," Deepa says to the driver wearing tennis shoes, her words rhythmic as a bulldozer's engine purring to life. "She mentioned she might give these photos to the paper. The kind of newspaper that, say, might be seen by the headmaster of the private school where you're trying to enroll your son. Which is a pity, because nobody wants to enroll the child of a man who bullies blind girls and their polio-stricken fiancés."

Turning to the driver with the maroon patch, she adds, "It's too bad about your daughter too. Who wants to marry a girl whose father is in the business of destroying lives? A girl's reputation is so fragile as it is. This won't help."

"It's true," Neelamma Aunty says, inserting herself in the middle of the men. "As a mother, I should know."

"As for you," Deepa says to the man with the wart, "allowing a foreigner into a demolition site to take photos of drivers fighting with women? To document government officials engaging in human rights abuses? That doesn't sound like leadership material at all."

"Not what the city's looking for," Fatima Aunty calls out, "that's for sure."

"Leave now and we'll tell her not to print the photos," Deepa says. "But if you stay, we'll tell her to print them. We'll personally deliver copies to that posh private school. Your neighbors—or, at least, the ones with eligible sons. Your managers too."

"You bloody women," the driver with the wart says. "You have no shame."

"We have no shame? What about you?" Selvi Aunty says. "Wrecking people's homes for a living. Your poor wives. How do you face them?"

"At least we *make* a living," the one with the wart says. "Where are your husbands? Maybe if they were more like us, you wouldn't live in a place like this."

Except we know these men's wives live in a place exactly like this. If they didn't, the men wouldn't be so afraid.

* * *

The night it was decided that Deepa would marry the boy with the crooked spine, Padma came to Deepa's house for dinner. For once, it wasn't because she was hungry (although of course she was). This time, Neelamma Aunty had asked her.

"I didn't want this. To marry her so early, to keep her from school. But you girls are all moving forward. She has to move forward too, doesn't she?" Neelamma Aunty whispered, clutching Padma's arms before she even stepped inside the doorway. "Plus you've seen the demolition notices, haven't you? If they go through with it—well. Then you know what will happen."

Then we can't protect Deepa any more, Padma thought. Without Heaven, we can't protect anyone. Not even each other. Not even ourselves.

Out loud she said, "I know, Aunty. I know."

* * *

On the main road, a cow bellows, a pack of dogs howls. Buses rumble by, brakes wailing and groaning. But Heaven is as still as a held breath.

"Let's go," the driver with the tennis shoes and the out-of-school son says.

"But what about the overtime?" The one with the patchy skin balls his fists into his eyes. Thinks of the dowry he hopes he'll still have reason to pay.

"He's right, *yaar*. Better we go now before things really get bad."

"Before you go, call your supervisor," Fatima Aunty says. Uses her union voice, which is also the voice she uses to scold Rukshana. "Tell him to honor the date of the demolition. Give us a month to deal with this the right way. Without bulldozers, without police. With our lives intact."

"Or what's left of them intact," Banu mumbles.

"This is too much," says the man with the wart.

"A man like you, up for a promotion," Deepa says. "You must know the right people, no? Or are you small-time, like your friends here?"

The driver looks stricken, trapped. Moves away muttering to himself and pressing the keys on his phone. The other men shuffle off.

When the one with the eligible daughter climbs into the bulldozer where Deepa is standing, his friend says, "Leave it. Don't want these people to get too comfortable."

Two of the bulldozers pull off, and the photographer keeps snapping her photos. Deepa leans back and closes her eyes. Sunlight ricochets against the mirrors woven into the fabric of her dupatta. She looks powerful, enormous. Like she is about to launch herself and all the rest of us into a kinder universe. A more generous sky.

"Is it over?" Rukshana asks.

"No," Fatima Aunty says. "There's still a demolition order. But we'll go to court on Tuesday and file for a stay. That should give you girls long enough to finish your exams. After that, we'll see."

"Do you want to come stay with us?" Deepa's fiancé asks her.

"No," Deepa says, leaning against his shoulder. "We'd rather stay home."

* * *

The foreign woman doesn't call the newspaper. She doesn't bring help. She doesn't do much of anything at all besides framing the photographs she took and hanging them in a gallery.

One of the photos features Deepa right in the center of it. Back against the tires of the bulldozers, toes bare and dusty. Crooked safety pin clinging to the dupatta falling off her right shoulder. She stares almost into the camera but off to the side a little bit. Just enough so you can tell she can't see.

The caption says, "Blind girl and Bulldozer."

But it's not just a blind girl and a bulldozer. Deepa's fiancé is there, staring at his future wife, pupils full of awe, wonder, love. Like he can't believe that this is the woman he's going to marry. Joy is there too. Neck long and proud as a swan. Hand on her hip, elegant and poised. Radiating strength even when she's trying to look weak.

And in the corner of the picture, the edge of a vest. A stained shirt, a stubbed-out bidi. The bottom of a letter *B*. The contours of the men entrusted with our destruction. Men whose worlds are as precarious as ours, whose powers are as fleeting.

Men who saved us. Who saved Heaven.

But only because we made them.

16

Heaven

THE WEEK THAT DEEPA GETS MARRIED, Vihaan's grandfather's brother's wife dies. Our mothers say that when an elderly relative passes away right after a wedding, it's good luck. But then, our mothers tell us being a boy is good luck, and being a girl isn't. So really, they don't know anything about luck at all.

We watch the funeral procession from Padma's roof. Deepa's father drives his auto-rickshaw in the front of the parade. Honks to part the traffic of two wheelers and pedestrians, compact cars and goats. The *nadaswaram* players look and sound like honking geese with thin brass beaks. Everything and everyone is covered in yellow and orange and white geraniums, petals as soft and thin as wings.

"What do you think heaven is like?" Banu asks. Leans back on her scratched-up elbows, fingers the paint staining the inside of her sleeve. "I mean, not our Heaven. Actual heaven."

"It's one long wedding," Joy says. "And I am always the bride."

"Like anyone would marry you," Rukshana says, but she doesn't mean it. Joy hits her anyway. Just so something stays the same.

"*Chee!* Forget the wedding. The wedding *night*. Now that's real heaven," Deepa says. Laughs a laugh that quivers with a secret knowledge her body now holds.

"It's a library full of big fluffy cushions," Padma says. Janaki Ma'am's gotten her a scholarship for eleventh and twelfth. Says Padma can keep it all the way through college.

Which makes us think that the scholarship is actually just Janaki Ma'am's bank account, but we're not quite sure.

"It's a riverbank and a jungle and a farm," Rukshana says.

"Wherever it is, there is always biryani, and there is plenty of music," Deepa says. "And there are never any chores, so you always have time to dance."

"If that's heaven, then I might actually start being good," Rukshana says, dangling her feet off the roof's edge. She looks like she's kicking the sky.

Heaven, our Heaven, stretches below us, its pathways buzzing with the histories we gave it. The tree where Rukshana fell in love. The church where Joy became herself. The thicket where Banu's *ajji* found out the truth about her husband. The truth that would save us the first time the city came for us, but not the last.

The funeral procession winds toward us. We can see the body now, covered in a white sheet, carnations the color of fire. The air is dense with beating drums, bleating horns. Noise to let the soul know that she's still home. That wherever she goes, this clutter and chaos will always be here. On the ground.

"What do you think, Banu?" Padma asks. "What's heaven like?"

"This," Banu says.

Our heads and legs are propped on each other's laps, stitched together like a quilt of girls—or, maybe, now, of women. Raised above the sagging sofas, the dry summer hum. On this rusty roof, we feel a little bit closer to the tops of the trees. A little bit closer to the sky.

"Yes," Joy says, "this."

Acknowledgments

THIS BOOK would have been impossible without the support of so very many people. Thank you to the Fulbright Foundation for funding the research behind this project, and to all the women and girls who allowed me to enter their worlds. Especially big thanks to the women of Kodihalli Circle, particularly Sumitra, Geeta, Sujata, Varalakshmi, and Yashoda. Thank you to Greeshma Patel, Perumal Venkatesan, and Devi Viswanathan for your help with Picturing Change and beyond.

Thank you to Chuck Adams, my editor, whose patience and insight made my first foray into literary fiction such a rewarding journey. Thank you to my early readers and friends Sally Campbell Galman, Zainab Kabba, Jill Koyama, Shabana Mir, Rohini Mohan, Cambria Dodd Russell, Lori Ungemah, and Bijal Vachharajani. Thank you to Ammi-Joan Paquette and Jacinda Townsend for judging early excerpts of the book for contests, and for their encouragement. Especially big thanks to Ishani Butalia and Maura Finkelstein for their repeated reads and support. Especially, especially big thanks to Minal Hajratwala, who gave me the professional, emotional, and literary support I needed to take this from a draft to a book. I couldn't have gotten here without you.

Thank you to Leigh Feldman, who is technically my agent but is actually my therapist. Thank you for believing in me and for always telling me the truth. Thank you also to Ilana Masad, who pulled this manuscript off the slush pile, gave me fantastic edits, and continues to be an invaluable friend. The two of you changed my life, and I will be forever grateful.

Thank you to Jayanti Akka, Malli Akka, Padma Akka, Savita Didi, Sujata Akka, and, most especially, Velu Akka for your help with domestic work and childcare. Without these women, many of whom come from communities like the ones in this book, I would never have had the privilege to write.

Thank you to my mother-in-law, Prema Narasimhan, for giving me the space to write. Thank you to Bamini Subramanian and Ram Subramanian for always believing in me, and for all of your love.

Santhosh Ramdoss, you are truly the partner of my dreams. Swarna Narasimhan, your presence in my life is the greatest gift I have ever been given. I love you both with all my heart. This, and every story I have ever written, is for you.